D0457522

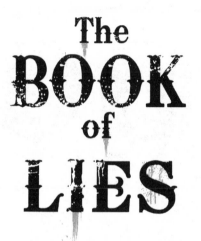

The BOOK

# of LIES

TERI TERRY

CLARION BOOKS
HOUGHTON MIFFLIN HARCOURT
BOSTON   NEW YORK

Clarion Books
3 Park Avenue
New York, New York 10016
Copyright © 2016 by Teri Terry
First published in Great Britain in 2016 by Orchard Books,
an imprint of Hachette Children's Group, part of The Watts
Publishing Group Limited, Carmelite House,
50 Victoria Embankment, London EC4Y 0DZ.
Published in the U.S. in 2017.

The text was set in 13-point Garamond 3 LT Std.

Library of Congress Cataloging-in-Publication Data

Names: Terry, Teri, author.
Title: The Book of Lies / Teri Terry.
Description: Boston ; New York : Clarion Books, Houghton
Mifflin Harcourt, 2017. | "First published in Great Britain in 2016
by Orchard Books, an imprint of Hachette" — Title page verso. |
Summary: "Twin teen girls with very different upbringings meet
for the first time at their mother's funeral. As they get to know each
other, it becomes clear that one of the sisters is driven by a secret
destructive power — or is it both?" — Provided by publisher
Identifiers: LCCN 2016035570 | ISBN 9780544900486 (hardcover)
Subjects: | CYAC: Sisters — Fiction. | Twins — Fiction. |
Good and evil — Fiction. | Supernatural — Fiction. | Blessing
and cursing — Fiction. | Families — Fiction. | Dartmoor (England) |
England — Fiction.
Classification: LCC PZ7.T2815 Bo 2017 | DDC [Fic] — dc23
LC record available at https://lccn.loc.gov/2016035570

Manufactured in the United States of America
DOC 10 9 8 7 6 5 4 3 2 1
4500671764

For my big sis, Sandy

A lie which is half a truth is ever the blackest of lies.
—Alfred Lord Tennyson

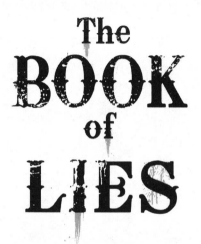

QUINN

There are things you know you shouldn't do. Like standing on the tracks when the train is getting close. Or holding your hand over an open flame—I can wave it across fast and be fine, but something inside makes me hold it there a second longer, then another, and another. Train tracks and mothers are much the same as flames: too close, too long, risk pain.

If I sat and made a list of all the things I shouldn't do and put them in order, starting with the worst, being here today would be near the top. But I'm drawn to things I shouldn't do. Is it just to see what happens, who it will hurt? Maybe.

So, no matter how much that inner voice of caution, of reason, said stay away; no matter how I tried to convince myself or lose my bus ticket and deliberately didn't wear anything even vaguely acceptable, I was never going to be anywhere else, was I?

I'm shivering under leafless trees on a hill above the crematorium, my coat a splash of red in a colorless dark day. Considering my options.

It starts to rain, and I'm glad. She hated the rain. Not just how most people grumble if they're caught in a shower or their garden party is ruined—she properly *hated* it. Almost like she was made of something that would wash away, not sinew, muscle, and bone.

Maybe she was afraid rain would wash away her mask —the one she's wearing in the newspapers, smiling, with a man I've never seen before. *Smiling?* I wonder if she smiles in her coffin, if they arranged her features into a pleasant lie for the afterlife. If they hoped it'd persuade whoever's in charge to open the pearly gates, instead of giving that final push for the long slide down. Or maybe there wasn't enough left of her face.

Cars start winding up the road. The first is long and black, a coffin in the back. When it pulls in front of the crematorium, it seems right that the rain goes from steady to *more.* It thunders down in sheets, and lightning splits the sky.

Even as I hang back and think about the things I should and shouldn't do, about how close to get to the flame, it's almost like the storm has made the decision for me. It says, *Quinn, you must step forward. You must seek shelter.*

But that's just the excuse. The truth is that I'm here to make sure she's really dead.

PIPER

The wind howls, rips the umbrella inside out as soon as I step out of the car. Cold raindrops pelt my face, my hands. In seconds, the wind whips my carefully arranged hair to a wild mess. Hard and furious drops sting my skin, and I focus on *that* pain, to avoid all the others.

Another umbrella is rushed over both of us as Dad emerges, but all I can think about is how the rain must pound on her coffin lid. Does it echo inside? Will she bang in protest, yell, *Oi, make it stop?* She who lived for sunny days shouldn't have her last outing like this.

The pallbearers take short, measured steps despite the freezing onslaught, and I want to yell, to shriek at them to hurry, to get her out of the rain. Dad's cold hand seeks mine, and I grip it a little too tight. Dad and I follow the coffin —follow her, follow *Mum*—inside.

One of Dad's aunts clucks and smooths my hair, and I'm pulled toward the row at the front, but like the rest of this, it doesn't really register.

I try the words on again inside my head. *My mother is dead.* My world is different; everything is different. I know it, but I don't *know* it in my guts. The coffin has been placed to one side at the front—dry now. Did somebody dry it? She's inside it, but it's not really her: just what is left.

Knowing all these things didn't prepare me for any of this. Something is shaking deep inside me; panic is building.

I want to scream, *Stop this, it isn't real! Stop pretending that it is!*

It can't be.

Focus on breathing: in, out, in, out.

They all think it's real. It's in their eyes — those that meet mine, those that shy away.

Breathe, Piper: in, out, in, out. I can't lose it. Not here, not now.

Focus on something else.

I turn and search the faces behind us, skipping over most of them. Dad's family, his work colleagues, his and Mum's mutual friends. Not many. No one from Mum's family. No one from her past, from before I was born seventeen years ago.

There is a good-size contingent of friends from my school. Apart from but near to them is Zak. His steady gaze echoes his words last night: *I'm here for you. Anything I can do, anything, just ask and I'll do it. No matter what.* And the touch of his eyes soothes me now, as it did then. The panic eases, just a little. But it's enough.

The service is about to begin when the doors at the back open, and the rent-a-vicar pauses to wait. A latecomer? I hear a disapproving *tch* under the breath from one of Dad's aunts behind us. I hazard a glance backwards. A slight figure, a girl in a red coat and muddy boots. She's moving toward the empty row at the back. A rainbow scarf covers her head, pulled low over her face.

Who could it be? Could it . . .

No. No way. Not here, not now. My pulse quickens.

QUINN

Rivulets of water run down my coat and my boots, and drip on the floor. The scarf wrapped over my hair is soaked, and I'm shivering.

I catch a movement as I sit down, a head turning away —a girl in the front row. Her hair is long, half pinned up and half escaping after the wind and rain, but that isn't what makes me stare: it's the color. A deep, fiery red.

Deep, fiery red hair—like mine.

Everything goes still inside; everything stops. Dizziness starts to overtake me, and I have to remind myself to breathe, to take air into my lungs in a gasp.

I didn't think of that. Could she actually have had another daughter? Never once did it occur to me that someone who was sort of the antimother, the embodiment of what a mother shouldn't be, who left me at the mercy of her own antimother and just came by occasionally to poke through my bars with a stick, could possibly have had another child.

The man the girl is sitting next to could be the one from the newspaper. I reach into my pocket. The newsprint is wet, the words running a little, but they're well memorized:

Woman Dies in Tragic Dog Attack
Isobel Hughes, 36, of Winchester was walking the
family dog late Friday evening when she was attacked

by a pack of dogs. She died later in hospital. The pack
of four was identified as guard dogs that had escaped
from nearby training kennels. The dogs have been
seized, and investigations are continuing.

Without the photo, I wouldn't have known it was her.
Her first name, Isobel, is the same, but she's always been a
Blackwood like me, like my grandmother.

It was a horrible enough end to be picked up by national
press and to kick off a whole debate about guard dogs and
control of dangerous dogs, or I wouldn't even have known my
own mother had died. She didn't visit often enough to give
me any sense of regularity or time. I assumed she couldn't be
bothered, and I wasn't bothered about it.

The man in the photograph is identified as her husband.
The image is blurred by water, but I study it, compare it
to the man in front. He finally turns his head a little: it's
definitely him. Her husband? He looks at least twenty years
older than Isobel. But there was nothing in this article about
her, this girl sitting next to him with hair like mine.

Finally the unheard words of the service are over. I will
her to turn around so I can see her, but there are quickly too
many taller heads in the way for me to catch any more than
a glimpse of red hair.

I keep my own scarf, saturated as it is, in place. This is
crazy. I'm getting out of here and far away as fast as I can get.

But she and the man with her—I'm guessing he's her
father; at least *she* has one—have gone to stand by the door.

They're facing away from where I'm sitting. There is a procession going by them—everyone stopping to shake his hand, to hug her. So many kind looks and words. So many people who care for them. The first ones appear to be family or family friends, then there is a long line of teenagers about my age, boys and girls both. There are so many of them, and they must all be the girl's friends—each with a word to say, a gesture, a touch. Then there is an older, dark-haired boy, tall, who'd hung back, waited for the others to go first. His arms go round her. He kisses her quickly and takes her dad's hand, leans forward to say something. Her dad is wiping his eyes. Someone gives him a handkerchief.

Wondering what would happen and who it would hurt if I came here today, I never thought that it could hurt *me*. Inside I'm clenched tight, twisting into knots of pain, pain tangled with *wanting*—what, exactly? Labels for things I've never had are out of my reach.

I can't do this; I can't shake their hands and look in their eyes, knowing what I know. I slide down in my seat and will myself invisible in the shadows.

Voices fade. There is the click of a door closing. Could they really be leaving me here, unchallenged?

Then there is the *click-click, click-click* of footsteps coming toward me. They stop.

"Hello? Have we met?" A girl's voice. It is a musical note to a dark day, warm and eager.

I turn toward her, somehow *knowing* who it will be.

The light from high windows catches the fire in her hair.

Her eyes are wide, curious—a clear blue-gray, the sort of eyes that change color with the light, with her mood, with what she's wearing. And I know this because they are *my* eyes. Her skin is pale, light freckles dusted across high cheekbones. *My* freckles; *my* cheekbones. It's like looking in a mirror.

Cryptic comments and overheard words—not understood then, but finding meaning now—are tumbling through my brain, crashing into each other. My head feels light, and I'm gasping, struggling to breathe.

"Are you all right?" she says. "Do you need a doctor or something?"

I stand up, shake the scarf off my hair, and step into the light.

PIPER

It's like looking in a mirror. Even the way her hair is tucked behind her left ear and falls across her face on the other side, damp and wavy from the rain, is the same as mine would normally be. The shock in her eyes is absolute. She didn't know?

"We're twins," I whisper, and can hear the wonder in my voice.

She swallows, licks her lips. "I don't . . . I mean . . . how . . ."

I hold out my hand. "I'm Piper." She stares at my hand. "And you are?"

She jumps a little. "Quinn. My name is Quinn." She gives me her hand; it is cold, ice-cold, and quickly withdrawn.

I look back at the door. "Dad'll be looking for me in a sec. We can't spring this on him here, not now."

"Not ever. Don't worry, I'm getting out of here," Quinn says, and she's half poised on the balls of her feet. She looks frightened, freaked out, but I can't let her bolt—not after everything that's happened.

"No! No, you can't do that. Please. Promise me you'll wait a minute. I'll get Zak to take you, and—"

"No. I don't belong here." She's backing away.

My eyes fill with tears. I want to reach out and touch

her, hold her, but I'm afraid she'll pull away. "You can't. Please. I don't want to lose you, too. Not again."

Quinn hesitates. "You don't know me. I don't know you. All we share is a face."

A tear trickles down my cheek. "And a mother. One we've just lost. Please don't go."

"A mother I barely knew." Her eyes flick to the coffin. "Is it . . . Is she really . . ."

And it's as if the disbelief in her eyes makes me finally able to admit it out loud. "Is our mum really dead? Yes. Do you want to see her?"

"What?"

"I'll arrange it if you want me to. Promise me you'll wait, right here. Don't move." My eyes are pleading.

There is a struggle behind hers. She glances at the door, and then she sighs. She finally nods. "All right."

Relief swells through me.

QUINN

The door shuts behind her.

Do you want to see her? Did she really just say that? I force myself to turn, to stare at the coffin on display at the front. Now that everyone is gone, now that I'm alone in the empty room, the coffin seems bigger, dominating the space in a way it didn't before. My eyes are fixed on the gleaming wood, and the more I stare, the more it seems to pull me in — to grow, to take over my senses, almost like it is moving closer. Then I realize that my feet have started taking hesitant steps up the aisle toward it.

Toward *her.*

Do I want to see her?

It would be the ultimate way to make sure she's really dead. My mouth is dry; I try to swallow.

Any moment now, *she* might come back — this Piper. We're *twins?* Piper said the word, but despite seeing her and registering how alike we are, I still can't believe it. How can I have a twin and not have known about her? We're identical, on the outside at least. Could even Isobel tell us apart?

Maybe that's why we were separated. I feel as though I've woken up and seen truth for the first time — a truth so unbelievable, so unexpected, and so all-encompassing that it will change me forever. But I'm afraid to focus on it too closely, on what it might mean.

Or *why* it is so.

I should leave now. Anyone could open the door, rush in, and find me here. They'd probably call the police if they saw me touching the coffin. Or worse, they'd look at me, realize whose face I share, and sell the story to one of those tabloid newspapers guests sometimes leave behind in the hotel where I work: *Twins Meet for First Time at Mother's Funeral!* Well, it's not the very first time, obviously. We must have had at least a first gasp of air moments apart when we were born. Before that we must have shared a womb for nine months, cuddled close together.

Her womb.

And what about Piper's dad? If we're twins, we must have the same father. Is he *my* father too?

The door behind me opens and I spin around, thinking too late that I should have covered myself again with the scarf. But it's Piper.

She walks toward me, stops close. Her eyes skip over me the way mine do over her, unable to stop myself from checking every detail, every curve, every feature, hunting for difference but finding none. She's a little taller, but then I glance down—her heels are higher than those on my boots.

"It's OK," she says, her voice quiet. "No one will interrupt us. I've told them I want some time alone with Mum. And anyhow, Zak is watching the door. He won't let anyone come in."

"Zak?"

"My boyfriend. Come on." She steps toward the coffin.

Her shoulders are straighter, like she's preparing herself for something, and I realize: whatever that woman was to me, she was *Mum* to her.

"You don't have to do this. It's all right."

She pauses, turns, and raises her left eyebrow: identical to a gesture I use, one that challenges. "Neither do you, if you'd rather not."

I straighten my shoulders like she did without thinking about it, then deliberately relax them. I take a step forward, and another, until we're both standing by the coffin.

She died from a dog attack. What is she going to look like?

As if Piper has read my mind, she shakes her head. "There were viewings earlier. The mortician sorted her out pretty well."

There are two handles on the coffin lid. She grips the one at the foot of the coffin, and glances at the other, near where her head must be. "You may have to help."

I slip my fingers around the handle. It's cold, smooth metal. "Ready?" she whispers.

My stomach is twisting, and I want to say, *No, not now, not ever,* but instead I nod. She nods back. We both pull.

The lid is solid and heavy, but easy enough for both of us to raise. It swings up smoothly, and we lower it down. The coffin is open.

Piper's eyes are unreadable, fixed on what lies inside it. "I'll give you a moment," she says, and turns her head by turning her whole body, almost like she can't stop looking where I'm not sure I want to. She walks away.

I stare at the floor, at the wall, at my hands — anywhere but in *there*. I've seen dead things before, like on the side of the road, or when Cat brings in mice or birds. Or the time a fox got in to the chickens, years ago — that was carnage. I'd had nightmares for months after I cleaned it up. Will she be like a chicken caught by a fox?

I steel myself to do this, and start to draw in a deep breath, but then choke it back. Will she smell? How many days has it been since she died? But Piper said a mortician sorted her out. Whatever it is they do, they'd make sure she lasted for her funeral.

I force myself to turn, to look. It somehow seems safer to start at her feet. She's wearing a long, heavy dress. Blue — was that her favorite color? I think back. She often wore blue on her infrequent visits, but I know so little of her, not even that much. Is the dress to hide what the dogs did to her?

My eyes travel upward. Her hands are sort of crossed; one looks normal, the other is hidden in the sleeve. I swallow, force my eyes to trail up and up. The dress has a very high neck. Did a dog rip out her throat? If dogs are like foxes, they'd go for the throat.

And now — it's time. Her face.

She looks relaxed, peaceful. If you didn't get too close, you might think she was asleep. High-set cheekbones, long lashes brushing her cheeks. Auburn hair — not as red or as bright as Piper's and mine—arranged about her shoulders. She was beautiful. I can see that, now that her face isn't frowning, suspicious, and twisted like it usually was when she looked at me.

Even with her eyes closed, there's no doubt. It's her. She really is dead.

Her face is heavily made up. She is—*was*—naturally pale, like I am, and the rouge on her cheeks is too much. It's almost clowny. The foundation is thick, and there are barely visible variations, as if it's been filled in in places. I shiver. Slavering dogs, four of them, isn't that what it said? They must have knocked her to the ground and attacked. They shouldn't have done so without a command, that's what their trainer said before he was charged. He couldn't understand how it happened, how they even got out. But somehow they did, and they killed her.

This is something I used to dream about when I was angry, which was a lot of the time—her dying. But now that I'm staring at her body, I feel sick with it, with the reality of the absolute, final end to her story.

She's really dead.

Outside, I'm shaking. Inside, something is choking— something has stopped.

There are footsteps behind me; they come closer. A hand touches my shoulder. "Come on. We'd better go." Soft words.

We swing the lid over and shut. I watch our mother's face as it disappears from view, the last time I'll ever see it. I stand there, my fingers still caught in the handle, unable to move.

Piper's hands are warm, gentle. She pulls my fingers away from the coffin lid, tucks my hair into my coat, then carefully wraps my scarf back around my head, knotted in front and pulled low over my face to hide who I am. She doesn't say anything about the traitor tears glistening in my eyes.

Tears I can't understand.

Why should I care? That woman never cared what happened to me. She was never there when I was scared and alone. She wasn't there when I fell and broke my arm when I was six. She wasn't there years later when I was ill and screamed in terror at fevered hallucinations, sure creatures of the night would rip me apart if the fire didn't kill me first.

She never loved me.

But even worse: now, she never will.

PIPER

She is quiet and pliable now, and when I tell her to wait a moment, she doesn't argue. Does seeing your mother like that make you a child again, even a mother you barely knew?

Despite my resolution not to, I couldn't stop myself from looking at Mum again. I'd wanted to study her, drink her in, climb inside the coffin and lay my warm body over her cold one. As if warmth could be all she needed to make her come back to me.

I open the door. Zak is there, like I knew he would be. Others are visible through the next set of doors.

He smiles, holds out a hand, and I take it. "Your dad's waiting for you," he says. "Are you all right?"

"Yes. But can you do something else for me?"

"Of course. What is it?"

I open the door farther so he can see Quinn standing in the shadows where I left her. "Could you take . . ." I say, then hesitate, not wanting to spring this on him with witnesses so close, not trusting him to hide his reaction. "Could you take my friend to your place to wait for me until after the wake?"

He's startled to see her. "I thought you were alone in there."

"I'll explain later. Will you do it?"

"Of course." Zak leans forward, slips his arms around me. I lean into him a moment, wishing I could go with them and not have to deal with all the rest. All I want is to be with Quinn: someone else I want to drink in, to study. As if being with her — focusing on her face — could make everything else go away.

I sigh, and look up at Zak. "Just wait until we're gone before you leave. All right?"

Unasked questions lurk in his eyes, but he nods. "OK. Sure, if that's what you want me to do," he says. "I'll take her to my place, and then meet you at yours afterward."

I frown. "No. You'd better stay with her. Make sure she waits for me." Despite how she is now, I don't trust her not to bolt once the shock wears off.

"What? No way; I'm coming. I have to be there for you, like you were for me."

I shake my head. "Listen to me, Zak. The best way you can help me right now is do what I ask. Take Quinn, and stay with her." I gesture toward her, still standing there silently, her head lowered and turned away. "I'll come as soon as I can. Please?"

His eyes search mine. "I don't understand, but OK, if that's how you want it."

"It is. Exactly how I want it."

"Your family will wonder why I'm not there." He rolls his eyes, and I know he doesn't care what they think, so long as they're not causing me problems.

"I'll tell them you're ill or something. Don't worry about it."

Another hug. I look through the doors; Dad is watching, impatient to get going. "I have to go now. I'll get them outside so you two can slip away."

QUINN

Their words reach my ears but float around, not understood, in my mind. I try to make myself listen. This is Piper's boyfriend, Zak: the one I saw kiss her earlier at the door. Is she asking him to take me somewhere?

Piper, my *twin*. Even said silently, the word is unreal. How could I not know this? What does it mean?

Piper slips away through the outer doors. I hear murmured voices outside that mute again when the doors shut. Zak turns toward me and steps into the doorway.

"Ah, hi," he says. "I'm Zak."

I feel frozen, unable to move or look up.

"Hello?" he says again. "Are you Quinn?"

I force out an answer. "Yes. That's me," I say, and I know the words are mine, but they sound distant, as if they belong to somebody else. I struggle to turn my eyes, to focus on him, to grab hold of something real.

Tall. He's tall. Dark, almost black hair, skin like milky chocolate, or coffee with cream. Nineteen or twenty. Wide, brown eyes with more dark lashes than a boy really has need of. Broad shoulders, but slim. He stands easily, like an athlete. If I wasn't in some sort of coma, I'd think he was gorgeous. He's looking back at me with a mix of curiosity and concern. He probably thinks he's had a crazy relative dumped on him—one with a strange scarf-based fashion sense.

A crazy relative? A smile pulls at my lips, and I stifle the hysterical giggle that wants to work its way up. What could be more true?

"Wait a sec," he says. "I'll check if they're gone." He walks over to the other double doors, peers through the glass, then turns back. "They're just leaving. Let's give them a minute."

When he judges enough time has passed, he gestures, and I follow him outside. It's still raining; it's steady, but not the manic downpour it was before. Once I feel the cold, fresh air, the raindrops on my face, and take another step and another, farther and farther away from that place of death, I start to feel more myself.

Not that I'm quite sure who I am now. One half of a set of twins?

He pulls out a key and presses it; a *beep-beep* sounds, and he holds open the passenger door to a battered blue car for me to get in.

He starts the car, drives slowly out of the car park and down the winding drive, even though no other vehicles are in front of us. As soon as he turns onto the road, he accelerates so hard that I check to make sure my seat belt is fastened.

He glances at me sideways, and I turn my head away. "So. Why are you being snuck out of there like some sort of spy?"

I shrug. "That was Piper. Not my idea."

He shakes his head. "That girl comes up with some crazy stuff sometimes, true enough, but even she wouldn't do this without a good reason."

I don't answer. I consider taking my scarf off in the car so he can see me properly, but he's driving fast enough that the shock might be dangerous. Do our voices sound alike —will that be enough to make him wonder? I resolve to say as little as possible, and keep my face turned away. At least, as far away as I can and still watch Zak.

"If you don't tell me, I'll just have to make it up. And I've got a great imagination."

"Have you?"

"Oh, yes. Let's see." He tilts his head to one side, then nods. "You are a famous actress, deeply in love with Piper's dad. You can't bear to be apart, but came to his wife's funeral in disguise to stop the scandal until a reasonable mourning period has passed."

"Interesting."

"Or maybe you work for the life insurance company handling her claim and were just checking she's really dead."

I don't say anything to that one. Cut the insurance company out of it, and isn't that exactly what I was doing?

"Sorry, was that insensitive? How did you know Piper's mum?"

"Stop asking questions—you'll find out soon enough."

"Or perhaps you've escaped from prison and fancied a funeral on your day of freedom?"

A smile tugs at my lips. A prison is close enough to where I came from, and it *was* an escape of sorts.

"Give up," I say. "There is a reason Piper had me snuck out of the funeral, and it's beyond anything you could invent. But can it wait until we get where we're going?"

"I may die from curiosity. But if you don't mind having that on your conscience . . ." He shrugs.

"I can live with it."

"Ouch. We're nearly there now, so I may just survive." He pulls in front of a block of terraced houses, expertly reverses into a tiny spot. "Here we are."

He dashes around to open my door. The rain has miraculously stopped, and the sun is shining. He stares at my face as I get out of the car, and this time I don't look down or turn away. His eyes widen.

He unlocks the front door to the house and holds it open. As I step through, Zak following behind me, I take the scarf off my head. I pull my wet hair out from under my coat and turn back to face him.

He shakes his head, confused. "Piper?"

"No. Not Piper. You saw her leave, didn't you?"

"I thought I did. But you . . . and she . . . I don't understand."

"Nor do I. I came to my mother's funeral, and there Piper was."

"*Your* mother's funeral? Are you *twins?*" he says, eyes wide. "I can't get my head around this." He glances at a door across the room, and as he does, I focus on the sound coming from behind it, a sound that started when we came in the front door. I was distracted enough to begin with that it didn't really register. But now it is louder: a high-pitched whining sort of sound. Then there is a *thump-thump* of something against the door. Is it . . . could it be . . .

"*Arf!*" It is. *A dog.* My skin crawls.

"Give me a sec," Zak says, and moves to the door, a few short feet away. Before I can unstick my tongue enough from my dry mouth to stop him, he opens it.

Out bounds a blur of black and white fur that starts to leap at Zak, then realizes someone else is in the room and stops in its tracks. It turns toward me and tilts its head to one side.

"It'll be interesting to see what she makes of—" Zak stops in midsentence when he turns and sees my face and notices that I've now moved to put a table between me and the dog. "What's wrong?"

The dog starts toward me, but Zak grabs its collar and picks it up in his arms. "Are you by any chance afraid of dogs?"

Now that Zak is holding it—*her*—and the dog isn't leaping at me, I see that she's smaller than I thought, and I'm embarrassed. But even as I try to hide the panic, my heart still beats fast.

"I don't really care for them," I say, making a massive understatement.

"Well, you needn't be scared of this one: she's a puppy, not a full-grown dog. Let me introduce you. This is Ness."

He picks up one of her paws, waves it at me, then puts his head behind hers. "Pleased to meet you!" he says. And Ness barks once as if to agree. He looks around her again. "Can we come a little closer?"

I shake my head.

"Ness is just a playful puppy. She's a Border collie, very intelligent and friendly, and not the least bit aggressive. She's only about four months old. She wouldn't hurt a fly; the only thing she might do is lick your face. Maybe you could walk toward us?"

The puppy and I study each other. Is Ness confused by me looking like Piper, or does that kind of thing not register with a dog? She's got black patches of fur over her ears and around her eyes, a white stripe down her forehead and nose, and big brown eyes that seem to be regarding me with eager curiosity. And my brain is saying, *Actually, not so scary, really quite cute and friendly-looking,* but my feet won't budge, and her eyes go sad.

"I'm sorry. I'd rather not."

"All right. Ness, want to play in the garden for a while?" Her tail wags furiously at the word *garden;* he takes her out the same door she came in through, which I now see leads to a kitchen, and then through another door to a garden on the other side. He goes out with her for a moment, clips her to a long, fixed lead, and she runs around in ecstatic circles. When Zak comes back inside, she flops down on the ground, head on her paws, and watches us sadly through the window.

"I'll have to keep an eye on her. Sometimes she gets

tangled, but the fence has gaps under it. If she's not on a lead, she's an escape artist," he says, and sits on the side of the kitchen table facing the garden, gesturing to the other side for me to sit down. But even with a closed door and a puppy, not a dog, I'm not sure I want to turn my back on her. I sit instead on the side next to Zak, where I can see both Zak and the garden.

"I'm really sorry. I just can't handle being around dogs."

"And I thought identical twins were supposed to be the same? Piper loves all animals, but especially dogs. Ness is actually her puppy."

"Oh? Why's she here, then?"

He hesitates. "I'm looking after her for a while," he says, then faces me. "I'm sorry about your mother." His eyes are full of warm sympathy, and it makes me uncomfortable. To accept it feels like lying.

I shake my head. "Don't be. I mean, we weren't close. I barely knew her."

Ness whines outside, and something clicks. "The news report said that Isobel was walking the family dog when she died. Was Ness with Isobel when she was attacked?"

"Yes. Somehow Ness legged it and got away. She went home, trailing her lead. Piper found her barking in the front garden in quite a state. She didn't think anything of it, just thought Ness had got away, that her mum would be home soon. But she never came. Later the police went looking for her, and, well . . . I'm guessing from your question that you know the rest. They found her. She was still alive, just.

Paramedics got her to hospital, but she died soon after. And that's why I've got Ness: they didn't want her in the house just now."

The whole time he is talking, he is staring at me, his eyes running over my face, hair, every bit of me in an intense way that makes me squirm and look away, a flush climbing in my cheeks.

"Sorry. Was I staring? You're just so like Piper. How come I didn't know about you?"

"I didn't even know Piper existed until today."

"But where have you been? Why weren't you together?"

"No idea. I was raised by my grandmother. Isobel only visited now and then. She never hinted that I had a sister somewhere else."

"I can't believe Piper had a twin she didn't know about." He looks shaken, much how I feel.

But then I realize something that should have struck me before. Piper *did* know, didn't she? She wasn't shocked that I exist, even though she couldn't stop looking at me any more than I could stop looking at her. She must have known. Did our mother tell Piper she had another daughter stashed away somewhere? She never told me, but she told Piper. Piper, the one she kept.

All the missing clues and connections I've been trying not to think about since I first saw Piper's face tumble into place. The way Isobel was with me. Things she said — that I needed to be kept away, the darkness contained, so I couldn't hurt anyone. And it didn't sound like Isobel was doing all this as a service to humanity; it was more personal than that. She never filled in the blank about *who* I might hurt, but it was my twin she kept me away from, wasn't it?

Isobel was making sure I was kept away from Piper. That's why I didn't know about her, and that's why Piper *did* know about me.

No wonder Isobel never needed me. She had Piper. A carbon copy, but one who smiles more. One who is nice, whom people like, whom her parents and someone interesting like Zak maybe even love.

Something that the day stirred and softened inside me shifts back and hardens. I was always right about my mother, wasn't I? Who cares if she's dead? Not me. I'm *glad.*

And no matter how Isobel wanted things, she's failed. I'm in Winchester, with her precious Piper, and there's not a thing she can do about it. In fact, *she's* the one who brought us together. Her death did this.

I cross my arms, holding myself in. "You haven't got that quite right. Piper knew. I didn't."

Zak doesn't answer, but I can tell he doesn't believe me. He doesn't think Piper could keep such a big secret from him. He doesn't know that I never lie. Except to myself, and I'm finished with that.

PIPER

My phone vibrates with a text; I pull it out of my pocket. It's Zak, with a single word, in caps: *WOW*. I'm guessing Quinn took off her scarf.

I slip my phone back in my pocket, and Dad raises an eyebrow, caught between my head teacher and his law partner. He extricates himself and comes over. "Was that Zak?"

"Yes."

"I can't believe he's not here, after everything you went through together last year. He seemed all right earlier. But maybe the funeral was too much for him?"

I sigh, struggling to focus on *now*, on hiding the wonder that moves through my veins: *My twin is close by.* "It's not that. He's ill, and you wouldn't want him throwing up all over the place, would you? Must be something he ate. He'd be here if he could." Dad squeezes my shoulder, and I droop against him. "Is it all right if I go check on Zak later?"

He starts to give me a dad look.

"You know he hasn't got anybody else. What if he's really ill? Besides, I need to get out of here." The bodies all around are too warm, the hands pressed into mine too insistent. The sense of unreality is back, even stronger than before. Mum should be standing there, next to Dad, but instead my mind is full of my last images of her—stiff and silent in her coffin.

He kisses my forehead, the empty space stark next to

him. "I haven't got anybody besides you now, either, Petal. But I understand. Go if you need to."

"I'll wait awhile and pretend to go to bed. Since, you know."

He nods. The terrible duo are in residence tonight. His two aunts have a definite sense of what one should and shouldn't do at all times.

Dad goes to the door to greet a latecomer; I go to my friends.

They're bunched together in a corner, a bit quiet and uncertain. Erin sees me coming and nudges Jasmine, who turns and slips an arm in mine.

"How are you? I mean, how are you holding up, Pip?" Jasmine says. "Is there anything I can do?"

I lean my head against her shoulder, and her arms close around me. "Just being here is enough."

Tim comes closer and smiles. "Pip and J in a clinch: it's like one of my dreams."

"Tim, honestly!" Jasmine says, and shakes her head, but he's broken the uneasy mask on their faces. They start talking more naturally, and I pull Jasmine away with me while the others continue to tell Tim off.

"There is something you can do for me," I say to her, voice low.

"Of course. Anything."

"I'm all in. Can you hint to get everyone to head out soon? I'm sure they'll be happy to go, anyhow."

"That's not true. They're just—*we're* just—a little

unsure what to do, what to say. But if you want them gone, I will make it so."

"Thanks, J."

The clock ticks slowly down. One by one, my friends and the rest of the crowd trickle out our front door, until it finally happens: the whiskey comes out of the cupboard. Dad is pouring, sitting between his brother and cousin, while both aunts look on disapprovingly.

"Should I start clearing up?" I ask Aunt No. 1, rubbing my eyes and stifling a yawn.

"No, no; of course not, duck. Get yourself to bed. It's been a long and hard day for you."

"Are you sure?"

"We're sure," says Aunt No. 2. "We'll take care of it." They both give me a hug and a kiss on the cheek, and I head up the stairs.

In my room, I swap my dark dress and heels—funeral look for family reunion—for jeans and trainers. I focus on Quinn, holding her face in my mind to stop seeing Mum made up and laid out in her coffin.

I head down the other stairs at the back of the house and step out into the night.

QUINN

I sip cautiously: my first-ever taste of red wine. "It's nice!"

"Go slow if you're not used to it," Zak says, but I have another sip, and then another. Warmth starts to slide through me, to replace the shivering that even a hot bath and dry clothes borrowed from Zak haven't dispelled. I'm curled up on a chair in his miles-too-big tracksuit bottoms, T-shirt, and fleece, while he clatters about in the kitchen. Something smells good, and reminds me that I haven't eaten today. Suddenly I'm ravenous. When he hands me a bowl of rice and vegetables with a lovely spicy sauce, I don't look up again until it's gone.

"Either you were very hungry, or I'm one hell of a cook." He grins, still finishing his on the sofa.

"Both. That was *good*. What is it?"

"Vegetarian curry—my mother's recipe." He looks at me oddly. "Haven't you had curry before?"

I shake my head. "It wasn't on my gran's list of approved dinners."

"Strange woman."

I nod seriously. Very true. And what she will or won't eat isn't the half of it.

He pours more wine into his glass, lifts the bottle with

a question on his face. I hold out my glass, and he half fills it. "Last call for you," he says.

"That doesn't seem fair." I raise an eyebrow at his full glass.

"I'm old enough, and as I'm guessing that you and Piper must share the same birthday to have the same face, you've got almost a year to go until your eighteenth. Your glass and a half tonight were purely medicinal."

"And how about yours?"

"Well earned. Not an easy day. Not an easy few weeks."

"Sorry to disrupt things for you tonight."

"Don't apologize. It's fine. And while I should be there for Piper, I was kind of relieved to miss the wake."

"Why?" I'm surprised I ask. But with the warmth of a full belly and the soft buzz of wine running through my veins, I'm relaxed, more than I usually am.

He hesitates. "I don't like big parties. Especially those associated with funerals."

"I can't imagine most people enjoy them. That was my first funeral, and I wouldn't exactly call it a good time." Is Zak a loner? I look around the room. Few personal things are in evidence, and what is—a cricket magazine on the table, a pair of trainers and a bike under the stairs—is probably Zak's. Books on shelves are neat, tidy. There's no hint of anyone else. "Do you live here on your own?"

"Yes."

"How old are you?"

"Nineteen. Do you always ask this many questions?"

"No. Where are your parents?"

A shadow crosses his face. "My parents split when I was little, and I lost contact with my dad years ago. My mum died last year."

"Oh. Sorry. Is that why—"

"I don't like funerals? Yes. Pretty much."

"How did she die?" I say, then wish I could bite it back. "I'm sorry. Don't answer if you'd rather not talk about it."

"Stop apologizing. And I don't, generally. But it's OK. We've got losing our mothers in common, haven't we?"

The warmth of the wine and food is fading. I pull my knees up and wrap my arms close around them. Can I lose something I never really had? "*Losing* sounds like we misplaced them, and if we look hard enough, we can find them again."

"One day, maybe we can. But for now, I know my mum is around me still. Watching over me." He says the words calmly, with quiet conviction. For me, any thought that Isobel might be here now, watching, is not soothing. Goose bumps rise on my arms.

"And to answer your question from before, it was a riding accident. Mum fell from her horse. Severe spinal and internal injuries. I rushed home from university just in time to hold her hand as she died."

"I'm sorry," I say, then start to say sorry for apologizing again, realize what I'm doing, and stop.

He leans back on the sofa, eyes half closed. "I felt like I shouldn't have gone away, shouldn't have left her alone.

Not that me being here would have changed anything, but I haven't been able to make myself go back to university." He shakes his head, looks at me. "Not sure why I'm telling you all this. I don't usually talk about it much. Maybe it's because when I look at you, I see Piper."

"What university did you go to?"

"Cambridge. I was reading human, social, and political science. They're losing patience on extending my leave. I'll have to go back soon or give up my place."

"What would your mother want you to do?"

"She'd want me to go back, of course."

"So go."

"It's not that simple."

"Sure it is. Why not?"

"What about Piper? I can't leave her alone. Not now."

As if mentioning her name again conjures her, the front door rattles, then opens. "Hello?" Piper calls out, in a voice that is eerily *my* voice.

Zak gets up, goes to the entrance hall. There are murmured voices, then silence. They come into the front room, their arms linked. When Zak looks at Piper, his face has a warmth it didn't have before. But Piper looks tired, drawn. He starts to lead her toward the sofa, but she lets go of his hand and turns toward me.

"I'm so glad you're here, Quinn," she says, and bends awkwardly, trying to hug me in my chair. She sits on the sofa with Zak, then looks around. "Where's Ness?"

"Asleep in the kitchen," Zak says, but as if either Piper's

voice or the sound of her name summoned Ness from puppy dreams, there is instant barking on the other side of the door. Piper jumps up and heads toward it.

"Wait," Zak says. "Don't let Ness out of the kitchen. Quinn doesn't like dogs."

"What?" Her face is incredulous.

But I'm feeling braver now. Is it the wine? "Let her in if you *promise* to keep her from jumping at me."

"OK, fine. I promise." Piper pulls the door open, and I tuck my feet farther up under me on the chair, but I needn't have worried. Ness is so full of joy at the sight of Piper, it's like I'm invisible. She runs around her in circles, and then when Piper gets on the sofa next to Zak, jumps up between them. She sits with her head on Piper's lap, gazing at her adoringly, and the feeling looks to be mutual. The more Ness wags her tail, the more the strain on Piper's face melts and fades.

"How'd you get away?" Zak asks Piper.

"No bother. Dad said it was OK to check on poor ill you. You've been throwing up, by the way, if anybody asks."

"What about your aunts?"

"I pretended to be sleepy, went up to bed, and snuck out the back way."

Zak shakes his head, in a what-are-you-like kind of way, but I'm shocked. "You lied to your father? And your aunts?"

She shrugs. "It avoided a lot of fuss. Besides, why worry them more when they're already stressed out? I was sparing them. And Dad knows where I am."

I stare back at her, not quite able to take this in. Lying was not allowed around Gran—not any sort, not even little ones designed to spare feelings. Exaggeration was enough to make me miss dinner. Anything resembling an actual untruth got me locked in a cold room in the dark for the night, or longer. And she *always* knew—she had a special lie-detecting sense. It's been years since I even tried; I have a built-in aversion to it now.

Piper raises an eyebrow. "Don't you ever lie?"

"No."

Zak tweaks her nose. "Maybe your sister will be a good influence on you."

She scowls, and I laugh. "Now, that's something I've never been accused of before."

Piper sits forward, head in hands. Her eyes stare at mine, mirrors of my own. "I'm intrigued. Have you got a dark side, Quinn?"

Uneasy, I shrug and don't answer her question. Isobel thought I did—why else keep me hidden away? And Gran did, too. She was constantly at me to guard against it, forever using charms to keep it at bay.

Now it is Piper's turn to laugh. "Just one of many questions I have for you. To start with, where do you live? Who with? Did you used to see Mum? How did you know she died? How did you get here?" The more questions she asks, the less I want to answer them.

"I have a question first," I say, facing Piper. "Why did you know about me when I didn't know about you?"

Piper looks me straight in the eye. "I didn't."

I stare back at her. Do I have the same lie-detecting sense as my gran? "Yet when you saw me sitting there with your face at your mother's funeral, you didn't seem shocked or surprised at all. You seemed happy. Straightaway you arranged things so I could see Isobel and got Zak to bring me here. Then you told lies to your family to rush here and ask me questions. And you didn't know I existed before today? I don't think so."

Her face starts to crumple. "I didn't know! I just . . ." She shakes her head, and Zak wraps his arms around her, making soothing noises. She pulls free moments later, tears shining in her eyes. "You don't understand. I was in this horrible, dark place. I felt so alone. And when I saw you, it was like some of it lifted. It took me away from where I was, what was happening. I might have lost my mother, but unexpectedly, there you were: a beautiful sister I didn't even know I had."

She holds out a hand to me, and I *want* to believe her. My hand reaches across to hers, without plan or thought. She grips it hard.

"I'm sorry I upset you," I say. "It's just all so *strange,* and you didn't seem to react to the strangeness. But I'm not some sort of replacement part for your family. I don't belong here."

"Then where do you belong?" Piper asks. "Where did you come from?"

Nowhere I want to be. But I'm not saying that, not out loud. I cross my arms.

Zak looks between us, at Piper's increasingly frustrated face, my closed one. "Look, it's late. How about we stick to the really big question: what happens next?"

That is the one I've most been trying to avoid, but it has crept into my thoughts again and again without permission. I left without packing any clothes, with not much more money than I needed to get here, without anywhere else to go. My only destination was Isobel's funeral. I hadn't thought past that. I don't want to go back; I can't stay here.

I look at Piper, with her curiosity and endless questions, and suddenly just want to get away from her. "I should go."

"What about your dad?" Zak asks. "Don't you want to meet him? He's not a bad old guy."

"My . . . dad?"

"That's how the twins thing usually works," Piper says. "He's my dad, so he must be yours, too."

"I . . . I don't know," I say. There is part of me that wants to meet him, but Gran's reaction whenever I asked about my father makes me scared. She seemed to think he was a cross between a lowlife criminal and the devil. Yet Zak knows him; *not a bad old guy,* he said. But my father is still a stranger. "How would you feel if your dad suddenly appeared after all these years?" I ask Zak.

Piper raises an eyebrow, looks between Zak and me. Is she surprised that I know about his father?

He shrugs. "I'd probably thump him one for running out on us. But it's not the same story."

"Isn't it? How do you know my father doesn't know

about me? Maybe he was in on separating us. Maybe it was his idea."

Piper shakes her head. "There's no way he knows about you. I can't believe it for a second," she says, her words so full of conviction that I somehow accept them.

"But *how* could he not know about me?"

"I don't know, but one thing I'm sure of is this: if he did, you and I would have been together. And if he met you now, he'd love you," she adds, as if responding to my thoughts. Is this a twin thing — can she somehow read the doubts in my mind? "You're his daughter; of course he'd love you."

"Isobel didn't. And I was her daughter, too." Piper starts to deny my words, but I interrupt her. "Don't," I say, my voice sharp. "You don't know; you weren't there. She *left* me. Sure, she visited now and then, but she never had a kind word to say. Not once. It was more like she was just making sure I hadn't got away." I wrap my arms around myself. I didn't want to talk about Isobel, yet I did — giving away more than I intended.

Piper shakes her head helplessly. "I don't understand. This isn't the same mum I knew that you're describing to me." Zak gives her a look, and she shrugs. "All right, I know she had some problems. I don't know your story, and I want to, so much. Just *don't* assume Dad will be the same. Despite that, he's definitely not fit to have this sprung on him now. The shock would be too much, after everything else. But can you stay, and wait awhile until we can tell him?"

"How can I? Where?"

"You can stay here, of course," Zak says. I start to protest that he doesn't even know me, but he shakes his head. "You're Piper's sister. That's good enough for me. You don't have to decide what you want to do yet, do you? Just stay and think about it. Time enough for questions another day."

"But I didn't pack any stuff. I wasn't planning on hanging around."

"You can borrow from me," Piper says. "I've got loads of clothes, and I'm guessing they'll fit you perfectly. We'll pick some up tomorrow."

"I don't know," I say. "I don't know what to do. I'm too tired to think straight."

"Stay," Zak says again. "You can think about it tomorrow."

I find myself agreeing. Everything they say sounds reasonable, sounds right when they say it. Or is it just that I have nowhere else to go? And I'm tired, *so* tired, right into my bones. The last week hasn't involved much sleep.

"Is there anyone you need to call?" Piper asks. "You can use my phone."

"No. No, thanks," I say, and she looks disappointed. Was she hoping to get a phone number to where I come from?

"Come on. You look exhausted," Zak says.

He takes me upstairs, lends me another T-shirt to sleep in, and shows me to one of two bedrooms. It's a beautiful room, in green and pink, a flowery duvet cover. Definitely not decorated by Zak. I call him back. "Was this your mother's room? I don't want to intrude. I can sleep on the sofa."

"It's fine. Really, it is." He hesitates, points at the bed-side table, the phone there. "If you want to call anyone, go ahead. I don't want anyone to be worrying about you; it can be our secret." He winks. "Good night."

He shuts the door. I hear murmuring voices and soft sounds from downstairs—are they kissing on the sofa?

Then there are footsteps below, leading to the front door. Piper's voice floats up the stairs. She has to go and insists he can't walk her home, that someone might see him and he's supposed to be ill. She promises to text when she gets there.

The door opens, then closes.

I hesitate, then pick up the phone and push the buttons for the number I'd memorized. It's late, but I'm pretty sure where Gran is will be open all the time.

It's answered with the ward name, the nurse's name. "Hello? This is Quinn Blackwood, Sybil Blackwood's grand-daughter. Can you tell me how she's doing?"

"Hello, Quinn. I remember you, I admitted your grandmother. She's doing well, much better than expected. Though she keeps asking for you." She runs through the tests they've done, the results. It was a stroke, as they'd thought. "But despite her age, she's very strong. Her speech and move-ment are still affected, but she'll be able to go home soon. If someone is there to care for her for a while."

I hurriedly thank her, and say goodbye. Leaving the implicit *When will you come?* question unanswered.

She's strong. She'll be fit again. It was the shock that did it. When I showed her the newspaper clipping, the one with the photo that said Isobel *Hughes* had died, Gran keeled over on the spot. I had to run the miles to the hotel in the dark to get them to call an ambulance. It was too windy for a helicopter, so Dartmoor Search and Rescue came up with the paramedics, to lower her down the rocks and scree past Wisht Tor, so they could get her out the fast way instead of going the long way around.

During the ambulance ride, her eyes were scared. She tried to speak to me, but couldn't. The paramedics thought she was afraid she was dying; they'd done their best to reassure her. But there was something else in her eyes. Was she scared I'd get away?

She's strong; the nurse said so. Does she really need me? If I go back, will she ever let me go again?

I curl up in Zak's mother's bed. This *feels* like a good place, a safe place. There is something reassuring about Zak, like everything will be all right if he's around. In contrast, there's something about Piper that scares me. Is she what I'm uncertain about, or is it all her questions? There are too many things I'd rather keep to myself.

Moments later, there is a faint *beep-beep* downstairs: Piper must have texted to say that she's home.

So her home — the one Isobel lived in, the one Piper still lives in with our dad — is close by. I try to imagine what it's like and how it felt to grow up there as a cherished daughter with both parents, with friends and extended family all around. But my imagination isn't that good.

PIPER

They actually did it. How could they?

It's on the radio news in the early morning, and now there's nothing to stop me from going back to the kennels. And then on to where Mum died.

I almost leave a note for Dad, but if he gets up early enough, he'll know where I've gone, and if my aunts found a note, they'd flip out. He came with me the first time, but I could tell he didn't want to go back again. He didn't want to stand there and think about what had happened. He knows I go, and thinks maybe I shouldn't, but isn't sure enough that it is a bad thing for me right now to try to stop me. Not that he could. Anyhow, I've already decided that today is the last time.

The woman in the shop knows who I am. I see it in her eyes every morning, the pitying glance at the poor mother-less girl. But she doesn't say anything, just sells me the flowers.

Today, I pick out not one bunch of flowers, but five. She wonders why, but doesn't ask. When you work in a shop that is open twenty-four hours, maybe you stop asking why people buy what they do before dawn.

This time I walk the long way around. I stop outside the kennels just as the first glimmer of sunrise finds it. All is quiet there now. It used to be that when I came past, there'd be a chorus of doggy hellos—friendly yips and barks. I'd go to the fence past all the DANGER signs, and they'd jump around and wag their tails and lick my fingers through the fence by their cages.

Now there's a chain over the gate, and silence. The other dogs have been sold or returned to their owners.

It's a mile or more from home, through the woods on a muddy path. Today it's so cold that the mud is stiff, half frozen.

The path leads down to a small clearing. The police tape is gone now. There are flowers scattered from other mornings, showing all stages of life and death—fresh, wilted, decayed.

I know the exact place where Mum was found. I insisted on knowing. I open the bunch of red roses first, but this time, I rip the petals off each one and scatter them on the ground —where I imagine her head was, her hands, her legs . . .

Her heart.

The other four bunches are colorful and mixed, like one Zak gave me once. Ness decided they were a puppy toy and ripped them apart before we could stop her.

What happened here wouldn't have happened if I'd been with Mum. The dogs that escaped from the kennels and did this horrible thing were my friends; they all had names I gave them, names they answered to. I should have been with Mum. Ness was my dog, as she pointed out often enough. I should have been walking her, not Mum.

And yesterday, the dogs were destroyed. That's the word

they used on the radio. How do you destroy a dog? An injection, or something more violent?

I'd asked them not to. You might think this coming from the poor motherless girl would go a long way. But the policewoman who spoke to me said the order was made, and that was it. Nothing could be done. I could tell she couldn't understand why I wanted to save them.

A bunch of flowers for each dog. I open them, spread them all around the outside of the rose petal outline, and lie down on the red petals.

Mum wasn't found until the next morning. She was still alive — just. What was it like, lying here, bleeding, in pain, all night long?

They called us, and we raced to the hospital, but she died before we got there.

I never got to say goodbye. I never got to say I was sorry that I left her alone.

I close my eyes and reach inside.

I'm sorry, Mum.

I'm sorry, Bob.

I'm sorry, Boo.

I'm sorry, Flapjack.

I'm sorry, Hobie.

You'd all still be alive if it wasn't for me.

The cold and damp seep into me from the ground. Is this what it is like to be dead — cold and still forever?

Mum could have found a way out of this. If she'd let herself, she could have stopped it all. I know this.

For a long time I'd known that there were things about Mum, about me, that were different from everyone around us. There were things we could do that other people couldn't, things we knew about those around us that we couldn't have known. But where Mum had turned her back on what she was, I wanted to embrace that part of myself. I *needed* to. Like a singer denied music, or a writer denied a pen—I needed to find an outlet for this hidden part of me, or wither and die.

She couldn't understand this in me; I couldn't understand her.

And she wouldn't help me. She'd hint about things, but never come right out and explain anything, or answer my questions. We'd argued again that day; that's why I left her alone. That's why it happened.

Today, for the first time in this place, my eyes stay dry. There has been enough crying.

I will find a way to work out who I am—what I can do, and how. It would be easier if Mum had helped me, but there has to be another way.

Quinn must know; she *must*.

I have to make her trust me enough to help me.

But when I get to Zak's place, it doesn't go well.

"No, thanks." Quinn looks at the mustard brown scarf in my hands like it is a dead snake I'd suggested she wind around her head.

"We can't exactly walk up the road together as we are. We're bound to draw attention." The curse of long red hair.

"Well, if you feel so strongly about it, you wear it."

I stare back at her. This is my home; I live here. I'm not the one who needs to be hidden. But then I make my face relax, and smile. "Fine. Sure. It doesn't really matter which of us we disguise, does it?" I fix it round my hair.

Zak comes into the kitchen, back from a run with Ness. "She should sleep well after that many miles." As if she's listening, she flops straight into her basket.

He looks at the clock. "Quick shower and then I'm off to work." He turns to Quinn. "See you this afternoon?" He bends to kiss her, and she squirms away, red creeping up her face.

I start to laugh. "Over here, idiot."

He does a double take. "I just assumed, with the scarf —oh, never mind. You two need to wear name tags or something. Here." He kisses me once quickly, then again, slower. Under my lashes I can see Quinn is watching us, her eyes wide. Then, like she realizes she's staring, she looks away.

Zak heads up for a shower. "Did that weird you out?" I ask.

"What? Zak thinking I was you?"

"Ha! That's weird, too. No, I meant us kissing in front of you."

"No. Why?"

"You were kind of staring."

"Was I? Sorry." Quinn shifts on her feet. "Where does Zak work?"

Changing the subject? "He's helping out at a friend's restaurant. Waiting tables."

"Not great for a possible Cambridge graduate."

I raise an eyebrow. "You're obviously better at getting information out of people than I am. He's just working there while he figures out what he wants to do next. Come on, let's go."

We head out. Yesterday's rain has gone, but the wind is bitter. I hug my arms around myself as we walk the short distance down Zak's road, then up the footpath shortcut to my street. Quinn's eyes dance around us. She was probably too freaked out when she arrived with Zak yesterday to take in her surroundings, but what she finds so interesting today is beyond me—houses, trees. That's kind of it.

I walk up the drive to our house, but turn when Quinn doesn't follow. She's standing on the pavement, staring at our house.

"What?" I say, and walk back to stand next to her.

"It's just . . . it's so . . ." Quinn shakes her head. "Never mind."

I look at our house and try to see what she sees, and fail. It's an ordinary house on an ordinary street in ordinary Winchester. Three stories, garage, extension that doesn't quite match. A bit hodgepodgy, Mum always said.

"Come on," I say. When we get to the front door, I flip the keypad open and enter the code.

"Is that instead of a key?"

"Yep."

Quinn's eyes are wide as we step into the entrance hall. She stares at the gleaming parquet floor, the shiny balustrade on the wide front staircase. She puts a tentative hand out to stroke it.

"You must have to spend hours polishing this."

"*Me?* No, there's a cleaner." I start up the stairs, but something in her eyes makes me pause. "Do you want the full tour?"

Quinn nods yes, so I take her all through the downstairs — the big, formal parlor we never use, the lived-in one, the dining room, the kitchen. When we go into the sitting room with all the photos on the walls, she walks up to a family portrait. I study it with her. Dad is smiling widely. I'm between him and Mum. She's got a half smile; her eyes are distant, somewhere else.

It was around the time this photograph was taken that I first started to suspect her of hiding things. Back then, I couldn't begin to imagine how many.

"That was taken on my thirteenth birthday," I say.

"*Our* thirteenth birthday," Quinn says.

"Yes, of course. What did you do for yours?"

She hesitates. "Nothing I'd want photos of," she says.

"Do you ever give a straight answer to *anything?*"

Quinn shrugs. "Depends what you ask," she says. Then, like she realizes she didn't even give a straight answer to that, she shrugs and rolls her eyes.

"So that's a no," we say in unison, then both laugh.

Quinn looks back at the photograph.

"There is something very wrong with this photo, and with all the rest of them, too," I say.

"Oh?"

"You're not in them. You should be in them; you should have been here. Why weren't you?"

"Isobel may be the only one who knew," Quinn says, her voice quiet.

"Quinn, I'm so sorry you weren't part of my life before, but I hope you will be from now on." I try to keep the desperation out of my voice. *I need you, so much.*

Her eyes are brimming, and so are mine. She blinks, hard.

I take her hand. "Come on. Let's raid my wardrobe. You can take anything you like."

QUINN

Piper's soft sky-blue sweater makes my eyes take its color. I stroke it as I stare into the mirror in Zak's mother's bedroom. I can't believe I'm wearing anything this beautiful; I can't believe Piper let me borrow it. She didn't seem to care at all what I took. And these shoes are so lovely, and they fit perfectly. I suppose that makes sense: identical twins —identical feet.

Can she really have so many fabulous things that a few more or less make no difference to her at all? Piper seemed almost bewildered by my reaction to her home and all her stuff. She has so much, and doesn't appreciate any of it.

This sweater is blue, but it should be green: green for envy. Her life should have been *my* life. I shouldn't be feeling grateful for a few gestures from Princess Piper. I should have a room like hers, with its own TV, laptop, sound system, bathroom, and walk-in closet full of beautiful clothes.

There are so many things in Piper's house I still want to see, to touch—not least Isobel's room. Piper skimmed quickly past it when showing me around. It was full of cupboards and shelves of books and other interesting things, a desk, and a funny piece of furniture that was half like a couch and half like a bed, where Piper said Isobel used to read stories to her when she was little.

Hunger to know more about my parents, about the life

I never had, consumes me. That should be my house. I have every right to be in it. I have every right to everything inside of it.

I should go there now.

There is an uneasy feeling in the pit of my stomach. Just because it *should* be mine, doesn't mean it *is*. And what if someone comes home? But Piper and Zak left to drive her aunts home twenty minutes ago. She said they were doing it because her dad—*our* dad—was out with his brother.

Before I can second-guess any further, my feet are flying back up the road to her house. *Our* house.

I hesitate at the door. The pattern of numbers Piper entered seems clear in my memory. But what happens if I get them wrong? Will some sort of alarm go off, and police swoop down? It looks the sort of place where police would come in a hurry if anything went amiss.

Stomach twisting, I flip the keypad open like I saw Piper do, and push the numbers: 8, 4, 1, 6.

Nothing happens, and I start to panic. Did it take this long when Piper did it? I'm just about to run when a green light comes on. There's a click.

I push the door open and step inside.

The house is so still, so quiet. Hushed. Again my hand touches the balustrade, strokes it. Now that Piper isn't watching, I want to go into every room, drink in every beautiful thing with my eyes, touch each of them with my hands. I can't stop myself from going into what she'd called the sitting room. There's a massive plush sofa in deep red I'd been aching to try. I climb onto it, tuck my feet up. It's gorgeous, so comfy, and faces a fireplace. I long to light a fire, but how would they explain that one when they get home?

Onward, Quinn.

Upstairs, I pause in her—*our*—dad's study door. There is the dark wood of a massive desk, bookshelves, filing cabinets. I know Gran didn't think much of our father. Apart from seeing him across the room at Isobel's funeral, and Zak's assessment that he's not a bad old guy, he's a complete unknown to me.

Isobel's room down the hall is light and bright, with big windows, a window seat. Bookshelves surround the window, and they're full. There are shelves of children's books, from picture books on up. Travel guides. Fiction. Nonfiction. My fingers itch to pull them out one by one, and sit here and read them, read them all. Books were in short supply at Gran's, and many of those that were there were on topics forbidden to me. Until I started working at the hotel with its shelves of books for guests to borrow, my choices were very limited. I glance at the watch Piper lent me: there's only about an hour before I need to clear out. What next?

There's a door at the end—one Piper hadn't opened. I go through it and switch on the light.

It's part dressing room, part wardrobe. One wall is lined with clothes racks, full of pretty things. The opposite wall has a full-length mirror in the center, with slots for shoes and hats either side—silly hats, mostly, more like a bit of decoration that would perch on your head than anything else. Where would you wear such a thing? I try one on, then another, and pirouette in front of the mirror, laughing. What will they do with all of this stuff now that Isobel is gone?

On the wall opposite the door is a beautiful dressing table with a carved chair facing a three-way mirror. I sit down. There's a switch: the mirror lights up at the top. On one side are combs and brushes and a box full of all sorts of makeup, and on the other, a huge wooden jewelry box with many little drawers. My curious hands open one drawer, then another.

This stuff is worth something, even I can tell that. There are earrings and necklaces, silver and gold, many with gemstones. They're too beautiful to be anything but real —sapphires, rubies, diamonds. And there is one heavy gold bracelet with serious diamonds set in the links, and a chunky matching watch.

Would anyone miss a few of these? I could sell them, get out of here, go somewhere new. Gran will be all right. She's strong—they said so. I could leave Piper, her wanting and her questions, behind.

But what about Zak? Somehow, leaving him troubles me more than the others. In short hours, I've come to trust him.

Madness, Quinn. He belongs to Piper. Those kisses said so, didn't they? You wouldn't kiss somebody like that unless you loved him.

Not that I'd know.

No. Forget Zak, too.

Isobel was my mother; I have just as much right to all of this as anyone else. But it would be best to take just a few things and hope they don't notice until I'm long gone. Now, which of them are worth the most? I try to judge based on weight of gold, size of stones. Diamonds are the most expensive, aren't they?

I open another drawer, and my breath catches when I see what is inside. Isobel always wore this bracelet when she came to visit. I take it out and hold it in my hands. Unlike the other pieces, it feels warm, as if it remembers her pulse against it. It's not heavy gold or silver like the others, with things that sparkle. It looks old, really old, like an antique.

I'd been fascinated by it as a child. Once when I reached out to touch it, she jumped like she was stung and smacked my hand away. Now I study it closely. It's made of metal rings of what looks like burnished bronze, looped together in an intricate pattern, with beads here and there in the loops. A stone pendant, like a charm, hangs from it. It's seriously heavy. The pendant's surface looks smooth as glass, but when I run a fingertip across it, it feels uneven. When I close my eyes and touch it, I'd swear there were symbols of some sort carved on the stone.

Holding the pendant in my hand, I have more of a sense of Isobel in this one bracelet than in all the rest of her trinkets. They were mere decoration. Somehow I know: this one had substance. It *meant* something to her.

More than I ever did.

Then I want to throw it across the room, smash it into a

million pieces . . . and hold it close at the same time. I clutch it to my chest.

One tear, two—angry tears or sad tears, I don't know. Two tears are all I dare allow myself. Any more than two can become a flood, and this thin edge of control will be gone.

As I sit, fighting to stop myself from giving in to the darkness, focusing on my breathing—deep and even, in and out—something nags for attention. Did something disturb the silence? I hold still, and listen.

A faint sound, another. Footsteps? And they're getting closer. There is a creak—a door? Is it the door to the room that leads to this one? I should have turned off the lights. It's too late now—can whoever it is see there is light under the door?

I should hide, dive behind some clothes. But I'm frozen in place.

Click.

The door behind me?

I spin round and jump out of the chair, heart thudding. Piper's dad stands in the doorway. Fear rushes through my veins.

"Don't stand there with a scared look, like I caught you at something, daft girl. Any of this you want is yours."

"I . . ." The apology for trespass on my lips dies away. He thinks I'm Piper? Of course he does. I try to take the panic from my face. "Sorry. You startled me, that's all."

He walks close. He's tall, almost as tall as Zak, and smells of mints, and aftershave, and the pub.

"Petal. You don't seem yourself. Is there anything I can do?" I shake my head, afraid: can he tell I'm not Piper? Is it the way I speak? *Stay silent as much as possible.* His hand gently brushes a tear from my cheek. "What do you have there?" He's looking at my hand, still clutched to my chest holding Isobel's bracelet.

I hold it out, dangling from my fingers.

He takes it from me. "She loved wearing this, didn't she? I had trouble getting it off her when I gave her that diamond watch and bracelet set for Christmas. Do you remember?"

He's waiting for an answer, and I panic. I can't lie. But if he's asking, maybe he doesn't expect me to remember. I shake my head no.

"I suppose not. You were very young. Anyhow, she eventually worked out she could wear this one on the top of her arm, above her elbow, and have the diamond bracelet on one wrist, and the watch on the other. She did that now and then to make me happy, but always seemed uncomfortable about it. I learned my lesson and never got her a bracelet again. She seemed to be almost afraid to ever be without this favorite one. She made me promise if anything ever happened to her, to give it to you."

"To . . . me? Are you sure?"

"Of course. She wanted her daughter to have it." He hesitates. "Do you want to wear it? It's all right if you don't."

I pause, part of me scared that something will happen to me if I wear Isobel's favorite bracelet, that she'll be so annoyed she'll make a special visit to the living just to take it off me. But the rest of me *wants* this bracelet around my wrist, more than I've ever wanted anything else. I nod.

"Here. I'll put it on you."

I hold out my right wrist; he does up the clasp. It slips warm against my skin, not as heavy as I expected it to feel.

"Thank you," I say, and hold out my hand, touch the bracelet with wondering fingers. It's a bit big, but not so big that it can slip off. Isobel's bracelet. I shouldn't take it; he means to give it to Piper. But what was it he said? *She wanted her daughter to have it.*

I *am* her daughter. Although a moment ago I couldn't decide whether to smash it or hold it close, now wearing it feels *right*. As soon as it went around my wrist, I felt calmer, more centered in myself.

My fingers close around the pendant.

"Come on. Downstairs for a cup of tea?"

He holds the door open. No choice but to comply. I step through, leaving the rest of Isobel's jewelry behind.

Luckily the phone rings almost as soon as the tea is ready. Piper's dad — my dad, but I can't seem to think of him that way — spends most of the time making apologetic faces to me, and talking about some legal case. It's an hour before I manage to get away, scared the whole time that Piper will walk through the door.

Once I'm out of sight of the house, I pause and study the bracelet. Piper may have said to take anything I liked when we were at the house together, but I'm sure her words wouldn't extend to this. I should take it off, hide it in a pocket, but somehow I don't want to. Shall I try Isobel's trick?

I push the bracelet up my arm, under the blue sweater. I can just ease it past my elbow without undoing the clasp. I slide it far enough to make it tight, so it won't slip down or move around and make clinking noises. There is kind of a bump under the sleeve, but the wool is thick enough that no one should notice.

I hope.

PIPER

When we get back to Zak's house, Quinn isn't there.

Cold panic spreads through me. She couldn't have left me, could she? I run upstairs to check her room again, and breathe easier when I see her things still in place. Surely she wouldn't have left without them. And then one worry replaces another as I walk back down the stairs.

"Where could she be?"

"Don't panic," Zak says. "She was probably bored and went for a walk or something. It's a nice evening, and we were ages later than we said we'd be."

"But what if someone sees her and thinks she's me?"

"What if they do?"

"Well, what if they talk to her, and she says something barmy, and then they think I'm crazy? Or worse, what if she says, 'I'm not Piper, I'm her secret twin'?"

Zak laughs. "You don't really think she'd do that, do you? Anyhow, if she did, no one would believe her. They'd go back to thinking you were crazy."

I don't answer. I don't think she'd do anything to expose who she is on purpose, when she seems very careful not to show anything of herself. But it's the unknown I don't like —having something so important not under my control.

I sigh and flop onto the sofa. Zak sits next to me, and I snuggle in against him. "She could be doing *anything*."

"Like what?"

"What do we really know about her? Apart from the obvious fact that she and I are twins. We don't know anything about where she's lived, or who with."

"Her grandmother. Quinn was raised by her grandmother—I guess she's your grandmother, too."

"Oh. So even *you* know more about my sister than I do. Do you also happen to know *where* they lived?"

"No."

"Maybe you could try to find out for me?"

"No way. I'm not getting between the two of you. If you want to know something, ask her, ask her nicely, and if you take her feelings into account, she might just answer. Anyhow, one redhead on my case is bad enough."

I pinch him, hard, on the arm.

"Ouch." He rubs the place. "That's exactly what I mean." He jumps back before I can get him again, and looks out the front window. "And guess who is walking up the path right now."

The gate rattles. The door opens. Quinn walks through the entrance hall and into the front room. "Hello," she says.

I get up and face her. "Where've you been?"

"Out." She raises an eyebrow in a way that says, *None of your business,* but it so *is* my business.

"Tea?" Zak says, smiling. He stands and puts himself between the two of us.

Quinn hesitates. "Uh . . . all right."

Zak draws both of us into the kitchen, and sits us down

at opposite ends of the table. He fills the kettle while I study Quinn. She's sitting awkwardly, not quite meeting my eye. Why? This isn't how I want us to be.

I sigh, and try a hesitant smile. "I'm sorry if I sounded cross. I was really worried about you."

Zak puts cookies on the table, gives me an approving glance.

"As you can see, I'm perfectly fine," Quinn says.

"So, where were you?" I say, still smiling.

She stares back at me. A muscle twitches in her jaw, and there is no trace of a smile of her own. "I can't think of one good reason why I should tell you what I do every minute of the day."

"I can," I say, trying to keep the anger rushing through me from showing on my face. "I think while you're staying here, we should establish some house rules. And include a discussion of where you can go, and when." I try to use my best reasonable tone, but my usual powers of persuasion don't appear to be working.

"Are you *serious?*"

"Come on, Piper," Zak says. "You're not her keeper. Don't be ridiculous." I glare at Zak, but he doesn't back down. "It's my house, and it's pretty much a rule-free zone. Apart from the put-the-toilet-seat-down one that you imposed and I accept. When I remember." He grins, but the tension is like a living, squirming thing in the room, filling it, and I start to panic. What if Quinn is so annoyed that she leaves?

My head drops on my hands. "I'm sorry. I'm just so

stressed out that I'm not making sense. Please forgive me?" I look up, pleading.

She seems off balance — is she confused by my changes in mood? When I say *forgive me,* people do — Dad, Zak, everybody. No matter what I may have done. Yet suddenly I'm less sure of Quinn than I've ever been of anyone.

Except Mum.

She shakes her head. "Piper, just calm down a little, and everything will be fine."

Everything will be fine. A generality, right up there with have a nice day. Yet somehow when she says it, I believe her. I shake my head, bemused. That is the sort of effect I usually have on people. It's almost like she's me, and I'm her.

"How about we start again?" Zak says.

I walk back late, Zak with me this time. He holds my hand. Before we go round the corner to my house, he draws me into shadows — our goodbye place, under some trees and away from streetlights. He puts his arms around me, but doesn't draw me in for a kiss. His hand strokes my hair.

"Is everything all right, Piper?"

"Hmm?"

"You don't seem yourself. I know, how can you, with your mum and everything, but I don't mean it like that. I know this twin situation is beyond weird, but it's how you're handling it. You have to get to know Quinn as her own person; she's not some sort of extension of you."

I stiffen. "Well, the next time an identical twin walks into your life, maybe you'll know how it feels."

"Tell me. I'm listening."

But there are things I can't tell Zak, things he'd rather not know. I reach up instead, pull his head down, and kiss him until he forgets.

QUINN

I ease the bracelet carefully down my arm, over my elbow, and back to my wrist. It was too tight up there; it left a painful imprint in my skin.

Piper could tell I was hiding something, I'm sure of it. But instead of homing in and asking more questions until I was trapped, she backed off, and I got the very definite impression that this isn't something she usually does. She is obviously a girl who is used to getting her way. Even Zak seemed surprised. It's almost like there's something she's afraid of, but what could it possibly be? She's the one who has everything. I have nothing.

Except this bracelet. I run my fingers over the links, spin the beads, and examine the stone. That's odd: the marks I could feel before with my fingertips but not see—now they're visible. Maybe the light is better in here; they are still quite faint. They're interlocking symbols. I don't know what they mean, but they remind me of something, and I search my memory, trying to work out what.

Goose bumps run down my back when it hits me. Gran had a book with symbols like this on the cover; I'm sure of it. It was high on a shelf in her room downstairs, the one where she did readings. I wasn't allowed in there, and she kept it locked. But once, when I was about ten, she forgot to lock it after a client left, and I snuck in.

I remember I stood there and drank it all in: the strange cards laid out on the table, the markings on the walls, the pretty crystals placed around the room and dangling from the ceiling. The books, including one that was clearly very old. My hands were drawn to pull it from the shelf, to stroke the faded red cover—and it had the very same symbols drawn across it as are carved on this stone pendant.

She found me standing there with the book in my hands. Her face went white. She took it away and dragged me out by the ear. The punishment was severe: I was locked in darkness, with no food and only a little water, for two days.

She never forgot to lock her reading room again. But I remembered every bit of it—a place that seemed magical.

Going into Gran's room was crazy. Keeping this bracelet is crazy, too, but sometimes crazy things must be done, and hang the consequences.

But our *dad*—I make myself try the word on in my mind—is bound to mention it to Piper, to ask why she's not wearing it. I should come clean. I *should* give it to Piper. Failing that, I should get the hell away from here.

But for some reason, I don't want to leave anymore— at least, not right now. I sigh. Is keeping this bracelet from Piper part of the darkness inside me that Gran was always warning me to guard against?

Somehow, I don't think so. This bracelet was *meant* to be around my wrist. Our dad gave it to me, as Isobel's daughter. I am Isobel's daughter.

As thin and as crazy as these justifications may be, I'm keeping it.

Late that night, I'm pulled from sleep. A whisper of a dream lingers on — of running, searching, drawn by a deep hunger for *something,* but I don't know what. It's somehow important to know what it is, but as I reach for the traces of the dream, they slip away.

This bed is too comfy, the blankets too soft, and I'm disoriented, confused. Then memory rushes back: Piper and Zak. I'm at Zak's.

There's a sound; and again. Is that what woke me? At my door — like something scratching. It must be the puppy, Ness. What else could it be?

My heart beats faster; I pull the covers up. *Scratch-scratch* again at the door. I'll never sleep now, unless I open the door and see what is on the other side.

Somehow I prod myself to get up, to walk across the room to the door. Now there is a faint whining sound; she must hear my approach. It is definitely Ness.

Should I ignore her and go back to bed? But then I remember the sad eyes she gave me when I wouldn't go near her.

I know how crazy I look to Zak and Piper, being afraid of a puppy. I know it doesn't make any sense, that it's some strange reaction I don't understand. We never had a dog; I've never been around dogs, other than very occasional chance encounters where I got away as fast as I could. So where does this fear come from?

The Hounds of the Wild Hunt: an involuntary whisper inside. They hunt the moors for the unbaptized, the unwary —murder them and carry them to hell. To hear them is a sign of disaster and death; to see them is worse.

I shake my head. Those are just fables, stories, and nightmares. Nonsense.

That's what I tell myself, but uneasy certainty inside says it isn't nonsense—not to Gran, not to me. But even if it isn't, I'm sure there is nothing supernatural or frightening about Ness.

And here is my chance to try to make friends—without witnesses.

She whines again.

She was really quite sweet, wasn't she? What was it Zak said? *The only thing she might do is lick your face.* She's not a full-grown dog; she's a puppy—like a small child—and she doesn't understand why I don't love her. I sigh. I can relate to that one.

I can do this. I take a deep breath, and open the door.

Ness is lying down now, her head between her paws. Her tail thumps and she lifts her head. But as if she knows not to scare me, she doesn't jump up.

I ease myself down onto the floor, not right next to her, but at a little distance. My heart is thudding like a wild thing; I'm breathing in, out, in, out.

She looks up at me with soft eyes, tail still thumping.

She's a sweet little puppy, not a huge scary guard dog like the ones that killed Isobel.

Ness was there, though, when it happened—when Isobel was attacked. How did she get away? How could this puppy with short puppy legs possibly have got away from big, mean guard dogs? Unless they weren't hunting for her, but only for Isobel. Goose bumps run up and down my back.

I reach out a hand. It's shaking. I pet Ness lightly on the top of her head. Her fur is soft, softer than that huge mongrel cat that sometimes deigns to visit at Gran's. Her tail thumps harder. She suddenly launches herself at me, and I almost cry out but manage to bite it back. She licks my face—an eager, warm, wet tongue and cold nose and soft fur against my cheek—and settles against me. My arms go around her; an automatic, natural thing.

Well. I guess that wasn't so bad.

A door creaks open across the hall. Zak stands there in boxers and a T-shirt, eyes half open, dark hair mussed —gorgeous and unreal, like a wish summoned from a late night dream.

He smiles sleepily. "I thought I heard something, but it looks like things are good here. Good night, Quinn."

PIPER

I run and run. I'm alone, but I shouldn't be. There are others who would join me.

But there is something I must find, something important. I don't know what it is. I hunger, but I don't know what I'm searching for.

I run through the night, past exhaustion, past will. Always running—toward something, and away from something else.

Something I don't want to know . . .

I wake up in tangled, sweaty sheets, caught between fear and anger. Despite the hours of sleep, I feel awful, as if some part of me really has been running all night.

Downstairs, Dad takes one look at me and says nothing about school.

I shake off the dream and bide my time, until at last he's gone.

There is this desperate hunger inside me, like in my dream. Something is missing from my life. I can't move on until I find it, but I don't know what it is.

Mum wouldn't help me. I was hoping that Quinn would, but she is so touchy if I ever try to ask her anything. If she isn't going to give up her secrets easily, I'll try another way.

There has to be *something,* some clue, in this house. If I can find out where Mum came from, will that lead me to an answer?

I'd tried searching when Mum was alive. Her careful eyes watched me all the time. But she's not here now.

The most likely place to start has to be her study and dressing room. She spent a lot of time in there on her own.

I stand in the doorway, caught by memory. There, on the chaise longue — Mum read to me.

She loved books, loved to read to me, the two of us cuddled together. Things were different then, when I was little — before I knew she had secrets.

I start on the bookshelves, and look inside every book, riffle through the pages, look under the dust jackets, then every shelf and drawer.

In the back of one drawer is her smartphone. I turn it on and go through her calendar, for months and months back, but there is nothing out of the ordinary. But she'd hardly have an entry like *Tuesday, 3 p.m., visit secret daughter,* would she? I turn it off, put it back in the drawer, and continue to hunt. I even peer under the chaise longue and unzip its cushions to look inside. But I find nothing.

Then I go into her adjoining dressing room. I feel along every shelf, inside every hat and shoe, every pocket. I don't know what I'm looking for, but there has to be some clue to where Mum came from.

Her dressing table next. I feel along under the drawers,

in them—even go through her makeup box. Then her jewelry box: I pull out every little drawer, examine them all. Nothing. Though one drawer is empty—that's odd. I frown and try to think what's missing, then dismiss it. *Focus on the task at hand, Piper.*

Mum and Dad's bedroom seems less likely, but I go there next, sticking to her stuff. Everything is still in place, as she left it. The aunts suggested to Dad that they could help go through everything to see what to keep, what to give to charity. I put them off so I could have a look through it all on my own first.

Once again, I come up empty. I sit on her side of the bed to think. What else?

Wait. A marriage certificate! If I can find their marriage certificate, won't it say where the bride and groom are from? Someone in history class brought their grandparents' one in when they were doing a family history exercise, and I remember laughing that it had her grandmother's "condition" on it as spinster. I'm sure it had addresses on it for the bride and groom, too.

Where would it be? Dad's study. He's a lawyer through and through—the king of filing. He has everything in alphabetical order in massive filing cabinets.

I race to the wooden cabinets in his study. I pull open the *M* drawer, and rifle through—no marriage certificate. It's not there. What else? *C* for certificate? *W* for wedding? Everything I try comes up blank.

Where did they get married? Maybe it is filed under the name of the church or something. I frown. I can't remember. Isn't that something I should know about my parents? Isn't that the kind of thing parents do—reminisce about their wedding?

Dad once started to tell me about when they met. I concentrate, trying to remember what he said. It was something about being on holiday, but I don't know where. Mum gave him a look when he started talking about it, and he clammed up. I tried him later when she wasn't listening, but he changed the subject: she must have warned him off.

How about her credit card bills? I find the file for her card and flick through the bills from the last year. No petrol or restaurant receipts from anywhere outside of Winchester. But there wouldn't be, would there? Dad would have seen it on the bill and asked where she'd been. She was more careful than that.

I flop into Dad's giant desk chair, defeated. These cabinets are huge. I could go through them from beginning to end, but it'd take me weeks. I've been at this so long now that Dad could be home soon; I need to clear out of here.

I start to idly flick through the in-tray on his desk. It's mostly bills: phone bill, credit cards, funeral bills. Mum's death certificate. And—

Wait. What does that say? I pull her death certificate out of the tray. Rub my eyes, and look again.

Excitement courses through me. Maybe I've been wasting time looking for a marriage certificate that changed my parents into Mr. and Mrs. Hughes.

The name on her death certificate isn't Isobel Hughes. It is *Isobel Blackwood.*

QUINN

Beep-beep.

Zak takes his head out of the fridge, where he was assessing options for dinner, retrieves his phone from the counter, and checks the screen.

"Ah. Piper says she needs to spend some time with her dad, so she's making him dinner. Poor man. She says I should *keep an eye on you.*" He laughs. "What should we do with ourselves?"

"I don't know. But I haven't seen much of Winchester. Are we allowed out of the house?" I raise an eyebrow in challenge.

He stares at his phone again, then assumes a fair imitation of Piper: "Under no circumstances are you to leave the house." He looks up, and grins. "Just kidding! They'll be at home, so no chance of us all bumping into each other. Let's go out. We can have an early dinner at my work before my shift begins." He hesitates. "Unless you want to put on a big hat and dark glasses, people will think you're Piper. I can handle things if anyone gets too close. Are you up for it?"

"Sure, why not?" I managed to get away with being Piper with her dad, the one who surely knows her best. I'm ready to try it with the people of Winchester.

I go up to get ready, find a shirt of Piper's with long sleeves, and shimmy the bracelet back down my arm to my wrist. It was uncomfortable up there, but I didn't dare have it on my wrist when Piper could walk in at any moment. If Zak spots it, he may or may not recognize it; I don't know how much time he spent around Isobel. But with him I'm prepared to take the risk.

When I come down, Zak is waiting in the kitchen. "We really should take Ness with us. Unless I dreamt the two of you making friends last night, that should be OK with you?"

"No problem."

He whistles her in from the garden, clips a short lead onto her collar.

I pause at the door. Pretty as they are, I've had enough of Piper's shoes. They pinch. I put my own boots back on, and we head out.

Zak has a long stride, but I'm used to walking, and walking fast. It was miles to anywhere from Gran's house, over rough footpaths, hills, tors.

Here it is all even, smooth roads, pavements, lovely houses and gardens. How many people there must be to live in all these houses! It's a completely different world, and my eyes drink it in.

Ness pulls at the lead, dragging Zak along, wanting to go faster and faster, then stopping dead to sniff something, before bounding on again.

I pause to get a pebble out of my boot, and Ness runs back around me. I jump, the fear reaction automatic, but I quell it. She noses into my leg to make me keep going, and Zak laughs.

"Border collies are working dogs; they herd sheep. In the absence of sheep, they herd people."

"Haven't noticed any sheep around your place or Piper's."

"No. I did warn her that Ness would need a lot of exercise, but Piper had her heart set on Ness once she laid eyes on her — love at first sight."

"Was it like that with you and Piper?"

"Kind of. Sounds lame, but the first time we met, she just looked at me — and she said that we knew each other. Even though I'm sure we'd never met before. And just like that, it was like something inside me recognized her. Like I was tuned in to her."

"Yeah, pretty lame," I say out loud, but inside, I wonder. Does it really work like that? She just spoke to him, and he knew? We look exactly the same. If he'd met me first, would the same thing have happened?

I shake my head. That is one question that will never be answered.

PIPER

When I finally hear Dad's car pull in, it's late — much later than he said it would be.

The front door opens. There's a pause, then footsteps head this way as Dad follows the lights to the dining room. He stands in the doorway, sees the table set and me sitting there, head in hands.

"Oh, Piper. Did you make dinner?"

I nod, and look down through my lashes. "I just thought we should try to, you know, do the family thing on our own, but . . ." I shrug my shoulders as my words trail away.

He puts his briefcase down, walks over, and pulls me from my chair, gathers me in for a hug, and kisses my cheek. "Sorry I'm late, Petal. First day back; things were a mess."

"It's OK."

"No. It isn't." He starts telling me how he'll make an effort to get out of work at a reasonable time, that I'm important, all the kind of stuff I've heard him say to Mum a million times, but then as if he hears the echo too, he stops and smiles wryly. "Well, I'll do my best, anyhow."

I smile back at him. "Fair enough. I'll go and see if dinner has survived."

He follows me into the kitchen. I lift the lid on the stir-fry pan — I've left it on low for way too long — and pull a face at the dried-out remains.

Dad looks over my shoulder. "We can still eat that. Looks yummy!" He grins.

"Cut the keep-calm-and-carry-on impression. No, we can't. It's tragic. Even Ness wouldn't eat it if she were here."

"Want to head out?" he asks, but I shake my head. "Or order pizza?"

I give him a real smile. "Yes, pizza! Let's do that. Why don't you go and change, and I'll order it." I hesitate. "Should I get the usual?"

He pauses. So many years of family-negotiated toppings — of avoiding anything one of us didn't like. But one of us isn't here anymore. He says finally, "You know, I don't think I could eat a pizza with onions on it. It wouldn't feel right."

"Me neither. Usual it is."

Once he's up the stairs, I shut the door and dial the pizza place we use — the one where a friend from English class answers the phone after school, the one that is never speedy at the best of times. I place the order, then ask her to sit on it for an hour. This may take a while.

When he comes back downstairs, the red wine and photo albums are open. "Do you remember this one, Piper?" Dad points at a photo of me on the bicycle I got for my sixth birthday, beaming from ear to ear. "You'd just pedaled the whole length of the drive for the first time."

"Of course I do. I think you took it just before I fell off and broke my arm."

He turns the page, and there is me with a cast on my

arm, and a quivery lower lip. Last page of the album. I close it, and pick up another.

"Your mother was so annoyed at me that I wasn't running alongside to catch you." He shakes his head. "One minute you were laughing and flying down the drive, the next it was like something had tripped you and thrown you in the air. I couldn't work out how it happened. I should have been nearer. I should have caught you."

"But I wouldn't let you help me, would I?"

"No. You were just as stubborn then as you are now."

I pick up another album and scan through until I catch a shot of me in bed, as pale as the sheets around me. I shut the album quickly. I'd had the worst flu in history. It seemed to come from nowhere: one moment I was fine, and the next . . . well. I'm sure I nearly died. I missed weeks of school, back when I used to like going. And thinking of the hallucinations that came with the fever can still make me shiver, even now.

"Dad, is there another album of you and Mum from before I was around? There don't seem to be any pictures of just you two from way back when."

He starts stacking the albums together. "Enough photos for today. I'm starving—where is that pizza? I'll go and call them again." He starts to get up.

"No, leave it. You know they're slow. Dad, where's your wedding album? I've been through all of them. I can't find it."

"We don't have one."

"Why not? Doesn't everybody want memories of the day they marry the love of their life?"

He shifts in his seat, pours more wine into his glass. "Well, yes, I suppose, but . . . er . . ."

"I'm starting to think you and Mum were never married."

He looks back at me, and confirmation is there, in his eyes.

Despite my suspicions, I'm shocked. "You weren't, were you?"

"Does it matter?"

"Isn't that the sort of thing I have a right to know about my own parents? How could you keep that from me?"

"That was how Isobel wanted it. Your mother had her ideas. You know what she was like."

"Do I? I feel like in a lot of ways, I never really knew her, and now it's too late. I never will."

"Oh, Petal."

"Even just simple things like where she came from, where she lived, who her family were. Her family are my family, too. Now that she's gone, I'd like to find them. But whenever I asked her about them, she wouldn't tell me anything."

"I can't help you much there. She was estranged from her family; I never met any of them."

"Well, you must know where she was from, at least!"

He shakes his head. "Honestly, I don't. I used to ask her now and then, but she would never answer, and somewhere along the way, I decided it wasn't important."

"Do you know why they were estranged?"

"Not the details. But it was something like Isobel not wanting to go into the family business, or do something that her mother wanted her to."

"Sounds like a lame reason to never see each other again."

"Maybe, maybe not. Perhaps Isobel knew what she was doing, and you'd be better off keeping well away from them."

I cross my arms. "Maybe I'm the one who should make that decision. You can't protect me from everything, any more than you could have stopped me from riding that bicycle."

"True." He takes another sip of wine. "I never fully agreed with your mother about keeping things from you. As I said, that was how she wanted it. But now that she's gone . . ."

"There's something you can tell me, isn't there?" I will him to keep going. "Please tell me, Dad. Anything you can about her. Tell me where you met, for a start."

"All right. Isobel was working at a hotel when I met her. I was there on a walking holiday with a few friends. She was so beautiful then, not that she wasn't still." His eyes are wistful. "She lit up the room. And I wasn't exactly a ladies' man."

"No, really?"

He mock-glares. "Don't be cheeky. But anyhow, there

was something about her—and, as hard as it is to imagine, she seemed to like me. Singled me out. She told me we knew each other. I had trouble believing it at first. I mean, she was gorgeous and fun, and there I was—years older, this stuffy lawyer who barely remembered how to laugh. She reminded me."

"And?"

"I guess you could say it was a holiday romance, but it was more than that to me. I went home believing I'd never see her again, and that was the way it should be, but I couldn't stop thinking about her. I called back at the hotel, but they said she wasn't working there anymore, and they didn't know where she'd gone."

"What hotel was it?"

He frowns. "I can't believe I can't bring the name to mind. The sign—it had a two on it. Two something. Two Rivers? Something like that, but that isn't quite right."

"Where was it?"

"Dartmoor."

"So how did you find her?"

"I didn't. She found me. She knocked on my door about ten months later, with you in her arms."

My mouth hangs open. This, I wasn't expecting. "Get out. You mean you weren't even together when I was *born?*" That explains how he doesn't know about Quinn. Mum had twins, but brought only one to him; Quinn she left behind. *Why?*

"No. She said she thought she could do it on her own,

but she couldn't. That the price she'd have to pay to stay with her family was too high. And that you were mine."

"And you just believed her?"

He looks askance. "Of course I did. How could I not? And the timing was right."

"You did wonder, then, if you were counting up the months."

"No. It was my brother and my partner questioning things — looking out for me. Once they met her, they loved her too. She had that effect on everyone around her."

"But why didn't you ever get married?"

"Oh, I asked her again and again. She didn't want to, for reasons I never fully understood."

"But you were always known as Mr. and Mrs. Hughes. You both even wore rings!"

"We went on a holiday, and when we came back, we told everyone we'd eloped."

"Let me see if I've got this straight: my parents weren't married, and they lied to everybody about it. Is Hughes even my real name?"

He shakes his head. "No. Your legal name is the same as your mother's. I wasn't there when you were born; she didn't name a father on your birth certificate."

"So what is my name, then?"

"Does it matter right now?"

"It does to me. It's mine." And I'm willing him to tell me, tell me the name. If I have to confront him with what

I saw on the death certificate, he'll know I've been looking through things in his office.

He drains his glass, fills it again. "Your name is Blackwood."

"Piper Blackwood." I say it out loud for the first time, testing it, tasting it, seeing how it feels on my tongue. "I still don't understand why she didn't want to get married but wanted to pretend that you *were*. I mean, no one would have really cared that you didn't tie the knot. Except maybe your aunts."

"I used to think she didn't want to get married because she'd just disappear one day. Of course she never did, so it wasn't that."

"Unless she meant to, but changed her mind."

"That did occur to me. Your mother could be a devious creature at times. Which worries me, as you are starting to be more and more like her."

"I'll *devious* you! But was there ever any hint as to why she wouldn't get married?"

He hesitates. "Well, there was this one time, she said something about an inheritance."

I look back at him and just manage to stop myself from saying, *Aha! I knew it.* I knew there was something; it was hidden in the things Mum wouldn't say. "An inheritance? Do you know what it is?" I try and fail to make my voice sound casual.

"I don't know. There was something in her family that

could only be inherited by a Blackwood. But I don't know what or where it is. I also think using my name was a way of distancing herself from her family. Or maybe making it harder for them to find her."

"But if she never meant to go back, why would she care whether or not I could inherit something? I wonder what it could be."

"I can't imagine it'd be anything more than what you'll inherit from me one day. Don't go looking for problems."

"Hmm. Can I even inherit from you, as I'm not actually Piper Hughes?"

"Oh, that doesn't matter. When you were very little, we did some legal paperwork to make sure. You're all legally adopted."

"But how can you adopt me if I'm yours anyway?"

"You are my daughter. There is not a shred of doubt on that score," he says, and I can tell he means it, but I'm not so sure. "But as I wasn't on your birth certificate, it was just to make sure things were all legal and proper—it's the lawyer in me, couldn't stop myself. I would have changed your name legally to Hughes at the same time, but Isobel didn't want it that way."

"So let me check I've got things straight now. Isobel Blackwood worked in a hotel, had a holiday fling with you, and appeared ten months later with me in her arms and said I was yours. And wouldn't marry you but pretended she had, getting you to live a lie to everyone you knew. And all to leave the name Blackwood attached to me for some possible inheritance, but you don't know what or where it is. Is that about it?"

"Piper, you make it all sound so crazy. It wasn't like that. Your mother was the best thing that ever happened to me. I adored her. When she walked into a room, it lit up; when she left, darkness fell. Where she came from, why she didn't want to talk about it, never mattered to me. And I've always loved you." He reaches out a hand and touches my cheek.

"I know, Dad."

"But how can I live without her? The sun has gone down, and it won't come up again." He leans back on the sofa, eyes closed, the almost empty wine bottle next to him. A tear squeezes out from behind a closed eyelid and trickles down his face.

I can't move, can't speak. I'm so *angry* at all the secrets Mum kept from me—furious to my core. Dad did it too, but I know why. He was completely under her spell. He had no choice.

I'm also excited—whirling with it all, inside. An *inheritance*. From a family like Mum's, like mine, the possibilities of what it could be? Well.

Mum turned her back on who she was, but that was her choice, not mine. She wouldn't tell me about her family, or where they were. The little she did say was warnings to keep away from them. Yet she made sure I stayed a Blackwood. Why would she do this, unless she knew I'd be drawn to find them? Or maybe this shows they were still linked somehow. I know she visited Quinn now and then—did she visit other family, too? Perhaps they weren't so *estranged,* after all.

I have to find out what this inheritance is. *I have to.*

And there is one person who can help: Quinn. She was raised by our grandmother. She *must* know.

Quinn Blackwood, somehow I will make you tell me.

Dad stirs, reaches for his wineglass.

I intercept his hand and hold it. "Dad, listen to me. You *will* be all right. You'll be sad, but a little less every day, and you'll be all right. And that's enough wine for tonight."

He nods, his eyes searching mine. "You're so like Isobel. When she said something, just that way, I always knew it was true."

Half true, at least. Because that is the secret, isn't it? I'd observed it with Mum and experienced it myself. Say a half truth, say it strongly enough, and they *will* believe.

QUINN

"Hello, beautiful!" This must be Zak's friend Giles, the restaurateur. He's pretty beautiful himself — blond and blue-eyed, almost as tall as Zak but otherwise kind of the opposite.

He rushes over, bends to kiss my cheek, and it's not an air kiss — warm lips linger on skin. Luckily Zak had warned me this would happen, so it doesn't freak me out. Much. I can still feel heat climbing my neck to my face, and bend to fuss Ness so he doesn't notice.

"Take your usual table," Giles says. "Zak, can we have a quick word about scheduling?" And he draws him toward a door at the back.

Our usual table? Zak doesn't turn, but points with his hand to one in the corner by the window. It's early for dinner, and the place is almost empty — just a few people with coffees here and there. There's a bored-looking waitress, a woman polishing glasses at the bar. She waves when she sees me looking, so I wave back. She bends behind the bar, and then walks over with a bowl of water in her hand. She gives it to Ness, who laps at it eagerly.

"Thank you," I say, with no idea who she is. I glance at the door at the back. *Come on, Zak.*

She sits in the chair opposite me. "Sweetie, how was the funeral?"

"Uh, fine." I mean what are you supposed to say to that sort of question? It was great? Anyhow, most of it passed me by as I stared at the back of Piper's head, unable to process that I might have a sister. Let alone a *twin*.

She reaches out a hand, puts it on mine on the table —gives it a squeeze. "Brave girl. Oh, what is that—has Zak given you some serious jewelry?" Her eagle eye has spotted the tip of the stone pendant on my bracelet.

I shake my head and try to pull my hand back, but she's already grabbed it and pulled up the sleeve I'd thought was long enough to hide it.

"Ooooh, this is really interesting. Wherever did it come from?"

"It belonged to my mother," I admit.

"Really? Do you know where she got it?"

She's still holding my hand, studying the bracelet in a way that makes me curious.

"I don't know. She always had it. Does it mean something to you?"

"I can't be sure, but I think I've seen something like it before. Maybe in my shop? Now, where was it . . ."

I hear the door open behind me, and footsteps: Zak? "I'll leave you two alone now," she says, and lets go of my hand. She pats my cheek and goes back behind the bar. I tuck my hands together under the table just as Zak sits down in the chair opposite.

"Is everything OK? What did Wendy have to say?"

I shake my head. "Nothing much. She asked about the funeral and stuff."

He looks at me closely. "But something's rattled you, hasn't it? Listen, don't let her faze you. She's always wanting to talk to Piper for some reason. Seems fascinated by her."

"She said something about her shop. What sort of shop is it?"

"It sells charms and crystals and all sorts of weirdness; she's really into the occult. She works here some evenings when it's closed."

"What does Piper think of her? Does she take her seriously?" something makes me ask.

"Piper nicknamed her Wacky Wendy. Mostly she avoids her. Wendy was probably delighted that you chatted with her. She's all right, really. Just a bit on the ditzy side, and Piper hasn't got a lot of patience."

Zak hands me a menu, and I look down at it without seeing the words. Spells and charms might sound crazy to Piper and Zak, but not so much to me. I've spent too much time around people who believe in them. Whether I do or not, I can't really say. I've seen some strange things, I guess. I know Gran completely believes in it all.

"What do you fancy?" Zak says.

I look back up at him, momentarily confused—at his warm eyes, eyes that are even warmer when he looks at Piper. What do I fancy? Oh. He means food.

Ness suddenly lunges at the window, barking, and my

heart leaps in fright. A woman is walking past with a big dog on a lead, which turns and regards Ness through the window without interest.

"Quiet! Sit," Zak says. "Sit!" he says again, more firmly. And Ness looks torn—glancing between him and the window—but then does sit. "Good girl," he says, and bends to pet her on the head.

Then he turns back to me. "Are you all right?"

"Yes. Sorry, I'm fine. When Ness started barking—well . . . It just really made me jump."

"What happened to you to make you so scared of dogs?"

"I don't know. I wish I did—"

Snarling. Evil, sour breath. Paws on my chest. Heavy paws, and I can hardly breathe. I'm crying silently, fat tears on my cheeks, too scared to make a sound, too scared to move.

"Aye-up." A man's voice. The dog gets off me. Voices—the man's and Gran's.

"That should do," she says. Then they move farther away, and I can hear them no more.

Piper, Piper . . .

Voices repeat a name. Who is Piper?

My sister. The voices think I'm her.

I stir, open my eyes. Zak is cradling my head, and Wendy is kneeling next to him. I'm on the floor?

"Are you all right?" he says.

"Uh, yes. I think so. What happened?"

"You went all white and slipped out of your chair. I think you fainted," Zak says. "Have you done that before?"

I start to say no, and then—

I'm dislocated. Fainting—not fainting. It's something else.

"We must put a stop to it." Isobel's voice, sharp with fear.

I shake my head, push it away—whatever *it* is. A memory? A vision? I manage to stay conscious this time—just. What is happening to me?

Ness squirms up to me and licks my face. I look at her with different eyes, eyes that understand. They made me afraid of dogs. *On purpose.* Why would anybody do that?

I choose not to be afraid of dogs anymore. I wrap my arms around Ness. Tears are springing in my eyes, and I can't stop them.

There are more murmuring voices.

"Come on, beautiful." It's Giles. "I'm giving you a drive home, and your lover boy the night off. It's not that busy. We'll cope."

Home? Piper's house isn't my home. We get him to take us both to Zak's. It's the closest thing to one that I've got.

Later I'm on Zak's sofa wrapped in a blanket, with Ness at my side. My shaking hands are wrapped around a big mug of tea.

"I'm sorry I wrecked your evening," I say.

"Don't apologize. Are you sure you're all right?"

"Yes. No. I don't know. But I will be. Thank you for looking after me."

"No problem."

"Piper will be furious. I've got everyone thinking she's crazy."

He shakes his head. "Nobody thought you were crazy. Your mother just died. You're allowed to faint and cry if you need to."

"Piper won't agree with you. She doesn't lose control." Somehow I know this, even though I haven't known her for long.

"That may be true most of the time, though she does actually have quite a temper now and then. But she'll get over it. So . . . do you want to tell me what happened?"

I put the tea on the table, lean back and sigh. "When you asked me why I was scared of dogs, it's kind of like I had this memory. I've never known the reason, but then it came back to me, like it was happening to me now. I was really young, maybe four or five. And this horrible snarling dog was standing on my chest. He was huge, and I couldn't breathe, and . . ." I shake my head, not wanting to go back there in my mind.

Zak gets up from the chair, sits next to me on the sofa. He takes my hand and holds it.

"I'm sorry I triggered your memory like that. That sounds absolutely terrifying."

"It's fine; I'm not sorry. Now I know why." But I don't

tell him the rest of it. That man and his dog and *my grand-mother* who did that to me.

How could she?

And what was it that I remembered after — the fainting that wasn't fainting — that had made Isobel so afraid?

Ness looks up at me and licks my face. Her body is warm and helps me stop shivering — that, and Zak's hand in mine.

That night, I'm afraid to go to sleep. Every time I close my eyes, I see that snarling dog, feel it standing on my chest.

And hear my gran's voice:

That should do . . . that should do . . . that should do . . .

I scratch the stick into the dirt — drawing the thing from my night-mare.

Teeth. Claws. Eyes. They should be red. How do you draw red eyes in the dirt?

I'm irresistibly drawn to the garden: Gran's special garden. There is a climbing plant on the wall with red berries.

No one is watching. Isobel is with Gran in the kitchen. They only just went in; they'll be ages.

I sneak around and grab a fistful of the berries, then run back behind the chicken shed. A thorn that came away with the berries cuts my finger. I suck on the cut, then squish and squeeze the berries into some sand to make eyes. They make goggle-eyes that stick up, bright red. Perfect.

I sit back on my heels to study my artwork. Do the claws need to be bigger?

Then the outline scratched in the dirt shimmers. The red eyes blink. The creature's muscles ripple and stretch, then strain to pull away from the earth.

The scream escapes from my throat before I can stop it. I run and plow straight into Isobel, almost knocking her over. She grabs hold of me.

Gran is beside her. "Listen to me, Quinn. You are the only one who can send it back."

I'm crying, struggling to run, but Isobel's hands are tight on my shoulders. She turns me around.

"Quinn, open your eyes!" Gran says, and I have to open them. I look at Gran, afraid to look anywhere else. "Put out your hand," she says, and she bends down. I put out my hand, and she puts dirt in it. "Throw this in its eyes, and tell it to go back to dust. Go on. You can do it, Quinn."

Shaking, I raise my eyes. My nightmare creature stands before us: horrible and tall, with long arms and huge claws dragging into the dirt, and I want to scream, to run. But it just stands there, like it's waiting for something. Waiting to be told what to do.

I throw the dirt. "Go back to dust!" I say.

The creature vanishes.

Then Isobel's fingers are in my hair. She drags me into the house and throws me on the floor in the hall.

Gran walks behind. She bends, takes my hands, looks at my fingers stained red, and shakes her head.

"You will never touch my plants again," she says. She says it

that slow, special way that winds through my thoughts and wraps around inside me.

"How did you know to mix blood with the berries?" Isobel demands. "How did you know the form to draw?"

"I didn't! I was just drawing something from a dream, and it needed red eyes, so I got the berries. I hurt my finger on a thorn." I'm crying. My head hurts where she dragged me; my knee banged on the door and it's bleeding.

"She must be lying," Isobel says.

Gran shakes her head. "I don't think so. She didn't command the creature, just made it."

But Isobel locks me in a cupboard for lying anyway. I hear their voices, but not the words. Angry voices. Worried voices. Angry again.

Later Gran unlocks the cupboard; Isobel is gone.

She stares at me very gravely. "You really didn't know what the berries would do, did you?"

"No. I promise, I didn't!"

"You've such a talent for trouble." She sighs. "Quinn, you must guard against the darkness inside you: it finds you so easily. It tricks you. You have to be vigilant and try as hard as you can."

PIPER

Clouds roll in as I walk, and the bare trees look almost black, like my name: Blackwood. I hug the knowledge close.

The rain starts as I reach Zak's front door. "Hello?" I call out, and step through. I timed this carefully, to be alone with Quinn; Zak should have left for work about half an hour ago.

"Hi," Quinn answers. She's on the sofa, Zak's throw blanket tucked over her knees—a book in hand and Ness curled up next to her. Her face is pale, tired.

"You look cozy." I come in, sit on the chair opposite, and pat my knees. "Hi, Ness!" She raises her head. Her tail wags. She looks from Quinn to me, an almost human expression of confusion on her face. But she stays where she is.

"Sorry," Quinn says, and looks abashed. "Want me to shoo her over?"

"No, of course not. Us being twins obviously has muddled her up." That's what I say, but Ness didn't seem to have any trouble telling us apart the other day, and I'm piqued. I shake it off.

"You said you had to spend time with your dad last night. Is he all right?"

"*Our* dad. He's OK. Ish. We just hung out and looked through some photo albums, talking about Mum. And the past. I found out a few interesting things."

She closes her book. "Oh? Like what?"

"We weren't born here. Our parents met at some hotel where Mum was working and Dad was on holiday. They fell madly in love! But he said goodbye and left her behind to go home and back to work."

"Not that madly in love, then."

"He always has been Captain Sensible. Then he realized his mistake and called the hotel. But they said she was gone, and they didn't know where. He was heartbroken. Ten months later, she showed up at his door, with me in her arms. And said I was his. So I was right: he never knew about you."

"Congratulations. You are the Hercule Poirot of Winchester." Quinn's leaning away, arms crossed; she doesn't want to talk about this. But you can't always get what you want.

"Why would she take me and leave you behind?"

"I have no idea," Quinn says. "Maybe it was too hard to carry both of us?"

I raise an eyebrow. "She had to have a *reason*."

Quinn remains silent. She knows something, something she doesn't want to say; I can feel it.

"Our mum was good at keeping secrets. She never told me any of this, and wouldn't let Dad tell me, either. But now that she's gone, he thought I had the right to know stuff." I watch Quinn carefully. "And there's more."

"Oh?" She's pretending she's not interested, but the desires to know and not know are doing battle behind her mask.

I smile. "Oh yes. Mum had a thing about not getting married. They told everyone they'd eloped, but they never actually tied the knot. For some reason, she wanted me to keep her name: Blackwood."

Quinn's eyes widen when I say the name.

"So I'm still a Blackwood: Piper Blackwood. And you are . . ."

"Quinn Blackwood," she says, confirming that she was raised with the same name. She shrugs.

"And now I know where you are from, too: Dartmoor."

She half smiles. "Really? Are you happy? Now that you have the answers to all your questions?"

Dartmoor is a guess, based on where Dad met Mum — one I was hoping Quinn would confirm. But does her smile mean that I'm right, or wrong?

"Not *all* my questions. Tell me, Quinn. About your life, where you grew up. We're part of the same family. I care about you and want us to be close, but how can we be with secrets between us? I want to understand you and why you haven't been in my life until now. Please."

There is uncertainty in Quinn's eyes. She *wants* to believe me, and that is half the battle. I make myself stay silent, don't press her. She looks down; hair falls across her face.

She sighs, raises a hand to tuck the strand back behind her ear.

Clink. Something clinks on her wrist with the movement. She's startled and quickly tucks her hand under the blanket—but not before I see a flash of brass and stone. Mum's bracelet?

"Where did you get that?"

"What?"

"I saw it—Mum's bracelet. It's on your wrist. You must have stolen it when we were at the house. She was *my* mother; it's mine!"

"Hang on a minute here. You were just telling me how we are all part of the same family—she was my mother, too."

"That doesn't excuse stealing. Give it to me; give it to me now." I hold out my hand, but she just stares back at me, defiant, and I'm shocked, unsettled, but most of all *angry*.

"I didn't steal it. *Dad* gave it to me—as you just pointed out, he's my father too, remember?"

"Oh, really? And when exactly did this happen?"

"Are we back to that again? I will not account for every minute of my day to you. He's my father, and if I want to see him, I will."

I'm shaking, actually shaking, with fury. "You mean you went there and pretended to be me to get him to give you stuff?"

Ness jumps down from the sofa, slinks into the kitchen.

The fury in Quinn's eyes matches my own. "Believe what you want. But he gave it to me, and I'm keeping it. What do you care? This is one thing, and you've got a whole house full of her stuff."

"That's not the point!"

"Then what is? That everything is yours, and nothing is mine? That you want me to be part of your family one minute, and don't want me to go near them the next?"

"You do know she never took it off, that she was wearing it when she *died*. Did you wash the blood from it, or was that part of the attraction?"

Her eyes are horrified and angry. Have I gone too far? Panic swirls into the rage. *I need her.* I stay silent, struggling for control. *Why* won't she do what I say? Something has gone wrong, so wrong, and I don't know what it is. My words aren't working.

Quinn's eyes unfocus. She nods to herself, her face quietens, and then her eyes meet mine. "I've had enough of this craziness. I'm either part of your family or I'm not. *You* need to decide. Either we go to our father, together, or I'm leaving and never coming back."

QUINN

Rain lashes down, stings my face as I stomp up the road. I'm soon drenched but past caring. The wild weather suits my mood.

Really, who does she think she is?

To think I was almost going to open up to her. I'm not sure just what or how much I would have told her, but I wanted to give her *something*—just to make her happy. And then she calls me a thief. A twinge inside reminds me that I had been thinking of being just that—of taking some of Isobel's fancy jewelry—before Dad came in. Before he gave me this bracelet. But she went too far, saying that I'd pretended to be her just to get stuff. I never wanted to pretend to be her. It's Piper who wants me hidden away, like a guilty secret.

Is that what I am?

Last night's dream lingers uneasily in my mind— another childhood memory I wished had stayed forgotten. Could I really make creatures from darkness, dirt, blood and berries, or was it just a dream, a hallucination? A guilty secret, indeed. I march on through the rain. Would I really leave if Piper decides she doesn't want me to stay on my own terms? This is still my family too. She doesn't have the right to say if I stay or go.

Piper wants me to tell her all my secrets; she wants me

to hide away and be good. I've spent too much of my life hiding away. I'm not doing it anymore.

And little does she know: I'm not made to be good.

She'll find out soon enough. But not because I'll tell her: show, don't tell. She can work it out for herself.

Before I marched out and left Piper, I told her she'd better stay put at Zak's, in case someone spotted both of us. It was about time she stayed in while I went out — about time she realized what it feels like to be a prisoner.

She didn't say anything; she just watched me go. Her face was white. She somehow can't comprehend that I won't do what she wants, how and when she wants it. Is she really so spoiled that she thinks the world and everyone in it should be slaves to her wishes?

Despite my anger, the cold is starting to sink deep into my bones. What now? I'm hungry, and I haven't got any money. The only place I have to go is Zak's house, and Piper is there.

Or Piper's house. I could go to our dad now and introduce myself. Though if I go there without Piper, he'll probably think I'm her and having some kind of mental breakdown. That's what I tell myself, but maybe I'm just plain scared to do it — to face him on my own and tell the truth.

There is one other place: Zak's restaurant.

I don't know where I am, and I wander some back streets, looking for the way to the main street. That's when I see it: the sign for WENDY'S WITCHERY. This has got to be Wendy's shop. I hesitate at the window. It's hung with all manner of trinkets and charms, crystals and colored stones. There is a warm light on inside, and an OPEN sign on the door.

Should I go in? This could be my chance to find out what she knows about Isobel's bracelet.

Lightning splits the sky; the rain intensifies. Yes.

A bell tinkles as I pull the door open. It's a small shop, and there is no sign of anyone until Wendy steps through a door at the back.

"Piper?" She's surprised, and so very pleased to see me —a warmth that feels real. Didn't Zak say Piper doesn't even like her? I'm teetering on the brink of telling her who I really am, just to have someone—*anyone*—sympathetic to talk to. Someone who might be my friend, not Piper's. But I just stare back at her, silent.

"Oh, poor thing, you're soaked. No umbrella in this weather? Take off your coat; here, sit." She pushes me toward the only chair. She chatters on while extracting my coat, proffering a towel for my hair, and making tea. She passes me a cup. "Now, what has you out on such an awful night?"

"Well, I was thinking about what you said at the restaurant. About having seen my mother's bracelet before— maybe here, in your shop."

"Ah, yes. Let me have a look at it again?"

I pull up my sleeve and hold out my arm, and Wendy peers at the bracelet.

She finally shakes her head. "I must have been mistaken. I don't think I've ever had anything like that here. It seems familiar somehow, but I can't put my finger on where I've seen it before."

"Do you mind if I have a look around?" I ask.

"Of course not! Do, do. I might have forgotten something."

I put the tea down, wander around the shop. There are charms and jewelry, but it's all modern stuff. Some of it is made to look aged, but there is nothing actually old, like my bracelet.

There is a bookshelf along the back wall. It's full of what look like secondhand books, all different shapes and sizes. I pick one up. Spells for love? I make a face. Though, maybe . . .

"Wendy, could it have been in one of these books that you saw the bracelet?"

"Oh, that's a good idea. There are a few, there—top shelf—that have photos of charms and so on." She points out which ones, and I get them down. I take one myself, and she starts leafing through another.

The one I have is mostly about stones and crystals. I flip through it, then pick up the next one.

A musty smell rises as I turn the pages. It looks to be handwritten; the writing is odd and mostly unreadable, but there are frequent drawings, and most are of jewelry. "This book looks more promising," I say.

I flip through the pages, then pause at a diagram of

a bracelet—one that looks very like Isobel's, but without a stone pendant. "How about this one?" I say, and Wendy peers over my shoulder.

"Oh, well done," Wendy says. "That must be where I've seen it before."

I pull my sleeve up again and hold out my wrist next to the drawing.

"You can tell it isn't the identical bracelet, but the pattern of links and beads is just the same. I thought I'd recognized it!" She's beaming.

"Can you read what it says here?" I ask, and point at the writing under the drawing. It's curly and oddly slanted; I can make out some letters, but not all.

She peers closely for a moment, then looks up. "It says that this precise pattern of interlocking rings and beads is the basis of a protection spell."

"A protection spell? What's that?"

"It's witchcraft! Or rather, antiwitchcraft. It stops the wearer from being susceptible to spells."

"Oh. I see."

"But I can't find any reference to combining a protection spell with a pendant of power." She touches the stone hanging from Isobel's bracelet. "I've never seen one quite like this before."

"A pendant of power? What is that?"

"They act to focus the power of the wearer—if they have any, of course—though I'm not sure about this one. It looks a little different from the pictures I've seen."

"Do you know what the markings on it mean?" I hold out my hand, and she studies the pendant closely.

"I can't see any markings on it. Can you?"

I look at it again. The lines are faint, but the pattern they make is clear. Wendy can't see them at all? I shake my head. "No, no—sorry, I must have been mistaken." Shock fills me. I *lied*.

"I've alarmed you, haven't I? Your mother probably just picked the bracelet up at an antique fair or something, without an inkling what it was for. And even if it works, it can't do any harm to stop witches casting spells on you, can it?"

"I suppose not." My mind is racing, my face carefully composed. Most people might look at it that way and dismiss it as being of little relevance to them or their lives.

But most people don't have a grandmother who is a witch.

"If you ever want to sell it—well, I think I could get a buyer very easily, for quite a lot of money."

I'm surprised. "Really? I didn't think it was worth much. I mean, it isn't gold or anything."

"It's the history in it. I've read about them but never seen one before. I probably would be a better businesswoman if I didn't tell you! But I'm sure I could get, oh, ten thousand pounds for it, before commission. At a minimum."

I stare back at her, open-mouthed. "No. Really?"

She nods. "Absolutely. There are collectors who'd kill to get their hands on something like this."

My mind is whirling. That would be quite enough to

get away from here, to start over again. Somewhere new, where nobody knows me, where nobody has any reason to search into my past.

I touch the bracelet, and sigh. *No.* I can't sell it. I don't know why, but I can't. It *must* stay exactly where it is right now — around my wrist.

I shake my head. "I'm sorry, Wendy. I can't part with it."

"I understand. It was your mum's; of course you want to keep it."

We finish our tea. I start to say goodbye, then hesitate by the door. "Wendy, could you do something for me?"

"What's that?"

"Could you not mention the bracelet to me again? I don't want to sell it, but it's hard to say no."

"Of course. I won't mention it unless you do. Now, are you sure you won't borrow an umbrella?"

I shake my head. "No, I'll be fine. I'm just going to the restaurant to see Zak. Are you in later?"

She shakes her head in turn. "It's my night off."

The rain is merely steady now. I almost asked Wendy the way to the restaurant — that would have confused her.

I wander up one street and down another and, after a while, find the main street. The restaurant is near. As I walk, I wonder: why did I ask Wendy to not mention the bracelet again? Do I want to hide its value from Piper, or do I care if she knows that it is meant to be a protection spell?

Maybe Piper already knows how much it's worth, and

that's why she was so upset to see me wearing it. If it was knowledge of its value that had her so furious, not just the fact that I was in the house and our dad gave it to me and not to her.

But despite the logic of that possibility, somehow I know it isn't true. I'm certain that she doesn't know about the protection spell, or the pendant. If she did, it wouldn't have been just left in Isobel's dressing room with the rest of her jewelry.

And for some reason, I'd rather she didn't find out.

PIPER

I'm pacing Zak's front room, but it's too small — it feels like a cage. My world is upside down and confused. The anger starts bleeding away, replaced by an intense feeling of solitude.

I don't understand Quinn. Why wouldn't she give me the bracelet? And why won't she tell me what I want to know? Until now, Mum was the *only one* who wouldn't do what I wanted, the only one who could ever have this effect on me — make me feel crazy angry. Out of control, so I might do *anything.*

Add Quinn to the list.

It's too quiet here alone. I want Zak. I could call him at work, but what if Quinn is there? She doesn't know many places around here to go. How could he explain to Giles that he has to go home to be with me if she's sitting there the whole time?

Or even Dad. He should be home by now — I could go see him.

But it's the same thing. What if Quinn is there? She went there on her own once; she could do it again.

I flop down on the sofa. Ness peeks in around the door from the kitchen. She's hesitant.

We scared her, being all angry, didn't we?

I sigh. "I'm sorry, Ness. I'm OK now. Please come here."

She shuffles into the room and up to me, and licks my hand. I lift her up onto the sofa, and she settles against me.

Everything with Quinn is so confusing. There's a lump in my throat, tears that want to come. With Mum gone, Quinn is the only one who might understand me, who might know what it's like to be as we are: different from those around us. Isolated. I want her in my life in a way I've never wanted anything or anyone before: *I need her.* But everything I do and say seems to push her away.

Stuck here on my own, I feel like I've been excommunicated from my life by somebody I don't understand. What does Quinn want? How do I get through to her?

Wait a minute. Is this how things have felt to Quinn — like she's caged and cut off? With me asking her not to go out without checking, to be careful not to be seen?

That could be it. And if she's angry about feeling cut off . . . then what she *wants* is to feel like she belongs to something.

She wants what I want. If only she trusted me, we could belong to each other.

"And that's how we get through to her, isn't it, Ness?" She licks my face.

QUINN

"Hello, beautiful!" Giles kisses my cheek. "Hope you're feeling better?"

"Yes, thanks — apart from being soaked."

Zak comes out of the back; he's carrying plates of food to a table. He sees me, and smiles — a very warm smile, one that makes me feel all warm inside. *Oh. He thinks I'm Piper.* My smile falls away.

"Are you here for dinner?" Giles asks.

"If that's all right?"

"Always. Let me take your coat and put it in the kitchen. It'll dry better there."

He eases it off my shoulders slowly, standing too close and running his hands down my arms with the coat. I'm confused. How would Piper react? Would she let him flirt with her like this? I don't know, but stop myself from pulling away. He points me at a table in the back corner. Our "usual" one is occupied; it's busy in here tonight.

A glass of wine arrives without request. It's white. Is this Piper's favorite? I sip it; it's cold and tangy.

Zak delivers some menus to another table, then stops by mine. "Is everything OK?" he asks.

"Yes. Just wanted to get out. And I'm hungry, and I can't cook."

He laughs, leans down low to my ear. "That comment doesn't help narrow down who you are." And he's off again.

He didn't assume I'm Piper. Maybe that smile *was* for me?

Again without being asked for, food appears, and it's good: lovely pasta with a garlicky sauce with fresh basil, like they grow in the hotel's kitchen garden. It could be a great benefit having a boyfriend who works in a restaurant — even if he should be at Cambridge.

Zak is *Piper's* boyfriend, I remind myself — not mine. He'll never be mine, just like Piper's life will never be mine. I sigh. That's really why I got so angry with her, isn't it? And it isn't her fault, just like it isn't her fault that Isobel kept her and left me behind.

I eat slowly and linger afterward, and the tables begin to thin out.

Zak finally comes to sit with me.

"So, have you figured it out yet?" I ask.

"What's that?"

"Who I am."

"Well. I'm pretty sure you're Quinn." Though he doesn't *look* sure as he says it.

"Why's that?" I ask, curious how he knew.

"You've been very polite. Though you could just be trying to trip me up."

"I see. Anything else?"

"You ate the daily special without comment. Piper doesn't like pesto."

"Though I could just be trying to trip *you* up."

He laughs.

"Can you really not tell?" I say, and my words are wistful. Somehow I'd like it if he could.

"You're Quinn." This time he says it decisively. "Piper would have hit me by now for being wrong."

I reach out and punch him in the shoulder, and his look of doubt returns.

I shake my head. "You're right; I'm Quinn. Sorry. I hope it's all right that I came here."

"Of course it is. Is everything OK?"

I shrug. "Piper and I kind of had a disagreement. I had to get out."

"Ah, I see. Was it anything to do with you not wanting to tell her stuff?" I raise an eyebrow. "Just a guess," he says.

"That was part of it," I admit. "Also, I don't want to be hidden away anymore. If I'm going to stay in Winchester, I need to be out in the open, and be myself."

Zak nods, his dark eyes full of sympathy. He's on my side about this, I can feel it. But what if he knew all the rest?

I'm not sure I want to tell him about the bracelet, but if I don't, she will. It may be better to get my version of events in first. So I tell him the whole story—about going to their house, and our dad giving it to me, thinking I was Piper. He just listens, doesn't comment. His eyes aren't judging, but I have to ask.

"Do you think I'm wrong to want to keep it?"

He shakes his head. "There's no easy right or wrong

with this one. I understand why you'd want something of your mum's, something you remember. It's only natural. It's not fair of Piper to get so upset over it when she has had so much more of your mum in her life, and as far as your dad goes, you are still his daughter."

"I'm sorry to put you on the spot like this. It must be hard to get caught between us."

"It's fine. I've known Piper for a long time. I know she isn't always the easiest person to get along with. She's stubborn, and she's always very . . . focused. On what she wants." A wry smile.

"And she wanted you." I can't believe I said that. Has just one glass of wine made me speak without thinking?

He laughs. "I like to think I had some say in the matter."

But you didn't. Unease prickles up my back at this unbidden thought.

"Not that I'm trying to change the subject or anything," he says, "but can I ask you something? Don't answer if you don't want to."

"All right; go." I'm expecting one of Piper's questions — the who, what, where, when, or why of my life.

"Apart from Piper being annoying about it, why don't you want to answer questions about where you come from?"

This is a new one. I stare back at his open, warm eyes. They don't hide secrets; at least, not megasecrets like mine do. Would he even understand? But I want to try.

"There are a few things mixed up together, so it's hard

to give an answer—there isn't *one* answer. My life hasn't been like Piper's. In a lot of ways, it hasn't been that great." I hesitate. "I'd have to really trust somebody to want to tell them about it, but even then? To be honest, there are things I just don't want to talk about."

He reaches a hand across the table. His fingers are warm, and lace between mine. "That's fine. Talk—or not—when you're ready. Do you want me to try to explain that to Piper and ask her to back off?"

"Would it do any good?"

"Probably not."

"Best to leave it, then, I think."

"Can I make a suggestion?" he says, and I nod. "Tell her what you just told me."

The light, warm pressure of his fingers is still on mine, and I add silent words: *If I ever was ready to talk, it'd be to you, Zak.* He lets go abruptly, as if he suddenly realizes we're holding hands, and not just in a friendly way.

"I've got a few things to do here before I can leave. Do you want to wait for me, or walk back alone?"

"I'll go. I think I need to face Piper on my own."

"OK. Try to make it up with her. Believe me: it makes life *much* easier." He gives me another wry smile, and then goes to fetch my coat.

The rain has stopped. As I walk, I think about what I said to Zak.

Is this an issue of trust—that I don't trust Piper? Is

that why I have this huge reluctance to tell her things? Or maybe it is because the things Piper wants to know are the *only* things I have that she doesn't. She has so much, and I have so little.

I walk slowly, holding my arms close around myself against the chill, coat still damp. I didn't tell Zak about my ultimatum. What will Piper say?

It was so tempting earlier to open up to Zak completely. But there are things I *must* hide. I can't let Zak, Piper, or anyone else learn the truth: the real reason I was isolated and kept away from my family — why I didn't even know Isobel had another daughter, or that she lived with my twin and our father.

Like Isobel told me many times: it's the danger, the threat, that I present. That Gran warned me about, over and over again.

The darkness inside me.

PIPER

It's late when the door finally opens. Ness lifts her head from my knee. "Stay," I whisper to her.

Footsteps in the entrance hall are slow, hesitant. Then Quinn stands in the doorway, the light from the hall a halo around her red hair. I still can't get over the weird feeling I have when I see her: like looking at myself from outside of me.

"Hi," I say.

"Hello," Quinn answers.

Silence stretches. As if Ness remembers the arguing earlier, she is poised, looking to Quinn, to me, and back again.

"I'm sorry," we say, in unison. Then both laugh — a little awkwardly, but it's better than nothing.

"We need to talk," Quinn says.

"Yes."

Quinn sits in the chair opposite the sofa, her back straight. "I'm sorry we argued. Maybe I could have been more tactful about it, but I meant everything I said."

"You were right. About some of it." I'd been practicing saying the words before she got here — the *you were right* part, so I could put conviction into the delivery, but never meant to add *about some of it.*

"Which bit?" Quinn is amused, and I try not to let it rankle.

"I haven't been fair. This is your family, too; not just mine. You should be part of it if you want to be. And it isn't up to me what happens, or how. It's up to you."

Her eyes open wider. "Really?" she says, voice hesitant. "Do you mean it?"

"Absolutely."

"So the two of us could just go to our dad right now, and say, 'Surprise! There are two of us!' And you'd be all right with that?"

"I wouldn't put it that way. But if you want to tell him, it's your decision."

"So you're *not* all right with that."

The tricky part. "It's just that Dad has really been struggling with things. Let me tell you what he said the other night. That with Mum gone, it's like the sun has gone down, and it won't come up again. It would destroy his memory of her to know she kept his other daughter away from him. I don't think he can handle another shock so soon after her death."

"Yet you're saying it's my choice. So if we go to him and he has some kind of nervous breakdown, it's my fault. And if we don't, you've got things the way you want them."

"I didn't say it was an *easy* choice. But there is another option."

"What's that?"

"What you've already done. You went to my house, and Dad thought you were me. You could do that again. You could get to know him a little and see for yourself if you think he can handle suddenly being the dad of twins. Then you could start to be part of our family. You belong with us."

"But I'd have to be there as you."

"Just for a little while. We can coordinate times and places between us so there is no chance of running into each other when we shouldn't. And you can check it all out and then run for the hills if you want to. If you don't want to run, if you want to stay, at least you'll know what you're getting into."

"What about the bracelet?"

"How about you keep it for now, and if and when we tell Dad about you, we'll leave it to him to decide who gets to have it." As I say the words, I struggle to keep my face neutral, to hide the anger that Quinn has Mum's bracelet. I know Dad will never refuse me anything. I'll get it back.

Quinn hesitates, then nods. "I guess that's fair. But there is one more thing we need to deal with."

"What's that?"

"There are things about my past I don't want to talk about. Letting me go to your house isn't going to change that." The way she says this, it sounds like she's thought about what to say and how to say it. Has she been rehearsing her lines on the way here like I was before she arrived?

"I won't lie — not knowing stuff makes me crazy with curiosity. But it's up to you what you want to tell me. I'll try to back off."

"Well, as long as you *try*." She's amused again; I ignore it.

"All right, then. Do we have a deal?"

A pause. And then she smiles, and it looks like a real smile. She holds out her hand and I take it in mine to shake. "All right. Deal."

QUINN

I feel like a secret agent, like George Smiley right out of a John le Carré novel on the dusty bottom shelf at the hotel. A long list of Piper's dos and don'ts is tumbling through my head as I walk over to her house. *Our* house: it's mine, too. Isn't it? Piper has even given me her fancy smartphone so I can call or message her tablet with any emergency queries.

There is a car in the drive and lights on upstairs, as Piper predicted. He always waits up for her, she said, and will probably be in his study this late. I'm to go to the kitchen, make two cups of tea, then take them upstairs — this is our evening ritual.

I enter the door code and pause. Which way is the kitchen? I start across the room, then retrace my steps to take my shoes off and leave them by the door.

Tea bags are in a canister in a cupboard near the kettle. Which cupboard? I open doors to find the right one, then lift lids off canisters to find the one with tea bags. The mugs are waiting by the kettle as she'd said they would be. Piper's favorite has a picture of a dog on it — Jinny, her dog since Piper could barely walk, who died of old age last year. Dad's is a massive red mug, a present from Isobel.

When Piper was telling me everything I needed to know to come here and masquerade as her to our father, she didn't mention that she might have doubts about whether he really is our father. Dad had told her that Isobel turned up with Piper and said she was his. When Piper told me this, she looked skeptical about whether Isobel was telling the truth.

But I can't believe Isobel could lie about that. After living so long with Gran and Isobel telling me lying is dangerous and brings the darkness, how could she herself possibly lie? He *must* be our father.

The kettle boils. My tea at night is weak and milky; Dad's is strong always, with only a splash of milk.

I walk up the stairs, carefully balancing the two mugs of tea. The treads are deep, a little deeper than most, and I concentrate to avoid stumbling, feeling like an idiot that I'm finding *stairs* tricky. It's the bundle of nerves deep in my belly that makes me feel like this. The last time I was here —when Dad gave me the bracelet—meeting him was an unexpected shock. I didn't have time to get nervous or think about anything. This time is different.

The hall carpet upstairs is plush underfoot. A door is ajar, light spilling into the hall—that is his study.

I hesitate, take a deep breath in, and square my shoulders. No; look relaxed. I deliberately relax them again and walk up to the door.

He's at the desk, tapping away at a laptop, files arranged neatly around him. He looks up.

"There you are," he says. "I was about to send out a search party."

"Sorry. I went out for dinner with Zak and got back a

bit late." I reach across to put his mug on a coaster next to his laptop.

"Enough of these delaying tactics, Petal. You need to get back to a normal routine. Go back to school tomorrow."

"All right."

He looks surprised. Would Piper have argued?

"Get off to sleep, then; an early start will do you good."

My stomach is in knots. This is where Piper said to put my tea on a coaster on the desk, walk around, and give him a hug. And I'm not sure I can do it, or that I want to do it, or what it will be like.

"Is something wrong?" he says.

"No. Yes. I don't know." And I'm frozen in place.

And he gets out of his chair and walks around the desk. He takes the cup of tea from my hand and puts it on the desk without bothering about a coaster.

He takes my hand. "Now, Piper. What did you tell me the other night?"

I stare back at him with no idea what she might have said, but he doesn't wait for an answer.

"It'll get easier. Day by day." He reaches to pull my hair off the side of my face. "And getting back to all your usual things — classes, friends, even some homework — will help. Won't it?"

"Does being back at work help you?"

"Ha. Caught out! Not really. But it fills the hours. And pays the bills, so no choice, really. And you need to go to school, so the same applies."

He leans down, slips an arm across my shoulders. I lean forward a little. Aftershave and coffee, and rough stubble on my cheek; seconds only, then released.

"Go on," he says.

I turn for the door.

"Wait. Your tea?"

I step back, pick it up, and hope I remember the way to Piper's room. I go there as fast as I can without slopping tea all over the carpet. Tears unaccountably fill my eyes; my hands are shaking. That was my actual *father.* Someone I thought I'd never know anything about, let alone meet.

Now I even know how he takes his tea. I know that he drinks coffee, too; he must be a caffeine freak. I know that he has stubble on his cheek this late at night, and calls me *Petal.*

No. He calls Piper Petal, not me. What would he call me if he knew who I was?

Not a bad old guy, Zak said — not quite the evil personified that Gran hinted at. It's so very odd to be masquerading as his daughter when I *am* his daughter — both are true at the same time. Not that he knows anything about it.

I shut the door behind me. Safe in Piper's room — my room, at least for tonight — and I want to throw off this strange mix of emotions. I want to see and touch every single thing in this room. I want to try on her clothes, figure out how to use the sound system. I want to feel what it would be like to be her.

I already looked in her closet when she let me go through and pick what I wanted to borrow. We didn't have much time, and Piper's eyes were on me. I felt apologetic, tried to choose plainer clothes, things she'd be less likely to miss. Now there are no eyes, no clock.

I pull out a beautiful red top with a plunging neckline, a shiny black wrap, a narrow black skirt—I try them all on. I find a cupboard full of boxes of shoes and laugh to watch myself in the mirror, tottering across the floor in the highest heels I've ever seen. I sweep my hair up and study myself: if it wasn't for my hair, no one at the hotel would even recognize me.

I try on outfit after outfit, then pile them high on the bed. Then in a drawer I find a furry, fuzzy all-in-one that looks like a giant puppy, complete with a hood with puppy ears. I pull that on and laugh again.

I sit at Piper's desk, still in the puppy suit. Schoolbooks and novels are mixed haphazardly on the shelves. Photos in frames on the wall, of Piper with friends, family. And one of a dog and a small Piper, maybe eight years old—it must be Jinny, the dog on her mug.

The novels are new; some even look unread. I scan the blurbs and choose one, cross to the bed, and push the clothes to one side.

Piper's bed is *so* comfy, and huge—as big as the four-poster ones I make up at the hotel. She's got, like, what—four pillows? I'm running my hands over the soft duvet cover when a buzz in my bag makes me jump. Piper's phone?

I take it out, and look at the screen. It's a text. From Zak.

Hi, gorgeous girl, I'm on my way. How did you convince your dad that you can stay the night? Can't wait xxxx

What?

Oh. Piper must have told him she's staying at his place tonight, but not that I've got her phone. I'm momentarily confused about how she got word to him without the phone, then remember — she'd showed me her messages go to both her phone and her tablet. That's how I can message her if I need to. She must be able to message from the tablet as well.

She knows I'll see Zak's message.

Gorgeous girl.

I couldn't figure out earlier why Piper was letting me do this. Just hours ago, she was furious that I'd been to her house and pretended to be her with her dad, and then tonight she's suggesting I come here and do it again?

Stay the night.

And she didn't set any conditions, didn't insist I'd have to tell her anything. I was wondering why she was letting me do this, what was in it for her, but it seemed too good to pass up, the chance to be here, to see what it is like to live her life, even just for a little while.

So. Basically, she's got rid of me so she can be alone with Zak. She's got me covering for her here, with her father, so she can be with Zak.

For the night. The whole night.

Will they be in his room, or will she sleep in mine? Or maybe they'll both be in mine.

I shake my head. It's not my room; it's Zak's mother's room, and I'm sure it's the last place he'd take Piper. That room isn't mine, not at all, any more than this one is. Nothing is really mine, is it?

Can't wait.

I try to keep my thoughts away from what might happen there tonight, but I can't.

PIPER

Ness jumps up and runs to the door: a puppy early warning system, something she only does for Zak. Somehow she always knows he is on the way well before he is within sight or sound. Sure enough, about five minutes later, I hear the gate.

He opens the door and steps through, a happy Ness bouncing around his feet. He smiles when he sees me. "Piper?"

"Who else?" I say. I sniff, and wrinkle my nose. "Let me guess. Garlic, basil. Pesto. Pasta night at the restaurant?"

"Right as always." He walks across the room, takes my hand—pulls me up off the sofa and wraps his arms around me. I let my body relax against his. He bends down, nuzzles into my neck. "I could shower." His words are muffled in my hair. He pulls away a little, looks around. "Where's Quinn?"

"She's not here. We are completely alone." I half close my eyes, and give him a slow smile.

His eyes sparkle. But he doesn't lean down to kiss me. "Where is she this late at night?"

"At my house. She's . . . me for the night."

He raises an eyebrow. "Does that mean that right now you are being *her?*"

I pinch his arm. "Don't be daft."

"I hear you two had a bit of an argument earlier. I hear she wants to openly be herself. So why is she at your house now as *you?*"

"It's called *compromise.* Apparently."

"Oh, is it? Sounds to me like you're getting things the way you want them. I don't think it's good for Quinn to be pretending to be somebody else."

"Oh, is that a fact? What makes you such an expert on *my* sister?"

"Well." He smiles. "I'm a bit of an expert on you." He runs a hand up my arm, but I yank it away.

"We're not the same person, no matter how we look."

He sighs. "Well, yes. I am well aware of *that.*" He turns, walks into the kitchen. I hear the clunk of the kettle, the tap running.

I follow him. "What is that supposed to mean?"

"I just think that you should try putting yourself in Quinn's shoes. Think what it might be like to be her. She's got this vision that you've had this wonderful family, all cozy with your mum and dad all this time. While she's been—"

He stops.

"She's been what? Do you know things you haven't told me?"

"No." But he turns away to pour the tea.

"If you knew something, you'd tell me, wouldn't you?"

"What I was trying to get at is this," he says. Evading my question? "She thinks you've had the perfect family, the perfect life. Something she hasn't had. Maybe you should tell her the truth. Tell her how things really were with your mum. How you weren't getting along at all, could barely be in the same room with each other. Maybe then she'd be more willing to open up to you about her life."

I shake my head. "No. No! It wasn't like that."

"Yes, Piper. I'm sorry, but it was."

I sleep on the sofa with Ness — furious with Zak for reasons I can't explain even to myself. How could he speak to me like that? It's Quinn, isn't it? He's taking her side against mine. And it's anger that makes me lose control. I know that, but I couldn't stop its heat.

And the things Zak said about my mum. We didn't always get along, but not the way he made it sound. *She loved me.*

All the same, there are doubts inside, which he stirred up. I know she loved me; she *did.* So many memories I can count and relive say it must be so.

But are they all from when I was small?

After I became aware of our . . . abilities, Mum looked at me differently. She watched me, almost like she was afraid there was something inside me that might get out.

It was when we were in a furious argument that she told me about Quinn. She said we could never return to our past because of my twin, that if we met, Quinn would destroy us all. That was why Quinn was kept locked away: she had darkness inside her. And the way Mum said it, it was like she thought I should be locked away, too.

Or instead.

Almost as soon as she said it, I could see she wanted to call the words back — to undo finally telling me something that was my birthright.

Our birthright — Quinn's and mine, to be together.

But I couldn't tell Quinn I knew about her when she didn't know about me.

Quinn must trust me. She must love me to trust me. I must be lovable, all the time.

I sigh, the pain Zak aroused raw and gaping inside. I tried that with Mum, but it didn't work, did it? She never loved all of me, not as I really am.

I turn and struggle to get comfortable on the sofa. I don't want to be in Zak's mum's bed — the one Quinn has been sleeping in. The pillow her cheek has rested against, red hair a stain like blood on white sheets. The blankets that have covered her body as she loses herself in dreams.

The space there now is more hers than mine.

Solitude hangs heavy on me; it weighs me down. No one who thinks they love me — Dad, Zak, my friends — really knows *me,* all of me, so no one has ever truly loved me.

Quinn is the only one who might.

"Come on, up you get." Mum holds out a hand, and I clamber up next to her.

"Story!" I say.

"Which one today?" She kisses my forehead, wraps an arm around me. "As if I need to ask."

There's a pile of books on the table next to her. She holds one up —something thick, grown-up, and boring looking.

"This one?" she says.

"No." I giggle.

"Are you sure? It's really very interesting."

"No. Puppy!"

"Oh, now there's a surprise. OK, then." She finds the picture book with the puppy on the front, draws me onto her lap, and begins.

I know the words and chime in, lean back into her as she turns the pages, her arms a warm nest. Her bracelet clinks against the book, and I reach for the pendant that hangs there to hold it in my hand.

"No, baby. That's not for you."

She pulls her hand away, but I don't let go, and then . . .

We are somewhere else. I'm not on Mum's lap; I'm not at home. I'm standing in front of her on a stone floor, and it's cold. Where am I?

Mum smacks my hand hard, and tears rise in my eyes. I let go of her bracelet.

I look up. Her eyes are dark and wild and looking at me, but not the way they usually do.

I step backwards. She steps forward.

"You must learn to behave," she says, and raises her hand.

QUINN

Bzzz. Bzzz.

I open one eye. Is that an alarm? I find the clock: 7:20 a.m. My head is pounding after a night of little sleep and unwelcome dreams.

The last one was so strange: one minute it was like I was in this house, but as if it were many years ago. I was little, and Isobel was reading me a story? What a fantasy! But then it went back to more the past as I know it—at Gran's house. A hard smack to my ear.

The clock is silent; maybe that was a dream, too. My eyes settle closed again.

Bzzz. Bzzz.

They snap open. That seemed to come from next to me: ah. On the bedside table—Piper's phone. I'm afraid to pick it up, afraid to look at the screen. What will it be this time? Zak, with *Dear Piper, thanks for a ravishing time last night.* Or maybe one from Piper for me: *Thanks for letting us spend the night together. Here's a photo of us in bed.*

Don't be an idiot, Quinn. I sit up and reach for the phone. It buzzes again; it's not a text. Someone is calling. According to the screen, somebody named EB.

I hesitate, then touch the screen to answer. "Hello?"

"Hey, Pip, was about to give up on you. Are you coming to school today? Do you need a lift?"

I pause, unsure what to say. Dad said to go to school. EB —whoever she is—will pick me up. Piper is probably very busy with Zak right now, anyhow.

If I go, I'll see what it's really like to be Piper for a day: school, friends, the works.

Piper wouldn't like it. That makes me smile: isn't it about time she feels what it's like to not get her own way all the time? But can I pull this off? I've never been to school before. This could be my one chance to see what it is like. I've always wanted to know. I push away the nerves.

"Are you still there, Pip?" EB says.

"Sorry, yes. Yes, I'm going to school. Thank you for the lift. What time?"

"Same as always. See you in an hour."

She says goodbye, and I head for the bathroom and a hot shower. I find fluffy clean towels in a cupboard. Then wrap myself in a robe.

Now, what does Piper wear to school? Last night when I was looking through Piper's endless closet, somewhere I saw a school blazer. But where?

There's a knock.

The door opens; Dad peers in and holds out a cup of tea. "I'm impressed. Up already? So you really are going to school?"

I smile. "Yes! Though it all feels a bit strange and confusing, like I haven't been there in years. I have a feeling I won't know what classes to go to. I'm not even sure what to wear."

"Not falling for the *haven't got a thing to wear* line. Though it was easier last year when you still had to wear a uniform." He puts my tea down on the desk, surveys the clothes all over the bed with a raised eyebrow, but says nothing. "Do you want me to drive you?"

"No, thanks. EB is coming."

"Give Erin my regards," he says, and leaves, shutting the door behind him.

So, EB is Erin. That's one question answered. And no uniform—a disaster averted. That blazer I saw must be from last year. Does that mean I can wear *anything?*

I rummage through the wardrobe, pulling out jeans, colorful tops, everything that catches my eye, and laying them across the bed.

There's another knock on the door. It doesn't open. "Come in," I call out.

A girl peers in: willowy, blond, and immaculate, in a very expensive-looking jacket. Could this be Erin?

"Aren't you ready yet? Erin sent me up to check."

Not Erin, then. "Sorry. I can't seem to work out what to wear."

"Good to see some things never change!"

"Help me?"

"*Really?* Cool." She smiles like I just gave her a prize and sifts through the stuff on the bed, then peeks in the closet. Low-slung jeans, beautiful leather boots, and a gorgeous pale blue top with matching jacket are held up for my approval.

"Looks good to me. Thanks!" She turns while I pull them on.

"Come on, then," she says, and I follow her toward the door. She pauses, looks back at me. "Where's your bag?"

"My bag? I'm sorry. Maybe school today is a mistake. I'm just not with it." My guts are churning in panic; what makes me think I can do this? Piper didn't brief me on school. I don't know where the bag is; apart from a few guesses based on the books on her desk, I don't even know what subjects she's taking.

"Oh dear, of course you're not." She hugs me, and a waft of lovely perfume follows the swish of her hair. "Don't worry. I'll help you, I promise. It'll be fine."

She turns back, looks around, then reaches under my desk and pulls out a school bag. She fishes around the shelves for a few books and puts them in, then hooks an arm in mine and pulls me toward the door.

Waiting in the front of the car is Erin, our dark-haired driver, and a blond guy, cute, with a cheeky smile. He jumps out when we approach and holds the door for me, giving me his front seat. Erin rolls her eyes.

We head off, and they are all being extra nice. Maybe they are always extra nice to Piper, or maybe they're not used to being around a friend with a dead mother. They seem a little unsure what to say to me, which suits me fine; hopefully they'll put any strangeness in how I am down to Isobel's death. And they seem happy to chatter to each other while I stay quiet, with glances and smiles cast my way now and then — ones that say they care for Piper and they're worried about her.

Piper's phone beeps in my pocket. I pull it out: think of the devil, and there is her text.

> Hi, it's me. How'd it go last night? Can you come
> here now so we can swap back?

No; actually, I can't. I smile. I bite my lip for a moment, thinking, then text back: *All was fine last night, just heading to school with Erin and friends. So you'd best lie low for the day.* I put the phone back in my pocket on silent. It starts vibrating furiously. She's calling? I ignore it. She had her fun last night; today, I'll have mine.

PIPER

I stare at Zak's landline phone in my hand. She's not answering? She's going to my school, with my friends? Pretending to be me? I'm not angry; I'm more . . . stunned. I can't believe it.

There's no way she'll get through a whole day without everyone thinking she's completely crazy—thinking *I'm* crazy. She doesn't know where anything is, what anyone's name is, nothing. How does she think she can pull this off?

"Good morning." Zak walks through past the sofa, Ness's lead in one hand and his jogging gear on. He pauses, turns. "Are you OK?"

I shrug. "Ish."

"Still angry?"

"Ish." I sigh and look down through my lashes, lean back on the sofa. Zak crosses the room and stops in front of me.

"I don't like it when we fight," he says.

I look up. "Then don't do it. Just agree with me at all times."

"That is *so* never going to happen," he says, with a ghost of a smile.

"Not when I get angry," I reply. "I lose my touch." Very true.

He leans down, gives me a quick kiss. "Breakfast together when I get back?"

I shake my head, the beginnings of a plan starting to form inside. "Nope. I'm going to school today."

"Good for you. Come by after?"

"OK."

He clips Ness's lead onto her collar, and they head out.

So. Quinn has gone to school. There's not much I can do about it now, but at least this means I don't have to. And there are other things I can do today.

I smile.

QUINN

So many eyes. So many nuances of feeling behind them—sympathy, curiosity, and some other thing that is well hidden and not entirely pleasant. So not everyone loves Piper, but they keep it to themselves: Her return after her mother's death and funeral—via her twin-imposter, me—is acknowledged by everyone, in a blur of words and faces that makes me dizzy.

The bell finally goes. Blond girl seems to have taken seriously her promise to look after me today. She leads me along, down halls and up stairs, through a claustrophobic onslaught of warm bodies rushing in all directions.

Erin and the cute guy from Erin's car all go to the same classroom as we do. I pay close attention when the teacher starts calling out names, trying to remember them all. So blond clothing advisor is Jasmine; cute door-opening guy is Tim. I'm so busy memorizing names that Erin has to elbow me to respond when the tutor calls out *Piper Hughes.*

"Sorry. Here," I say. Not my name, but it's not Piper's, either, is it? It should be Piper *Blackwood.*

The teacher is in the sympathy camp. She smiles. "It's good to have you back, Piper." She carries on with calling out names, and I continue trying to remember them all and the faces they belong to.

Just as I'm wondering what subject this will be, the bell goes again. Was that just to see who is here? Everyone rushes out and I start to follow Erin, but Jasmine pulls my arm. She shakes her head. "You really aren't with it today, are you? Come on. We've got English now."

I follow her down more endless halls into yet another classroom. Other students file in.

There are student presentations today, so it is easy to sit back and just listen. They're doing Sylvia Plath: who is she? Sounds like she had some serious issues, and I'm drawn into wanting to know more about them, to read her work and find the hidden threads inside her poems. Around the room some faces are interested, some are puzzled, some are masks as minds wander.

There are so many things they all seem to know that I don't; things I itch and burn to read, study, and figure out. Even though many of the students seem to find being here a torture, they don't know what they have — what is being given to them in this place.

So this is school. I often wondered what it was like.

When the bell goes again, I start to follow Jasmine out of the room.

The teacher stands by the door. "Piper? Stay a moment." She waits until the others file out. "I don't want to put any pressure on you now, but you need to do your presentation as well. You are on the schedule for tomorrow. I can leave yours to the end and juggle things around if you're not ready?"

I wonder if Piper has done her assignment. Somehow, I doubt it. She's been far too busy with Zak.

I smile. "No problem. I'll do it tomorrow."

PIPER

From the bottom of our road, I check our drive; Dad's car is gone. I walk fast to the door and enter the code, hoping no nosy neighbors watched me leave in a car and return on foot dressed differently moments later.

Upstairs, the door to my room is ajar, and I step in, close it behind me. When I turn, my eyes open wide. There are clothes flung all over the bed, spilling onto the floor, too —even that silly onesie my aunts got me for Christmas last year.

Has she been through *everything?* All of my stuff? I look through my desk and drawers, and nothing seems to be missing. But it all somehow *feels* different, disturbed. Her eyes and hands have been over all my belongings, and I'm as creeped out as if a burglar had rifled my room.

But she's my *sister.* I try to make myself calm down, but can't stop the anger simmering inside. A sister that just now I'd like to slap, but I can't because she's with *my* friends, at *my* school, pretending to be me.

Focus, Piper.

What do I know so far? The other day, I couldn't find any trace in this house of where Mum came from. Dad said Mum's family name—and mine—is Blackwood. Quinn confirmed this is also her name. Dad said there is a Blackwood inheritance, but that he doesn't know what or where it is. Quinn told Zak she was raised by her grandmother, and she told both of us that Mum visited her.

So the only family I know for sure we have is this grandmother. Somehow I have to trace her, and the only way I can do that is by finding out where Quinn lived, or where Mum visited. Then I hope this will lead me to our family and our inheritance.

Next step? The internet.

I open my laptop. Has Quinn been on here, too?

No. She wouldn't know the password—unless she guessed it was NESS.

To start with, I type *Isobel Hughes* into the search engine. The first hits are reports of her death. Her eyes look at mine from the screen, and my fingers reach out to her, to touch her image. An image that is somehow both her and not her.

Like that dream I had last night. First she was the way I remembered her, from when I was small; and then she was someone else, someone horrible.

This photo was taken at some law firm party and was one she hated. She was looking down a little, distracted and sad —she'd have smiled if she'd seen the camera, projected what she wanted to be seen. It had caught her in an unguarded moment. What was she thinking? Did I ever really know?

I make myself scroll down until the photo is gone, but once I'm past recent events, a random collection of people and places with no connection to her or each other comes up.

Next, I search for *Isobel Blackwood,* then *Quinn Blackwood.* With both searches, endless pages scroll past; none of them seem to relate to Mum or Quinn. No Facebook, no Twitter, nothing. I know Mum wasn't into social networking, and I'd be surprised if Quinn was online much—she's not very tech-y. I even had to show her how to use my smartphone. But it is somehow more surprising that nothing Quinn has done has ended up on anyone else's radar, either. Wherever she's been, she's not turned up on the internet—at least, not as Quinn Blackwood.

How about *Blackwood* and *Dartmoor* together? I don't know that my relatives are definitely from Dartmoor; or if they are, that they are still there. All I know is that Mum was working there when she met Dad. But if they are from Dartmoor, that could bring up something. I type the words in, not really expecting anything much, and hit ENTER for search.

Vast numbers of hits fill the screen.

Blackwood is an ancient name for Dartmoor's black peat, which was cut for fuel. Garth Blackwood was the brutal master of Dartmoor prison, until he was murdered by an inmate in 1895. He apparently came back from the dead to take revenge. Nice move.

Then there are all sorts of random, apparently unconnected links between Dartmoor and an old-fashioned version of our name: of-the-Black-Wood. There are hauntings, myths, and all sorts of supernatural things.

Now, the internet can be weird. Can't it? Sometimes searches throw up all kinds of odd things that have nothing to do with what I'm looking for. But a lot of this is weird with extra weird stirred in, and there is something about it all that just *feels* like it means something.

But nothing is specific enough to be definite. Nothing says it must be about my family and Dartmoor or gives me a clue where to look or what to look for if I go there.

I sigh and frown at the computer. What next?

If Quinn lived on Dartmoor, she must have gone to school there or near there. I search for every secondary school in the area, and make a list with addresses, phone numbers. I start at the top.

"Hello? I have an urgent personal message for one of your students. Yes, I'm a family member — her sister. Sadly, there has been a death in the family. Her name is Quinn Blackwood . . . Oh? You don't have a student there by that name?"

I cross off the first school and carry on through the list. Each time some variation of the first call takes place that amounts to no Quinn, right through until I cross the last one off the list.

How does someone live in the world and leave no tracks, no traces? Quinn must be a ghost.

QUINN

The bell goes at the end of an incomprehensible math class, but at least I wasn't alone in not understanding any of it: a scan of the room earlier suggested most of the others were in a similar fog of confusion. Everyone runs as if the very Hounds of Hell are on their heels before the bell has even stopped ringing. But when I go to follow Jasmine, the teacher bars my way at the door.

"Piper, have you got your coursework that was due last week?" His words have none of the softness of the English teacher's.

"Sorry. I don't."

"I can't grant you any more extensions."

"How about I bring it tomorrow?" I say, anxious to get away from him and follow Jasmine. If she disappears, I've no idea where to go.

"See that you do."

Luckily Jasmine is waiting outside the door. "Have you got it done?" she asks, evidently having overheard.

"Ah . . ."

She raises an eyebrow. "Tim will want *something* if you keep getting him to do your homework for you, you know. And I don't think even he is lovesick enough to do your actual coursework."

I'm shocked. Piper has Tim do her work?

I follow Jasmine to the cafeteria—time for some lunch?
—and the reason everyone bolted is apparent. It's packed.
But Jasmine walks confidently through the masses, and they
part before us. A large table has two empty seats with bags
across them that are moved as we approach.

I sink into the one next to Tim, Jasmine on my other
side.

"Poor Piper, you look all in," Tim says, and slips an arm
over my shoulders. He gives me a squeeze, and I see Erin at
the other side of the table giving me an odd look. Does Piper
normally not allow this? I smile and lean on his shoulder,
and her eyes widen.

"Let me get your lunch," he says. "What'll it be?"

"You decide. Thank you." I smile at him as he gets up
and heads for the endless queue.

"Darling," Jasmine says in a low voice by my ear, "when
I suggested he'll want something for helping in math, I
didn't mean to start right *now*." I wink, and Jasmine titters.
"Not entirely sure what the divine Zak would make of that."

"I can handle him." I shrug, and wonder as I say the
words. Can Piper really handle Zak? Surely not even Piper
could get away with flirting with other boys when she has a
boyfriend. Someone is bound to tell Zak.

Jasmine smiles approvingly and winks back, and there
is a feeling of warmth and belonging. This could be my life.
It would have been, if Isobel had picked me instead of Piper
when she left Gran and came to Winchester.

It *should* have been my life.

If only Isobel hadn't left me behind. How could she do that to me? It is too late to ask her, and none of the conclusions I can reach on my own are comforting.

Lunch arrives with Tim—salad and a yogurt for me, fries and ketchup for him. Is that the sort of thing Piper eats for lunch? Lettuce?

"Is that all right?" Tim is concerned.

"It's fine. If I can steal a few fries?"

"Have these. I'll get some more." He's so eager to please, he reminds me of Ness. I shake my head, and when he starts to stand, I take his hand to pull him back to his seat.

"Really, it's fine—don't," I say, and his smile is absolutely delighted—that I touched his hand?

"No, I insist." And he's gone back to stand in the queue.

What is it about Piper that makes her friends behave like this? I study the others at our table.

They are all in the sympathy-for-Piper camp and defer to what I—*she*—says, some in a faintly odd way.

Some of Piper's friends seem to genuinely care for her, like Jasmine. And Jasmine reminds me of the fancy car types who come to the hotel and never notice anyone who works there. She's beautiful; everything about her hair and clothes screams money, and the way she interacts with many of the other students and even teachers is much like they're the help, beneath notice. Yet she seems to be Piper's sidekick and happy to do what she wants.

Piper seems to inspire love and obedience in equal measure in her friends, but why? How does she do it? It's not by her goodness or sweet nature. She lied so easily to her dad and aunts; she probably does to everyone in her life. Gran would be horrified.

And as if I'm really Piper, the lies seem to fall easily from my lips when I'm her.

Gran would be horrified at me, too, a voice whispers inside. At me pretending to be Piper, deliberately making promises for her that can only land her in trouble, flirting with Tim just to create mischief. Why am I doing these things?

My belly squirms, uncomfortable. One large Zak-size reason. I wanted to get back at Piper for how she made me feel when she spent the night with Zak. Some twist inside says she knew the whole time that I'd be upset.

Gran was always right about me, wasn't she? Isobel, too. The longer I keep up this charade, the more I prove them right.

Jasmine leans in close, voice low. "Are you all right, Piper? Is there anything I can do?" Her eyes are soft and concerned. Her arm links in mine, and suddenly, unexpectedly, something chokes inside me. I look down and shake my head, unable to speak. Her arm goes around my shoulders.

She's Piper's friend, not mine. None of these people know *me*. None of them would want to.

I look up, and the sense of claustrophobia I felt earlier rushes back. So many people, so many eyes, and they are all focused on me—wanting me to be who they think I should be.

"I'm sorry. I have to get out of here."

When I get up and start heading for the door, Jasmine follows. She shakes her head at the others, and they stay where they are.

"Let's cut. Go out for a Coke or something?"

"No. No, sorry. I just need to get out of here and be alone."

"Are you sure?"

"Yes."

She looks inclined to argue, then finally nods. "All right. But call if you want me, and I'll come. OK?"

"Yes. Thanks. Apologize to Tim for me. Do I need to tell anyone I'm going?"

She shakes her head. "I'll cover for you. Just go." She leans in and gives me a quick hug. And I bolt out the door.

PIPER

There's a knot in my neck. I roll my shoulders forward, then backwards. How do you find a ghost?

I think for a while. Maybe there is a flaw in my approach. Quinn never confirmed she was from Dartmoor, did she? All I know is that Dad met Mum in a hotel on Dartmoor. Despite all the interesting weirdness a combined search of Blackwood and Dartmoor generated, they could have nothing to do with anything. Mum really could have been from *anywhere*. This is a complete waste of time. I can't phone every school in the country.

But what else can I do? I sigh, head in hands. *Think, Piper.*

Take a step back. What do I *know* to be true about Quinn?

She's my twin; we have the same mother, Isobel Blackwood. Quinn told Zak she was raised by her grandmother. Mum used to visit Quinn occasionally.

I already tried all of Mum's bills and records that I could find, and there were no stray trails to a place she visited regularly. She must have deliberately hidden her tracks —whether from me or Dad or both of us.

Then pieces click into place, and I sit bolt upright. Quinn lived with her grandmother. Mum's mother. So if I can find Mum's past—where she lived as a child, with her own mother—maybe I can find Quinn's present.

The only thing I *know* about Mum's past is that she worked in a hotel on Dartmoor. Dad said he'd contacted them; they'd said she wasn't working there anymore and they didn't know where she'd gone. But did he ask them where she *came from?*

It's a long shot. So many years have gone by—even if I find the right hotel, it'd be lucky if anyone who remembers her still works there. Even if I find out where Mum came from, our grandmother could have moved with Quinn long ago. But I can't think of anything else to try.

Back on the laptop in my room, I search for hotels on and around Dartmoor, and generate another list—names, places, phone numbers. I try the first one.

"Hello? I'm doing a family tree for school and trying to trace my relatives. Apparently about eighteen years ago, my aunt worked in your hotel—her name was Isobel Blackwood? You only opened ten years ago? Oh. OK, sorry."

I phone another one, and another, but come up with nothing. There must be a way to narrow this down. Dad said he couldn't remember what the hotel was called—Mum probably "suggested" to him that he should forget the name of the place. But he told me the sign said something like *two rivers.*

I scan the list. There is a hotel called Two Bridges. Could it be that one?

All right: one more try. I dial the number. It rings: once, twice, three times, four . . . "Good afternoon, Two Bridges Hotel!"

"Hello! I'm an A-level student doing a family tree for history class. I'm hoping you can help me trace a relative who used to work there?"

"How long ago?"

"I think about eighteen years."

"Oh, sorry, I've only been here a few years. I don't think there's anyone working here from back then who'd know, though I could ask some of the regulars. What was her name?"

"Blackwood. Isobel Blackwood."

"Did you say Blackwood? That's funny, we've got a cleaner by that name now! Quinn. But she's been off because her grandmother is ill. And you want someone from years ago. I'll just check at the bar . . . Hello? Hello?"

I stare at the receiver in my hand; her voice becomes faint. I click End Call. Quinn Blackwood. Quinn worked at this hotel. Whether or not Isobel ever did no longer matters. If Quinn worked there, they must have lived close by.

I've found her.

QUINN

Clouds are drawing in. Shivering, I wrap my arms around myself as I walk away from the school. Piper's jacket may be cute, but it's not up to October weather. I shift her heavy book bag on my shoulder and sigh. Why didn't I pay more attention when we were driving here? I have no idea where I am.

The cold I feel isn't just from the dropping temperature; it's more. It's deep inside. For a moment, just a fleeting instant, I'd let myself forget. I'd felt like this could be my life: I could have friends, go to school, be normal. But Piper's friends are forming ranks around her, not me. They don't know me. If Piper told them about me and what I've done, masquerading as her, they'd be angry.

But it's not just that. They were right—Gran and Isobel were right. The words are echoing through my head. The darkness will find me. It has found me; it will claim me soon. I'm weak. I could have stopped it, but I didn't. Ever since I left Dartmoor, I've taken the wrong path: jealousy, lying, deliberately causing trouble. What will I do next?

Walking isn't enough to calm me, and I start to run, faster and faster, down streets I don't recognize—but I can't run away from what is inside me. Wherever I go, it comes along. Tears start to blur my vision. The heat from running, from gasping air in and out of my lungs, warms my skin but not the cold dread inside.

After a while I realize that my feet have found the way, that I know where I am again. I'm heading straight for Zak's house. I slow to a walk when I reach his road, and stop outside the house. His car is out front. I know he's working today — he must have walked to work.

I find the spare key Piper gave me when I left last night and open the door. Ness bounds around the corner. I drop to the hall floor on my knees and wrap my arms around her, bury my face in her fur. Any attempt at control long gone, I'm crying in great, gulping sobs.

The door to the front room opens. A hand, a warm hand, is touching my hair. Stroking it. I look up through my tears: it's Zak. Of course it is.

His hand finds mine, pulls me to my feet. Arms wrap around me, hold me close. And the cold starts to go away. Just a little at first, but then there is a rush of heat through my whole body, heat that starts inside and rushes through my arms, my legs, flushes my face.

I open my eyes and look up at him. He leans down, kisses the tears away from my cheeks. I close my eyes again, and he kisses my eyelids. I tilt my face back, and his lips are on mine — gentle, sweet, warm, but that isn't enough. My hands weave through his hair and pull him closer. And I kiss him back, desperate for more. His hands are on my hips. I'm pressed into the wall, his thumbs stroking around my hipbones, just above Piper's low-slung jeans.

Piper.

Reason fights to return. He must think I'm Piper. I try to pull away, but his hands are tracing slow circles of fire on my skin.

The front door opens.

PIPER

I just stand there, mouth hanging open, like an idiot, staring at Zak and Quinn. Full-on *kissing?* And not just kissing.

Quinn springs away from Zak, her eyes wide, panicked.

He looks between us, confusion taking over. He shakes his head. "What's going on here?" he says.

I swallow, and manage to find my voice. "By the looks of things, you were making out with my sister."

"I don't . . . what . . . Quinn?" He turns to her. "Is that you? Why didn't you say?"

She's shaking her head, backing away — lips red from kissing, cheeks' violent flush fading to pale.

"How could you do that?" Zak says to Quinn.

Her heart is breaking; it's mirrored in her eyes. Just there — it cracks, with an almost audible snap. Broken.

"I'm sorry, I'm sorry." She runs up the stairs; the door slams.

Zak is rubbing his eyes, as if that will make this go away. He turns to me. "You have to believe me, I thought it was you. Jasmine texted me that you'd left school upset. I tried calling, but you didn't answer. I left work and drove to your school but didn't see you anywhere on the way. Came home, and then the door opened, and she was there — crying. She even had your school bag. You told me you were going to school." He gestures; the bag is on the floor. "I thought it was you."

My arms are crossed, but I'm strangely still and calm inside. "You really seriously couldn't tell the difference? Does she kiss just the same as me?"

He doesn't answer, but it's there, in his eyes. Some part of him *knew.* At some point he felt the difference, but he didn't stop.

"I'm sorry, Piper. I'm truly sorry. I thought it was you. I thought it was you." Words repeated to make them more true? There is shock and disbelief mixed with something else: guilt.

To start with, you did. I look away, shake my head a little, and lie. "I'm not angry with you, Zak. It's Quinn. She knew you made a mistake but didn't set you straight."

There are hesitant footsteps coming down the stairs.

Quinn is back in her own clothes. Her face is white and determined, but she doesn't quite look up, doesn't meet our eyes.

"I'm sorry for all the trouble I've caused. I'm leaving," she says.

QUINN

"Wait," Piper says. One word, just one. I want to run out that door before the will to go leaves me, before her angry words can find their mark.

My steps slow; I look back. After everything I've done, I owe it to her to listen to what she wants to say.

"Give us a moment," she says to Zak, and he goes into the front room and shuts the door. I watch him go, hurting inside. Could this really be the last time I ever see him? Can that be true? I force myself to turn my eyes toward Piper. She looks calm; how can she be so calm? She leans against the wall, the same place I was, when Zak . . .

No. I mustn't think about that; not now, not ever.

"Where are you going?" she asks, voice quiet.

"I . . . I don't know. Home, I guess. Where else is there?"

Then she says words I'm not expecting. "Don't go. Not like this."

"What did you say?"

"No matter what, Quinn, you're still my sister. Obviously if you go near Zak again, I'll have to kill you." A trace of a smile. "But you're still part of my family. Don't go."

I shake my head. "I don't understand. After what I did." I swallow. Kissing Zak was about the worst thing I could have come up with to do to Piper, but I didn't plan it. I wouldn't have—not just for what it would do to her, but what it would do to me. "And that's not all I've done," I say, wanting to push her to make me go.

"Go on."

"I was you at school today. Your English presentation is tomorrow, and I said your math coursework would be done by then, too. And I kind of flirted with Tim."

Annoyance crosses her face; she shrugs. "No matter. I'll wiggle out of all of that mess."

"What is with you? I don't understand. You should hate me." *I do.*

"We're family. That's it. That's enough. Don't you get it?"

My tears are back again, and I ignore them, just let them fall as I stand frozen by the door.

"Quinn? Please stay. At least until we can make things right between us."

"After everything I've done?"

She shrugs her shoulders. "If you knew half the stuff I've done, you wouldn't be so freaked."

Piper's words ring true, and I stare back at her: my sister, my twin. Every inch the same—my face, my lips—just the same as the ones Zak kissed.

What stuff could Piper have done? Maybe we have more in common than I thought. But if we're the same, then why were we separated? I don't understand.

"You have to tell me what happened with Zak," Piper says.

"I didn't mean for it to happen. I just—I was really

upset, and crying, and he held me. I wasn't thinking about being me instead of you. I wasn't thinking at all."

She stares at me while I talk. My words are true, but they sound lame, so lame.

But she nods once. "I believe you. I wish it hadn't happened, but I forgive you. The next time you need a shoulder to cry on, try mine." And she holds out a hand.

I hesitate, then take a trembling step toward her. Her arms go around me. They're softer than Zak's — his arms that I won't feel again. And I'm crying because she is holding me despite the things I've done. She knows the darkness, and she still holds me — something that Isobel never did, that Gran never did. Not like this.

Maybe Piper is the only one who can ever really know me, understand me. Just as I am.

And I'm crying because of Zak. She's forgiven me, so I can never go near him. Not ever again.

PIPER

The door opens, and there is a throat-clearing sound. "I've made tea," Zak says.

Quinn buries her face in my shoulder. I gesture for Zak to go. "I can't face him," she whispers.

"Let me talk to him. I'll tell him what you told me. Just wait here a minute. *Don't* go. Promise?"

"All right. I promise."

I leave her in the hall. Will she still be there when I get back? Somehow I know she will be.

I step into the kitchen and close the door.

"Hi," Zak says. "OK out there?"

"I think so." I sigh, hold out a hand, and he takes it.

"OK in here, too?"

"Yes. Though you're obviously an idiot. And will need to be suitably punished at some point."

"Is Quinn still leaving?"

"She needs to, I think. But not just yet, and not alone." He raises an eyebrow. "She's afraid to face you."

"I'm a bit weirded out myself."

"The thing is, Zak, I should have listened to you. You were right all along."

"Was I?"

"All this has been too much for Quinn. I don't know how things were where she grew up, but she's pretty messed up. And now it's all bubbled over, and she's kind of lost it. I don't think she meant what happened with you to happen. She was just so upset, and you were a shoulder to cry on."

"You're amazingly understanding."

"Aren't I?"

He kisses my forehead. His lips are warm and soft, but they've changed. They've changed forever. There is a well of hurt, deep inside me, and I don't know what to do with it.

But one thing I am certain of: Quinn can't leave. Not without me. We *must* be together.

"So, what happens next?" he says.

"That's up to Quinn. Shall I bring her in?" He nods, and I open the door. She stands where I left her, same position, as if she hasn't moved or even breathed the whole time — forlorn, face streaked. Scared: she looks scared.

I hold out a hand. "It's OK. Come on."

QUINN

My hands are wrapped around a mug of hot tea. My eyes are looking everywhere but at Zak's face. His shoulder —that's all right. His hand, there on the table. Not his face.

A shoulder where my head rested; a hand that traced fire on my skin. I shiver.

"Quinn," he says, and despite my resolution not to, my eyes are drawn up to his. His gaze is steady. "It's OK. Piper explained, and I understand what happened. But we've devised a secret handshake now, so we can't have any more confusion."

A trace of a smile crosses my face, but words are slow to come. It will never happen again. No secret handshake needed.

"It's my turn to say something," Piper says. "It's not something I generally ever say, so feel honored."

"What's that?"

"I'm sorry. I see how upset you've become. Zak did warn me that this situation wasn't good for you, and I didn't listen to him. I was wrong. And I think it's time for us to be completely honest with each other, and with everyone else."

Can Piper, who lies so easily, ever be completely honest? But I owe her trust. She's my sister. My family. Today she's shown me what these things can mean.

"Do you mean that you are going to go to your dad, together?" Zak says.

"Yes," Piper says. She looks at me. "If you want to."

Panic is rising. Do I know how to be part of a family? Do I know how to forgive someone just because they're related to me, like Piper has done? A whisper inside says that if things were reversed, if Zak were my boyfriend and Piper had kissed him, I wouldn't forgive her. I'm ashamed.

"But that's not all," Piper says. "The other half of the picture is that I want us to go to your home together, too: where you lived."

I stare back at her. "I'm not sure you'd like it."

"Is it the place where our mum grew up?" Piper asks.

I hesitate, then nod. "She was born there; our gran was born there. Me too, so I guess that means you as well."

"You see — it's all part of my past, of who I am. I want to go there. And I want to meet our grandmother."

"She's not there anymore."

"Even so. Can we go there together? To Dartmoor, isn't it?"

Something inside shifts and gives, just a little. I nod.

She smiles. When Piper is really happy about something, she is radiant in a way I never have been, no matter how alike we are otherwise. Something catches in my throat; it's hard to look away, and I feel warm inside. This is why her friends and everyone else want to make her happy; they want her to look at them like she is looking at me, right now.

"Thank you for being honest with me," she says, and I want to tell her more.

"My grandmother's house is on the moors, near a small place called Two Bridges. I've lived there all my life. When I came here, it was the first time I'd ever been away from home."

Her smile somehow deepens; her hand reaches out and holds mine. "Where is our grandmother?"

"She had a stroke. But she's all right. She's in hospital."

"We could visit her there?"

"I guess."

"Quinn? Should we go to Dad first, or Dartmoor?" Piper says, and there are two sets of eyes on me, wanting a decision. For one who isn't used to being allowed to make decisions, this is frightening.

"Well, as we're here, we could go to Dad first . . ." A slight frown lurks between Piper's eyes. I owe her, don't I? But what she wants is to go to the one place I never want to go to again. I push my fear down inside. "But not yet. Are you sure you want to meet Gran? She's not an easy person to be around. Even worse than me."

Piper laughs. "Family put up with each other's faults, right?"

I'm not sure Gran's issues are quite in the category of *faults*. I'm afraid to go back, to face her, afraid I'll never be allowed to leave again if I do. But if Piper is there with me, it'll be different. There'll be somebody on my side for a change—and not just anyone. Knowing it is Piper makes me less afraid.

"All right. Let's do it!" I say.

"One thing, though. Until we've told our dad that we are twins, we can't let anybody else know there are two of us. It's not fair to him."

I look back at Piper. So, she wants me to stay a secret. She has a point about it not being fair to tell anyone else before our family. Still, there is part of me that wonders: is there any other reason why she wants it this way? But what other reason could there be?

"Agreed?" Piper says, and holds out her hand.

"Agreed," I answer. We shake on it, and that is that.

Later we talk it through. Zak says he'll take us, but only if our dad agrees Piper can go. He seems to think that'll never happen. Piper looks confident, and I'm starting to understand why. She has a way of making things happen how she wants them to, doesn't she?

We're sitting on the sofa, the three of us. Piper is in the middle, one arm linked with Zak's, the other with mine.

And somehow that feels all right. There isn't such a gulf between Zak and me, not with Piper the bridge between us. She's my *sister*. Maybe I'm starting to get a sense of what that is supposed to feel like?

Piper is telling us stories from her childhood: funny moments, significant ones. Her first bicycle, her broken arm when she fell from it. Her voice is warm and lively and lulling me toward sleep, but then a few details snap into place, and my eyes open wider.

"Piper, how old did you say you were when you broke your arm?"

"Six. It was the spring after my sixth birthday."

"How did it happen? Did you lose control, or hit something, or what? Can you remember?"

"Actually I do remember, partly because it was so weird. I was absolutely fine and then I just flew off the bike. Like somebody had plucked me off it and thrown me on the ground."

"That was in April. Wasn't it?"

"Yes. It was Easter—"

"Easter Sunday. In the morning."

Piper twists in her seat a little to look me in the eye. There is intense curiosity on her face, and on Zak's, too. "How on earth did you know? Did Mum tell you about it?"

"No. She never even told me you existed, remember? But I broke my arm when I was six, too. On the morning of the same day."

"How?"

"I was climbing a tor, and I fell."

"Wow," Zak says. "Is that, like, some sort of weird coincidence, or what?"

Piper and I are staring into each other's eyes. We both shake our heads slowly. "Not a coincidence," we say at the same moment.

I shake my head. "You go."

"It can't be a coincidence," Piper says, "that the same moment you fell, I flew off my bike for no apparent reason."

"Do you think this is some freaky twin linkage thing?" Zak looks skeptical. "Has either of you had any other major injuries or anything?"

I shake my head no; so does Piper. "Just the usual. Bumps and scrapes. Though . . ." And I stop. Some things I don't like to talk about.

"What?" Piper says.

"When I was thirteen, I was very ill. I thought I would die."

Piper's face goes still. "So was I. They said it was flu, but it wasn't the usual sort of flu."

"I had these horrible dreams. They went on even when I was awake."

"Hallucinations from the fever? Me too."

"You've never mentioned that before," Zak says to Piper.

"I don't like to think about it," she says.

"Me neither," I say.

"What were the hallucinations? If they were the same, that'd be way bizarre," Zak says, clearly very intrigued. I don't want to say, and I can see by Piper's face that she doesn't, either.

"It's too late at night for that," Piper says. "Let's change the subject."

"All right. To what?" I say. All traces of my earlier sleepiness are gone. I can feel the cold fingers of memory, and need to focus on something else, anything, to make them go away.

"I've gone on enough," Piper says. "Let's hear some stuff about you."

"Like what?"

"Where did you go to school?"

"I've never been to a school. Before I went to yours today, that is."

"You mean you were homeschooled?"

"Not exactly."

Zak and Piper exchange a glance. "Surely the authorities—" Zak begins.

I shake my head. "The authorities were scared of Gran."

PIPER

Two cups of tea: one for Dad, one for me. I carry them upstairs and pause at the study door.

He looks up from his laptop and glances at the clock. "It's a bit late for a school night."

I walk across, put his tea in front of him, and keep mine in my hands.

"Well, yeah, about that. I don't think I was ready to go back."

"Petal. School is important."

"I know. But there's no point being there if all I'm doing is messing things up. Besides, it's just one more day, and then it's half term next week. And there is something I want to do."

"What's that?"

I put my tea down, walk to the other side of the desk, and sit on the edge of it next to him like I used to do when I was much younger.

"You know how I said I wanted to find where Mum is from? I found it."

He's surprised. "Really? How?"

"I called hotels on Dartmoor and found the one she used to work at: Two Bridges Hotel. And the house she grew up in is close by." I leave out the links that led me there, and the other daughter who confirmed my guesses and brought it all together.

"Impressive detective work."

"I want to see where Mum grew up. I want to meet my grandmother."

He takes my hand. "Petal, I understand how you feel. But I know your mum was estranged from her own mother, and I'm sure she had good reason. I always got the impression that your grandmother was somehow dangerous. I don't like to think of you meeting this woman. Who knows what she is capable of?"

"My grandmother isn't in her house anymore. The hotel said she's had a stroke and is in hospital. She may not live much longer," I add, embellishing further.

He takes that in, the change it presents. "I see." He pauses, has a sip of tea. "What is it you want to do?"

"I want to go to Two Bridges, see the house where Mum grew up. And visit my grandmother in hospital. No matter what may have happened between them years ago, you don't need to worry about an ill old woman in a hospital bed."

He stares levelly back, finally nods. "All right, then. I'll see if I can get some time off." He opens the calendar on his screen, surveys it silently, but I know he has trials. "It'll be at least a month before I can get away."

"Let Zak take me."

He gives me a dad look. "You are only seventeen. You're not going on a trip with your boyfriend."

"Honestly, Dad! This isn't a romantic adventure. I want to find Mum's past, my family. My grandmother is old, alone, and in hospital — what if she dies before I get there?"

A long pause. "I'll think about it."

A bit later there's a knock on my door. "Yes?" I say.

Dad peeks in. "I've spoken to Zak." So very predictable. "You can go."

I smile to myself as I get ready for bed. Everything is working; everything is coming together.

I'm burning.

I throw the blankets off, stagger out of bed, and open the window. It's night, and I'm alone. The moon is full and fuller; then it is red, on fire, and falling from the sky.

I scream and crouch on the floor, arms over my head, but there is nowhere to hide.

Arooooooo! There is howling in the distance, faint but terrifying. Then louder, and closer — in the garden below.

They're creeping up the stairs, then into my room. Their howling — arooooooo! — is so loud that it fills my head, turns my insides to liquid. I'm afraid to look, afraid not to.

They're with me, in the flames: huge black hounds, with red eyes, foul tongues dripping over sharp fangs. They smell of death, despair.

They crouch at my feet, waiting for me to die.

Somewhere there is a voice: one that soothes. Mummy? She tells me it will pass, that I'll be all right—that she lived through this, and her mother, too, and there was nothing to be done but survive.

But still I burn.

QUINN

In Zak's car, Ness is licking my face with great attention, not used to having someone lying down on the back seat in her zone. "I don't think you missed anywhere," I whisper to her, and wrap my arms around her a little too tight. She squirms until I let go. The car stops; Zak gets out. Ness runs out of the open front door behind him, and Zak calls her. The door shuts again.

I'm supposed to keep my head down until we're gone, but I can't stop myself from peeking through the window. The front door of the house opens, and Ness bounds across the lawn, Zak trailing behind. Piper stands there, and I duck down again before she can see me.

The phone rang late last night, not long after Piper had left. I heard Zak's door open and imagined him crossing the hall in boxers and a T-shirt, like I saw him wearing that one night, and opening my door to answer the extension in this room—the one next to my bed. I imagined him sitting on the bed next to me, his body heat spreading to mine. Instead he went downstairs to pick it up there.

The house was still, quiet. His words were clear enough, and his half of the conversation was enough for me to catch the meaning. So before morning came, I knew we were going to Dartmoor the next day, that our dad had wanted to speak to Zak before agreeing. I heard Zak promise to take care of Piper and make some other promises that I'm sure equated to Piper not seeing him in his boxers any more than I will.

So just hours after I'd somehow promised to go there with Piper, it was all arranged. I lay there in bed last night, hour after hour, almost rigid with fear. Like an escaped convict, I've been caught. If I go back to my prison, will I ever get away again?

No, Quinn. Bad Quinn. All the times I'd been punished without even knowing why or what I'd done wrong. All the times my will was twisted, and I was made to do or say things I didn't want to, didn't believe. There was something about being there that crushed who I was. I'm only just starting to feel, away from that place — feel things that are my own. Even if they hurt, like with Zak, I'd rather pain that is mine than feeling nothing at all.

But apart from all the fear from the past, there is a deep sense of foreboding twisting in my gut. Going there could be dangerous for all of us. But how can I back out now, after what Piper has done for me?

I can't.

After an almost sleepless night — and what sleep I did have, disturbed by nightmares — here I am: in the car. We're about to head to the one place I was sure I never wanted to return to, ever again.

Time passes. A door opens at the house. There are voices. Footsteps. The boot opens; the car drops slightly as something is put in. The boot shuts.

The driver's-side door opens; Zak gets in. "All right?" he says in a low voice.

"Yeah," I say, just to agree with him rather than because I actually resemble *all right*. It's all I can do to not jump up, rip the door open, and run.

"Piper said she wanted to have a word with her dad on her own. I think mostly to avoid him walking over to the car and seeing you." His voice is quiet again, his head turned as if to adjust the radio.

"That'd be hard to explain."

"Here she comes."

There are footsteps. "Bye!" Piper's voice calls out.

The car door opens, and Piper shoos Ness into the back seat with me, then gets in. The car starts. Her hand is waving.

The car reverses out of the drive and heads up the road. Piper laughs. "I didn't think I'd ever get away. Road trip!"

"Can I sit up?" I ask.

She twists around. "Really sorry, do you mind just waiting until we at least clear Winchester? Someone might see the two of us."

The radio is on low. The car sways back and forth. The lack of sleep is catching up with me, and I yawn, stretch, ball up my jacket under my head.

And with every heartbeat we get closer and closer to where I come from.

• • •

It's dark. I'm running and running across the moors — taking risks on the uneven ground to fly as fast as I can.

Arooooooo! The mournful cries of Wisht Hounds follow behind, and the fear makes me dig deep and go even faster.

But I can't keep up this pace much longer. Panic twists my guts.

They are getting closer.

There is a chorus of howls — not just behind me now, but around me as well. They are herding me to the most haunted place — the twisted place where deals are done, and hope is lost.

I scramble up a rocky slope, desperate to find a way to escape them.

I stop dead when I see her.

Her eyes are a brilliant blue, her coat thick, her long tail black. The black brush fox. She stares at my wrist — at Isobel's bracelet hanging there.

The cries of the hounds freeze my blood. They are very near now, near enough that I can smell rank death on their breath, feel my own death getting closer.

The fox's eyes are intelligent; she cocks her head to one side. She knows I am hers, that she is mine. With the hounds behind and the fox ahead, there is no real choice, but she wants it made freely.

PIPER

I'm cold. Shivering starts from deep inside; all the hairs on the back of my neck stand on end. The sun is shining on my face, the car is warm, but the shivering continues. Ness whimpers, and I twist around to look at the back seat.

Quinn is asleep. Her face is pale, her lips moving silently, her body shaking, skin goose-pimpled. Ness is next to her, licking her hands as if trying to help.

I snap my seat belt open, turn, lean over the seat, and shake Quinn, hard.

She jumps violently, breathing in gasps; her eyes open — wild and unseeing.

"Quinn? Quinn!" I say. Ness barks, and Quinn's eyes finally turn, focus first on Ness, then on me. Her breathing starts to calm. As her shivering subsides, so does mine. "Bad dream?"

"Something like that," she says. She sits up, and I drop back into my seat in the front and do up my seat belt again.

I study her in the mirror. She's still sitting up, but collapsed back against the seat. Pale, head turned as if she's looking out the window, hand absently stroking Ness, but her eyes are almost glassy, as if she is not really registering anything in this world.

So Quinn had a nightmare — or should I say, daymare?

—and I had a physical reaction to it. *What the hell is that about?* I shudder. Is it like the so-called flu we both had, and the broken arms? What would happen if one of us were ever seriously hurt? Or even died?

"Is everything OK?" Zak asks, with a quick glance from me to Quinn in the mirror, then back to the road.

"All right now. Are we there yet?"

"Just like the ninety-nine other times you've asked, no."

"Is anyone besides me hungry?"

"Me!" Zak says. "Quinn, how about you? Want something to eat?"

She turns her head slowly. "Sure."

The sun is still shining, and it's warm for mid-October. Zak goes to fetch some lunch, and I pull Quinn and Ness to one of the picnic tables at the motorway service station, the one at the end — not too close to anyone else. We sit next to each other, and Ness bounces about as far as she can on her lead.

"Your hands are so cold," I say to Quinn, holding them between mine. Her head droops against my shoulder. "Are you all right?"

Her shoulders shrug. "Mostly. Sort of."

"Is it where we're going, or something else? Maybe that dream that you had in the car?"

"A bit of both," Quinn says, denying neither. And warmth rushes through me: she finally trusts me a little — maybe even enough.

"What was your dream about?"

"I don't really want to think about it."

"What's weird is that I knew you were having a nightmare. I got all shivery, and turned around and woke you up. I *felt* your dream."

Quinn straightens up. "That is on the side of strange."

"So that's why I'm wondering what it was about. I can think of a few other times when I've had weird feelings or reactions that didn't seem to line up with what was happening to me at the time."

Quinn looks at me properly now, thinking. She nods. "I've had experiences like that, too."

"Is this a weird psychic twin thing? Or just a weird *us* thing?"

"How can we tell the difference? All we are is who we are."

"Good point. So, will you tell me about your dream?"

Quinn shrugs. "It was just a stupid nightmare, of being chased on the moors, with dogs barking in the distance. As if I were the fox in a hunt." She looks surprised as she says the last line. She thinks a moment. "Yes. Just like that."

"Is that all?"

Quinn nods, but I get the feeling there is more she isn't saying. She's not trusting me enough, then; not yet.

"Piper, have you ever had dreams like that?" she asks.

"I don't know about on the moors; I haven't been there before, so I don't know what it's like. I've had dreams where

I'm running over rough ground at night. But it's not a night-mare—it's exhilarating. I'm running and running."

There's more I'm not saying, too. *In my dream, I'm the chaser, not the chased.*

"How about last night?" Quinn says, voice hesitant. "Did you dream last night? I did."

Now prickles run up my back. I nod. "I thought it was because we were talking about it at Zak's, about—"

"When we had the fever," Quinn interrupts, finishing my sentence. "That's what I thought, too."

"What did you dream about?"

"I was sick. Burning up, in bed. I got up, and there was a full moon, and—"

"And the moon was on fire. And there were these hounds there."

"Yes," Quinn whispers. "Wisht Hounds."

"What are Wisht Hounds?" I ask her the question, but somehow know the answer without having to be told.

Quinn shivers. "Witches' Hounds. The legend is that they run on the moors at night. If you see or hear them, death or worse is close by. There have been reported sight-ings—and deaths attributed to them—on Dartmoor for centuries. But how can we have the same dreams?"

"I don't know. Quinn, do you know what that was about? The fever and the nightmares we had back then, what they meant?"

She looks at me, confused. "I thought it just meant I

was sick. But things seemed somehow different afterward. Gran was different, and I . . . I don't know. I started fainting a lot. Do you think it meant something more?"

"Mum said she went through it, too, and so did her mother."

Quinn nods, thoughtful. "They never told me that."

"I think it's something about becoming aware of who and what we are."

Quinn's brow wrinkles. "What do you—"

Zak walks up behind her, and I elbow her to be quiet.

QUINN

I wrap my hands around a big cup of soup, soaking up the warmth. Zak brought sandwiches, too; potato chips and cookies all around. As I make myself eat, I start to feel better, to warm up. But somehow the dreams are still with me.

Piper sensed the one I had in the car; she woke me. What would have happened if she hadn't? I've had that dream before, but have always woken as soon as I've seen the fox. Not today. I had a sense that I was about to finally understand something, to face something I didn't want to.

And soon we're back in the car, getting closer and closer. Dread deepens in my belly as we begin the drive over the moors — there is no hiding in this place, and the closer we get, the more I feel as though I am naked, lost, and pinned down under watchful eyes. It's only late afternoon, but as if it reflects my feelings, the sky is darkening. Clouds are pulling in.

Zak has Two Bridges on his GPS, but before we get to the hotel, I point out the turn. It leads to what is more a spindly track than a road.

"Are you sure this is OK for the car?" Zak asks.

"Yes. It's a bit rough, but we haven't far to go. Just about a mile."

He crawls along, and we jolt around in the ruts. "Hope no one comes the other way," Piper says.

"There are passing places. But it's not likely." Few came here before. None have a reason to now, with Gran in hospital; apart from Isobel, I never had any visitors. Until today.

The road narrows, and I point out an almost invisible cut in the moor. "Park here."

Zak looks skeptical, but pulls in. The ground slopes up around us, strewn with mossy rocks, boulders, gorse, and bracken. Seeing it through their eyes — city eyes — it is desolate. Wild.

"There doesn't seem to be a house anywhere," Zak says.

"No, you can't see it from here. This is the closest we can get by car. We've got to go the rest of the way on foot. Looking at the sky, I'd say we should hurry."

We get out. Piper looks around, eyes darting, her face lit up with excitement. "How far is it?"

"About an hour's walk the hard way, or about two and a half hours the easy way."

"An *hour?* The hard way?" Zak says.

"How hard is hard?" Piper asks.

I shrug. "I used to do it twice a day."

"What about Ness?" Zak says.

"She'll be fine. There are just a few bits we'll have to help her over."

"Come on, then. Let's get going," Piper says.

Zak opens the boot. Next to Zak's backpack and the one he lent me is a massive suitcase. That is what made the car drop at Piper's house. I shake my head. "I told you to pack light!"

"I did," she says, eyes surprised.

"You won't be able to bring that unless we go the long way around. Not sure we'll beat the storm either way."

Piper shakes her head. "I want to get there! How about I just take some stuff out? Zak, can we share your pack?"

She starts digging through her bag, and Zak takes some stuff out to make room for hers. She turns to me. "Have you got any room in yours?"

I shake my head. "No. Mine is mostly full of food raided from Zak's fridge. We'll need that." I suppress the urge to say *hurry* again. The sky is getting darker, the wind picking up. "Look, the weather is pulling in. Maybe we should head to the hotel and come out in the morning?"

"No way. We're so close now." Piper's eyes are dancing, red hair whipping about her in the wind and strangely lit in the dim light. It's hard to take my eyes off her when she is like this, full of excitement. She laughs. "Lead the way!"

Zak locks the car. With a last uneasy look at the sky, I head up the narrow path, Ness at my heels. I set a hard pace. It must only be about three p.m., but it's so dark the path is hard to see. Though I know the way well enough to find it in complete darkness — and have done, at top speed, when I had to: when Gran had her stroke.

At first it is just a rough track, fairly level. It skirts around rocks and along the bottom of a slope of loose scree. Then we join up with a more gentle, even path — part of a regular footpath used by walkers that goes to the twisted woods they all seemed to want to visit: a compulsion I could never understand.

There is a mournful sound in the distance, and it takes me back to my dream. I stop in fright. Was that a dog or the wind?

Then Ness growls deep in her throat.

There it is again, nearer and definitely not the wind. Piper and Zak catch up.

"Did you hear that?" I ask. Zak shakes his head.

Piper cocks her head to one side as it sounds again, louder and nearer, and now very definitely a dog. She smiles.

"There!" Zak says, and points at a moving smudge on the hill. It stops and looks toward us: now it is running this way. As it gets closer, I can see that it's not a puppy, and not a friendly looking dog, either. My fear is coming back. Zak picks up Ness, and I involuntarily step back.

Zak puts a comforting hand on my shoulder. "Don't be scared; watch."

Piper strolls out toward the dog. It slows to a walk. It is slavering like it has been running for a long time — eyes wild, teeth bared, and a *grrrrrrr* deep in its throat.

"Don't be silly," Piper says. She walks right up to it, and I'm scared for her. "You're just a friendly puppy, aren't you?" she says, her voice warm, musical. The dog looks at her, and . . . its tail starts to wag. It drops on the ground at her feet. She bends to pet it, and its tail wags harder.

There are some distant voices now—calling. Two figures crest the hill where the dog appeared. Piper sees them and waves, and they hurry to us. A man and a woman in walking gear.

"There you are, you naughty dog," the woman says, and bends to fuss him.

"He took off chasing a fox. I hope he didn't scare you," the man says.

"Not at all—he's lovely," Piper says. His tail thumps as if to agree. "He was a little spooked at something, I think."

The woman straightens up. "You're not heading out *now,* are you? It might rain."

No might about it.

"We're going to—" Piper starts to say, but I interrupt her.

"We'll be fine. Thank you for your concern." And I start marching up the path. I hear them say goodbye. Ness bounds up after me when Zak puts her down; Zak and Piper follow.

We soon leave the marked footpath for a barely-there trail that climbs up—gradually at first, then it gets steeper. The wind has picked up enough that I stop to knot my hair, tuck it inside my sweater. I look below; Piper is straggling, Zak behind her. I have to make myself wait for them to catch up, fighting the urge to run, to leave this place. Ness stays close to my feet as if she senses my fear.

Now I've stopped, I'm aware of how the temperature is

dropping; hair is standing on end on my neck, my arms, but it doesn't feel like it is just from the cold. I cast my eyes around, but everything is as it should be. Yet there is something about this place that has me on edge.

This place: is it where I saw the fox in my dream this afternoon? My stomach flips. Dreams aren't real—most of the time. *Calm yourself.*

Those walkers said their dog chased a fox. But it couldn't have been my fox, the one with the black brush tail. They'd have said if they'd seen anything that unusual.

Piper finally reaches me, gasping. "Where's the fire?"

I stare at her, shocked and uncomprehending.

"I mean, why are you in such a rush?"

As if in answer, the rain starts, and not in a gradual gentle way, but in the way it can only on the moors. It goes in seconds from nothing to absolutely lashing down, until it is like we are standing in a waterfall. Ness whines mournfully.

Piper struggles to get an umbrella out of the pocket of Zak's pack, but I shake my head. "It's too windy. Don't bother." I have to raise my voice to be heard over the wind and rain.

"How much farther is it?" Zak asks.

"Up this hill and over. Not far, but it's a hard climb in the wet. We could go back to the car?"

"Not a chance," Piper says. Her voice is determined.

Zak looks worried. "Is it dangerous?"

I hesitate. "I've done it in the rain many times before, but I know the way and know where to put my feet. If you go wrong, it could be dangerous."

"I'm not sure about this, Piper," Zak says. "I promised your dad I'd look after you."

"We'll be careful; it'll be fine," Piper says. Water is dripping down her face. "Let's get going before we freeze to death."

"All right," I say. "Watch and follow where I walk. Some of the rocks are unstable if you stray. Try to avoid the moss; it's slippery."

Walking on the steep path soon changes to scrambling up rocks. A few times I stop so Zak can pass a miserable-looking Ness to me over the bits that are too steep for her short legs. I want to hurry, both to leave this place and to get out of the pounding rain, but I worry about Piper and Zak. Making them hurry to keep up could be risky. I force myself to stay slow and steady, making sure they're only just behind.

A brilliant flash of lightning dazzles my eyes. A still figure is outlined in light on the edge of the sky, the ungainly pile of rocks that is Wisht Tor beside it. A fox? I blink, but the lightning is gone; I'm dazzled, can't see. The crack of thunder afterward is so loud I jump and nearly lose my footing.

"That's close," Zak calls.

I look back. Did he see it? But he's looking at the sky.

Another flash and crash soon follow, this time almost

at the same moment. I turn forward quickly to see if the fox is still there, but the place is in darkness before my eyes reach it.

Piper and Zak huddle behind me, Zak holding a whimpering Ness. "Is it safe to go on?" he says, just as another dazzling display splashes across the sky. Instant thunder drowns out his words.

"Just as safe going on as staying here or going back."

"Onward!" Piper says.

The rain intensifies. Rivulets are running down through the rocks, trickles turning to waterfalls. Even I'm anxious about finding safe footing, in a place so familiar I know every rock.

I look back at Piper. She grins widely. She's loving this. I shake my head and carry on, feet soaked even in my boots, hands needed for scrambling and holding on completely numb.

One last clamber, and I'm over. Zak passes Ness up to me. Then I turn to hold out a hand to Piper. She takes it; her hand is warmer than mine. Her foot slips, but between my hand and Zak helping behind, she rights herself and is over. Zak, with his long legs, follows more easily.

A string of flashes once again crosses the whole sky — it would be beautiful, if I were inside looking out at it. Thunder follows almost instantly, so loud it is in my bones, shaking and reverberating deep inside.

"Should we be standing on a hill?" Zak's face is alarmed.

I try to be reassuring, even though it is not how I really

feel. "Don't worry, that's the worst of the storm. It's heading away from us now."

As if to reinforce my words, another, lesser flash of lightning is followed seconds later by a crash of thunder, not as loud. I glance back, and the fox is once again outlined against the sky.

PIPER

We trudge the last steps across the top of the hill, around a haphazard pile of rocks that towers above us. Quinn identifies it as Wisht Tor, and stops in its shadow.

"*Wisht,* as in make a wish?" I ask her.

Quinn shakes her head. "*Wisht,* as in witches. Like the Wisht Hounds."

The ground slopes down more gently on the other side. The rain is slowing; the light increases as black clouds begin to pull away.

"There it is," Quinn says.

"What?"

"Gran's place." She gestures to the bottom of the slope, and my eyes now pick out the edges of a gray stone house, hard to see between straggly trees that surround it and the rocks of another tor behind it.

I pause to take it in, this most isolated place where my mother was born and raised, where Quinn and I were born. The place my mother fled from with me, leaving Quinn behind.

The stones of the house seem to blend into the tor behind it, almost like the house is part of the tor, or the tor part of the house. There is a rambling, crumbling stone wall around the house that almost hides it from sight, and there are stunted, twisted trees that weirdly appear to be not in front of or behind the wall, but part of it. It all looks old, really old. There are a few ramshackle outbuildings tucked around one side of the house, and what looks like a well. Really? An actual well?

"So, what do you think?" Quinn says. I turn to face her. Her cheeks are pale. Depths shimmer in her eyes, but I can't see past a surface of pain. She didn't want to come back here, not ever, did she? But she did it for me. I take her hand, and she clings to mine, tight.

"It's like a fairy-tale witch's house," I say — testing, prodding. She raises an eyebrow, and nods. "Without the fairy tale."

"Come on, ladies!" Zak says. "Let's get into the warm."

"Not much of that in there," Quinn says. "But let's go."

We trudge the rest of the way, and I discover that the distance was deceptive. The house is both farther away and bigger than it looked from above.

When we reach it, I see that my eyes didn't deceive me: the stone wall around the house *does* have trees growing out of it. Their roots twist down among the stones.

We follow Quinn to the far side of the wall, where a narrow wooden gate hangs open, covered in moss, half decayed. We go through, then follow as she picks a path around the edges of stones that seem to outline a crumbling ruin in front of the house.

The walls of the house are made of interlocking small slabs of rock, edges round with age. They look as though they are part of a puzzle that holds the house together without mortar or cement, like a farmer's dry-stone wall. There are only a few narrow windows, set deep into the walls. Through them, I see that all is darkness inside.

There is a wide, wooden double front door, like a barn door—is the house a conversion? If so, it was done a very long time ago. Quinn pauses when she reaches it, as if waiting, though we are right next to her now.

"Shall we?" I say, and she is still for a moment more, then nods. She turns the handle. It opens.

"Not locked?" Zak says, surprised.

"No one would come here," Quinn answers. She breathes in and steps into the house, with us close behind her.

We're in an entrance hall, with one door to the left, two smaller doors to the right, and stairs leading up at the end of the hall.

Zak pulls the door shut. Despite a small window over the door, it seems dark, and I blink to adjust my eyes. It feels even colder than it did outside. Quinn is shivering.

"Where are the lights?" I ask.

"We don't have electricity," Quinn says. She takes off her pack, rummages in a drawer under a table against the wall, and finds some candles and matches. She lights three candles, hands one to Zak and one to me, and keeps one herself. They're smoky, thick, and uneven—homemade?

"Follow me," Quinn says. She opens the door to the left and steps through, Ness close to her feet. We hold up our candles as we walk in, and thin pools of light struggle to show a large room with a huge fireplace so big you could roast a cow in it.

"I'll start a fire," Quinn says. "But it'll take a long time to take off the chill, since it hasn't been burning for days."

Quinn kneels and reaches into a box to the side of the fireplace for kindling and paper. She deftly lays and lights the fire in a fraction of the time it'd take Dad to do it at home in our small fireplace, which is more for atmosphere than heat. She tilts her candle down to hold the flame against the paper.

The paper catches in a bright flash of flame; the kindling soon starts, snaps and crackles, and lights up the room with dancing flames. Quinn adds coal, and the three of us hold our hands out as the fire gradually catches, but I can't keep my eyes still. They dart about the room.

"This place is kind of wow," Zak says, his eyes doing the same.

Hangings cover the walls. Scenes sewn into them are blurred with time, smoke, and poor light. A huge stuffed sofa made of heavy leather, with a blanket thrown on top, looks like a museum piece. There is a rough wooden rocking chair—was it carved by hand?

A massive freestanding sideboard has shelves on top and cupboards underneath. The shelves are covered with books and interesting things, every book and ornament like nothing I've seen before.

Quinn sneezes.

We turn and look at her; she's shivering violently. "You need a hot bath," Zak says. "We all do."

She shakes her head. "No hot water unless we lug it from the well and fill that to warm by the fire." She gestures; tucked in a corner is an actual tin bath.

"How about dry clothes for all, then, for now?" Zak says, and brings in the packs that we'd left by the door. "Are there any towels?"

Quinn nods, finally moving from where she's stood motionless since she lit the fire. She reaches into one of the cupboards under the sideboard and throws him a towel. Zak fishes in his pack for some clothes, then leaves the room.

I walk over and rummage in the cupboard: towels, but not as we know them—thin, patched, and darned. I toss one at Quinn and keep one myself. "Come on, frozen girl. Towel your hair and strip. I'll find you some clothes."

Her pack is, as she said, mostly full of food, and I go to Zak's instead for some of my clothes. There—a heavy sweater. Pants. Sneakers. I throw them at her; she catches them, hesitates, then starts shucking her wet clothes off while I do the same.

Quinn's skin is so white, so pure, in the firelight. Goose pimpled. She's shy, turns away, pulls the jumper over her head. She turns back, and she is—as I did with her—studying my skin, the same wonder in her eyes as in mine that everything is so alike.

There's a knock.

"Decent?" Zak's voice calls at the door.

"That's a matter of opinion," I say. "But you can come in." I pause, wait until the door opens to slowly pull a shirt over my head.

Quinn turns to hide a look of shock. Zak grins and shakes his head. "Don't start something I'm not allowed to finish."

I walk over to him and slip my arms around his waist. He's uncomfortable; is it because Quinn is in the room, or because of what he said to my father?

I nestle against him and whisper, "Promises were made to be broken." *Like the ones you made to me before you kissed my sister.*

QUINN

Once we decide to sleep where it is the warmest, I set blankets and cushions, gathered from different rooms of the house by candlelight, around the fire. Piper dances excitedly around me all the while like she's on some adventure; Zak more usefully ferries things back and forth.

Piper disappears out into the hall again and then calls back to me, "Quinn, this door won't open."

I was wondering how long it would be before she noticed. I get up and go to the hall.

"No. It's locked."

"Well, have you got the key?"

I shake my head.

"What's in there?"

I shrug, hesitate. "I don't really know. I've only ever been in it once, and that was a long time ago. It's Gran's reading room, where she sees clients. She has the only key."

"Wouldn't she have left the key here?"

"No. She always wears it around her neck."

"How intriguing." She tries the door again, rattles it a little. It's a heavy, thick, wooden door, hung so the hinges are inside the room. No easy way in.

Yowl!

Piper jumps, looks at the front door. "What the hell was that?"

"Probably Cat."

Piper hands me her candle, outrage on her face. "You left your cat on its own all this time?" She turns for the door.

"Be careful, it's more feral than friendly. And it's not our pet, or anyone else's; it just comes by now and then when it feels like it."

Piper opens the door. He is sitting in front of it and stares back at her in that regal manner cats have. A big black cat with battle scars from fights. "What's his name?" Piper asks.

"Cat."

"How imaginative." She bends down, holds out a hand, croons to him, starts to move closer, and I'm expecting her to get a few well-aimed scratches.

"Be careful," I say again.

"Ah, he's just an overgrown kitten, isn't he?" Cat looks cautious but doesn't move, sniffs her hand. She pets him, and he leans into her hand, then winds round her legs, purring so loudly I can hear even from a safe distance.

I shake my head. This is the cat I tried over and over again to make my friend when I really needed one, but he'd only ever accept my company if I came bearing food. Even then he drew blood if I got too close.

Later the three of us are full of sandwiches and snuggled up around the fire. Cat moves from the hearth to Piper, and Ness slinks away from her to me. Smart dog. Cat meows imperiously until Piper pets him, then drops down on the blanket next to her, curls up, and goes to sleep.

"*How* do you do that?" I ask her.

"Do what?"

"Make friends with the unfriendly." I gesture at Cat, who opens one eye enough to glare at me, then goes back to sleep.

"Honestly? I don't know."

"She's soft about animals," Zak says, tapping on his skull as he says it, and Piper throws a pillow at him. Cat protests grumpily at the movement. "Even to the point of not wanting the dogs that killed your mother put down."

I stare at her, surprised.

"It didn't matter what I wanted," Piper says. "They still had them put down."

"Weren't they dangerous?"

"What is dangerous? I'm dangerous. So are you. So is this cat to the unwary, but I wouldn't have him put down, either." Piper's eyes glint oddly in the firelight, Cat's yellow eyes close to her own, and I shiver. Dangerous? Her and me both?

Zak yawns. "Good night, danger girls. Time for some sleep." He leans across and tries to kiss Piper good night, but a flash of Cat's claws makes him retreat. "I think that cat is a secret agent of your dad's," he says.

Ness alongside me, I'm warm at last. The lack of sleep the previous night, the warmth, and the exercise all combine to make me drowsy, but something doesn't want to let go. My eyelids do that fluttering down thing, then open again. The flames blur as my eyes focus in and out, then seem to take over until the flickering, dancing light is all there is.

Flames flicker and dance, bringing both beauty and pain. I'm caught in their searing heat, and there is nowhere to run. The house is razed to the ground.

Bare, dead ground is left behind: only ruined stone marks the burning place, outside Gran's front door.

It is forbidden, like so many other things and places.

But then it shimmers and changes. The flames are gone, and I'm crouched behind Gran's chair. It's too late to run; if they find me now, I'm in deep trouble.

"Where is she?" Isobel says.

"I'm pleased you are so eager to see your daughter. Be patient." Gran's voice is mild, but it stings me. I know Isobel doesn't want to see me; she just wants to know where I am.

"You need to keep closer track of that girl now that she's aware."

Aware of what? I listen harder.

"Careful who you speak to in that tone," Gran says. "You know what is at stake." The warning is clear in Gran's voice now, and even Isobel must hear it.

"I'm sorry, Mother. I didn't mean to question you."

"Fetch me some tea, and I'll let it go."

I make myself small behind the chair. Isobel walks past, heads for the kitchen. The kitchen door shuts.

"Quinn!" I spin around. Gran stands behind me, face like thunder. "Go. Get out before she sees you."

I scamper out into the sunshine and hide behind the chicken shed, unable to believe that Gran knew I was there and let me run. Maybe the punishment will come later.

The sun is warm. I lie in some straw, wondering what they are talking about now. What did Isobel mean about me being aware? Aware of what? I wish I could listen.

I close my eyes . . . and drift.

I'm floating out of myself, back inside the house. Gran and Isobel are below; I can see and hear them.

Then Gran looks up. She sees me, although there is nothing to see. She throws something into the air that fills me with pain —pain that increases when I slam back into my body.

Uneasy dreams shift to wakefulness. I pull the blankets close; the temperature has dropped.

What brought those memories into my dreams tonight? Piper had said something about us being aware; maybe that is it. Then Zak arrived with our lunch, and I didn't have time to ask her what she meant by it.

Traveling to eavesdrop without my body happened not long after I'd been sick. Later on, I decided that it must have been another hallucination from the fever, like the ones that had me in our ancestor's house as it burned down. I frown. Perhaps I was wrong, and it really happened. I thought Gran was being uncharacteristically nice when she let me go after catching me behind the chair. Perhaps she let me go to tempt me, to see if I could come back to listen without my body.

Or to see if she could prevent it.

This is all completely *crazy*. It must have been a hallucination, or a dream.

I shiver; the fire is down to embers. I sigh, and slip out of the covers to put more coal on before it goes out, moving slowly and carefully to be quiet. Ness stirs, opens a sleepy eye, and burrows back into the blankets.

Somehow I don't want to look at Piper and Zak. Have they shooed Cat away and met in the middle? Do they lie in each other's arms? But I can't *not* look, either.

In the faint glow of the fire Zak's face is a dark promise. He smiles in his sleep, but he is alone.

Where's Piper?

Arrrooooooooo!

My skin crawls. Dogs, or worse, faint, in the distance — like in my dream this afternoon, but I'm standing here, wide awake. There's a cold draft along my feet; a chill whisper pulls across the room to escape up the chimney. It's coming from the door to the hall. The door is ajar.

I walk slowly across the room to the hall door and pull it open a little more. The front door is wide open. I step into the hall, teeth almost chattering with the cold. Is Piper out there? Late at night in the dark on the moors, when Wisht Hounds are howling?

I want to run back to the fire, wake Zak, let him look

for her. But something makes me walk to the door: one hesitant step, another. I reach the door and look out into the night.

The sky has cleared, and the stars are out. The moon is almost full; it will be in a few nights.

Piper stands in the moonlight by the gate. She's dressed only in pajamas, but she's not shivering. Cat is curled against her feet. Both she and Cat stare off into the moors, as if their eyes can penetrate the darkness, transfixed and not moving.

I should call out to her. I should draw her in, latch the door, shut the night and dark things out.

But there is something about the way she is standing, the curve of her neck — something wild. Whatever her thoughts, she won't welcome interruption.

Or so I tell myself, but is there something else about her that makes me back away, afraid?

I slip back inside, unobserved.

PIPER

"Let's make a plan for the next few days," I say.

"What do you want to do?" Quinn asks, and takes another bite of her jam sandwich. Breakfast of champions.

"Well, I want us to go visit our gran, of course. But how about today we just hang here?"

Quinn readily agrees. She's not looking forward to seeing Gran; that is clear.

The three of us step outside. The sun is shining, and there is no sign of yesterday's mad weather.

Cat trots up and deposits a dead rat at my feet — a sizable rat for a cat.

"Oh, aren't you clever?" I bend to pet his head and check out the rat. "Good job, but I'm not much into rat. How about you keep him for your breakfast?" I straighten up again. "Zak, I think we need more of our stuff from the car. Maybe you and Quinn could empty the packs and fetch some of it?"

"Right away, Princess Petal," he says in a fair imitation of Dad.

I stick out my tongue. "There are only two packs anyhow, and I want to explore the house. And could you call my dad, tell him we got here OK? There's no signal here."

Quinn looks uneasy — at going alone with Zak, or

leaving me on my own in the house? Either way, they soon go, Ness at their heels.

I should have at least two uninterrupted hours.

It's hard to look for something when you don't know what it is. I know there is *something* in this house — something only a Blackwood can inherit. Mum took care to make sure I remained Piper Blackwood; she did it for a reason. Even though she wouldn't answer my questions, she must have meant for it to be mine.

Gran's bedroom upstairs seems the likeliest place to begin.

I open the door, and there is something about being in here on my own that makes me uneasy. "Don't be silly," I tell myself, out loud. "It's only a room." With my words, the tension eases, and I step inside.

The light is dim; I hold up my candle. A large room. Square. A four-poster bed in the middle of it, a chair, a dressing table, and a chest of drawers.

There are hangings on three walls of this room. There are hints of patterns on the fabric, stitches that outline symbols I cannot quite see in such dim light.

Behind the hangings are bare stone walls — no plaster or anything — and no matter how tightly the stones interlock, the walls radiate cold. I look behind each hanging, careful to keep the candle away from the fabric. Hidden behind one of the hangings is a window.

There's a candle holder on the dressing table. I fix the candle on its spike and leave it there, then slip behind the hanging to look out. It falls around me, heavy on my back, and I have to fight a sense of enclosure that makes me want to get out, and now.

The walls of the house are so thick it is hard to see out the window. The wide window ledge is like a seat. I hoist myself up and sit on it with my back against one side, knees drawn up.

It looks out over the front of the house. The way down the hill that we must have walked in the rain yesterday is indistinct; no path can be seen on the uneven slope littered with rocks. Quinn knew the way; she'd barely looked at her feet, her eyes fixed on the house once it was in sight.

Below, between the house and the ancient wall and its sentry trees, the pattern on the ground made by crumbling rock is more definite. It outlines the walls of a small ruined house. The ground is bare between its boundaries; nothing grows there.

When I went outside last night, I walked around the edges of the ruin, like we did when we got here, without questioning *why* I'd go the long way around—it seemed somehow wrong to cut through. And I stood by the gate for hours, staring into the night. There was *something* out there —something calling to the wild places inside me—despite whatever weird dream Quinn was having that prickled at the edge of my awareness. When Quinn woke up and came out looking for me, I didn't turn or acknowledge she was there, and she soon went back inside.

I drop back down to the floor and push my way past the

hangings and into the bedroom. Now the air seems too dark and stuffy. I'm all for being warm, but that is the largest window in a house lit only by candles—forever closed and obscured.

The chimney breast from the fireplace downstairs is along the only bare wall, the bed close to it. I touch the stone there; it's warm.

Next to my candle on the dressing table is a hairbrush, a few white hairs caught in its bristles. No perfumes or lotions. What looks like a very old carved wooden jewelry box has odd things inside: a feather with a darkened end, a small knife, a few shells.

The chest of drawers is half empty. There are random bits of clothing, mostly worn and darned. There are a few fine things also, and I hold up a colorful skirt and shawl. I'm not sure of the fabric; it feels both light and warm.

Sparse at best, Gran's room doesn't take long to search.

Next, I go to Quinn's bedroom. It is on the other side of the chimney breast, but her walls have no hangings or windows, and despite the warm stone from the fire below on one wall, it feels markedly colder than Gran's. There is a hard, narrow bed, a small chest of drawers. I can't imagine that what I'm looking for could be in here, but I can't stop myself from going through every drawer, touching everything that Quinn must have touched over and over again—as if clues to who and what she is could have seeped into her things.

She has more clothes than Gran, nothing nice. There are jeans that look beyond vintage, and work-type clothes

—blue tunics and trousers. She worked as a cleaner at the hotel, didn't she? So probably had this stuff for that.

On top of the chest of drawers is a chipped china dish with dried flower petals in it, a pretty but cracked empty photo frame, a strip of velvet trim that doesn't match any of her clothes.

There is so little here, and what there is says next to nothing about who Quinn is. Seeing her room now, I understand why she was awestruck by my house, my stuff. But there must be more; there must be *something*.

Impatient, I feel under the mattress, and my hand connects with something hard. I lift up the corner of the mattress. Books? But they're the boring variety. Novels and plays. Nothing interesting, and they look years old—decades, even—and secondhand. Why hide them under a mattress? *Wuthering Heights* may be a favorite—it looks like it's been read and reread a hundred times. And *Romeo and Juliet,* too.

And that's it.

There's a small third room upstairs, next to Quinn's —the place where we'd got extra blankets by candlelight last night. It has a little uncovered window letting in natural light and is kind of a workroom, with a table and a half-made quilt that Quinn said she was working on. I stroke the joined-up squares, the tiny stitches, and the intricate pattern that is emerging from scraps of fabric. Next to it, there is a trunk full of odds and ends, fragments of material, clothes with bits cut out—the source of the squares.

I head downstairs, back to the massive front room where

we'd slept. I'd pretty much covered it last night, but go through it methodically again. The cupboards of the sideboard have odd bits of crockery and towels. There are a few ancient books and odd-looking ornaments on the shelves above. Nothing looks valuable or interesting enough to be an *inheritance.*

The kitchen across the hall is next. It's cold, with a bare flagstone floor. There is a smaller fireplace with a cooking arrangement of sorts, dark and chill. I rattle through the pots and pans. Nothing is interesting, unless you are an antiques collector.

The toilet is out back: not the sort that flushes, not fun in the dark, and full of spiders. There are also two other outbuildings. Quinn said they used to keep chickens in one of them. It's dark and musty, old straw scattered about. A dim scurrying suggests this may be where Cat caught his breakfast.

The other building has a bench, garden implements. There is a vegetable garden between the stone sheds, ravaged by the cold and yesterday's storm. Nothing much is growing there now.

That leaves the locked room inside next to the kitchen. Gran's reading room, Quinn called it. It—whatever *it* is—always had to be in there, didn't it?

I head back inside and examine the door again. There's no way to get in, not without taking serious action—a hefty ax, or fire.

I walk around the outside of the building, counting windows. The downstairs ones are small and far between, and there isn't one in that room.

There is only one answer. We need Gran here, don't we? To unlock the door.

QUINN

Our steps are light and quick today, even on the way back with packs full of supplies and Piper's clothes. Ness is happy to bounce along with us.

"This place is so different in the sunshine," Zak says.

Most things are. Zak, for instance. His skin has a warmer glow. The more brilliant the sun, the easier he seems in my company. I can almost pretend he is as he was before I kissed him. Even though I'm different. And there are no sounds of distant howling, no chance sightings of foxes, normal type or otherwise. Just bird calls, bracken rusty with autumn, yellow flowers bright on gorse.

When I was a child, I loved walking on the moors— exploring, climbing, making friends with the earth and the sky. Even after I fell that time and broke my arm, I couldn't stay away. But something changed when I got a little older. I started to feel the weight of the place, that somehow I was always watched—in a way that made it difficult to breathe.

I'm breathing more freely again. Is it because of Piper and Zak being here? Or maybe I'm the one who has changed. Maybe being here is OK, and nothing bad will come of it. Maybe all those premonitions I had were just nerves about coming back.

We take a break at the top by Wisht Tor, above Gran's house. On a clear day like today, it's a good vantage point to see all around. Zak shades his eyes and peers into the distance.

"What's that over there?" He points at the gray-green smudge of far-off trees. Even from here, they feel cold and impenetrable, seeming to soak the sun from around them to leave a dark stain on the moors—a wicked place, according to Gran. One she warned me to avoid.

"Wistman's Wood," I answer tersely.

"I haven't seen many other trees around here, just the ones in the wall by your house."

"No. Not many trees on the moors, especially as high as those." I start walking again.

"How far away are the woods from your gran's house?"

I shrug without turning back. "An hour's walk or so. Parts of it are dangerous and boggy, especially after all that rain. Anyhow, I should think we've had enough walking for today."

When we get back, Piper pounces on our packs. She empties them out and exclaims over what we brought, what we left. Then she sighs and flops down on the front step. She gestures and I sit next to her, Zak leaning on the house by her side.

"Quinn, what is there to *do* here?"

"Not much."

"Well, how did you used to fill the day?"

"Walking over an hour to work at seven a.m., cleaning for six hours, and walking back again stopped me from getting bored."

Zak looks appalled.

Piper shakes her head, impatient. "No, I mean what did you do around *here,* without any TV or internet or anything?"

"Let's see," I say, arms crossed. "Cooking, tidying up. Sewing. Gardening. Sleeping. Repeat."

"No wonder you liked Winchester so much."

"Yes, I did. But you're the one who wanted to come here, so what do *you* want to do?"

"What do tourists do who come here? Like the ones who came to stay at the hotel where you worked."

"Mostly eat and drink and complain about the weather. Admire the view, walk over the moors, and get lost and need finding by Dartmoor Search and Rescue."

"I know, let's go for a walk!"

"*We* already did," Zak teases her. "Seems to me you didn't want to come. But if you really want to head out, there are those woods we saw. How far away did you say they are, Quinn?"

"An hour if you go fast. It's a boring walk bog-hopping, though, just to see a bunch of trees." I turn away, trying to hide the tension on my face, to keep it from my words. I fail.

"Quinn doesn't want to go there, which makes me instantly curious," Piper says.

"It's a creepy dark place, full of snakes. Part of the walk is boggy, and after all the rain yesterday, you could find yourself up to your neck in mud. Still want to go?"

"Sounds perfect. Let's take a picnic!" Piper says. "You don't have to come; just tell us the way."

I sigh. "The path branches, and the first part isn't obvious. I'll come so you don't get lost. Ness can't come; she might get stuck in a bog."

Piper skips off to pack a lunch, dragging Zak with her. I study the sky: it's clear today. No sign of dangerous weather. But though things can change fast on the moors, the twist in my belly isn't about that. It's something else. Some misgiving about going to the woods, beyond Gran's warnings or my own wish to stay away from that place—something to do with Piper.

I'm resolved to refuse to go, to fake an illness, to argue.

But when they appear with lunch in Zak's pack moments later, Piper is so happy, so excited. Zak is with us. The sun shines, and that and Piper's smile melt my resolve.

I'm sure my misgivings are imagined from Gran's dark hints and warnings about the woods. Who cares if she said not to go there? If I'd listened to everything she said, I'd never have left this place, never have met my sister, or Zak.

Even when she's not here, it's like Gran is still controlling my thoughts and decisions. It's time to put an end to her tight grip on my life, once and for all.

We set out, Ness tethered to her lead at the house and mournful behind us.

"There—see, the patch of bright green?" I say.

"What about it?" Piper asks.

"Don't go near. It's a bog." I heft one of the sticks I brought, go closer, keeping my feet on solid rock, and push the stick into the green. It goes down, down. Then I try to pull the stick back out. I wiggle it, and there is a vague slurping sound; it sinks deeper. I let go, and it slowly disappears.

"Don't go there or anywhere that looks like there," I say. "Got it?"

"What happens if you get stuck in it?" Piper asks.

"The more you struggle, the more you get stuck, and the more you sink. What happens depends how deep the bog is. You might drown if it's deep enough. More likely it won't be, but if no one finds you to pull you out, you'll die slowly of starvation and exposure."

"Cool," Piper says, and Zak and I both shake our heads.

"The path we have to take rambles about and isn't always the same. The bogs seem to shift to catch the unwary. Follow me, and be careful where you put your feet."

It's easy to see the bogs in the sun, at least for me, but this is Dartmoor and there is no guarantee the sun will stay with us. I keep my other stick in case I want to test anywhere, and we're soon through to solid ground. After a while our path links to a main footpath.

"Nice," Zak says, pointing at the warning sign by the way we just came: DANGER — HIDDEN BOGS.

As we walk, Piper is chattering and laughing, more dancing than walking, going forward and then back again. Zak is laughing with her. I walk silently. They're on holiday —that's it, isn't it? This isn't a real place to Piper. It's a curiosity, something she can look at and remember when she's back home, warm and looked after.

As if she can feel my scrutiny, she skips over, links an arm in mine. Her skin is warm where mine is chilled.

"Why are you so happy?" I ask, unable to stop myself.

"I'm with you and Zak. The sun is shining. What's not to like about being right here, right now?" She smiles and laughs, and the sound almost melts the cold knot of apprehension inside me.

Zak has stopped ahead. I know why. We reach him, and Piper's mouth forms an O.

Wistman's Wood seems to rise out of the moors like an unexpected apparition — twisted, stunted oak trees, like souls caught in the chase, frozen in terror for all time. "It's beautiful," Piper murmurs.

It sort of is; I can see what she means, and why people walk to this place to experience it for themselves.

But *wrongness* runs deep in Wistman's Wood.

PIPER

I take Quinn's hand when we approach the trees. There's something about them, drawing me closer, a magnet to my steel, urging me on.

We're all silent, as if that is the way to be in this place.

We step under the first trees. They are twisted and misshapen, and under them, tumbled about as though they were thrown there and stayed where they fell, are big rocks covered in green moss. It is hard to pick my way, and I have to let go of Quinn's hand to keep my balance.

The light is muted, not just from the way the trees block the sun — the canopy overhead admits enough light — but it is the *quality* of the light. It seems somehow diluted. I stop in front of a strangely shaped tree. A few branches extend forward, like limbs. The trunk is bent toward them, as if frozen in the act of running.

I wander farther in, following no particular direction or pattern, just wherever my eyes and then feet take me. Zak is my shadow, with Quinn a little farther behind.

I pause by one of the twisted, stunted trees, oddly drawn to lay my hands on the bark.

Hunger, horrible desperate hunger.
Running in the darkness.
The smell of prey.

Images rip through my mind, and I gasp and take my hand away. I hesitate, and reach my hand back to the wood.

Red, red blood, hot, delicious. Wanting, needing more.
Always more.
Desperation.

"Piper? Piper?" Zak says. He puts a hand on my arm, and I jump. It breaks my connection with the tree.

"What?"

"Quinn thinks we should go." She walks up now, and I turn to look at her. Her eyes are fixed on the trees above.

White fingers of mist, cold and searching, are encircling us. At first the mist is thin and lacy, drifting around the trees; then quickly it's so thick I can barely see past Quinn, a few feet away. Zak's hand finds mine; his other hand reaches out and finds Quinn's. He draws the three of us together.

"I can't believe how fast the weather changes on Dartmoor," Zak says. His voice is quiet, muffled by mist that is heavy and wet around us.

"Should we stay put for a while?" I say. "It'll be too hard to see where we're going."

I lean against the tree without thinking, and terrible hunger and blood fill my mind again. I take Quinn's hand, and press it against the trunk. Her face is close to mine. Her eyes widen, and she jerks her hand away.

So this is something else we twins share.

"What is this place?" I ask her.

"There are many legends about the wood, some more true than others."

"Tell us."

"This isn't the place to speak of them. We need to get out of here, *now*."

But her voice is faint and drifts away. I'm still *there*, hand on the trunk — *tasting the fear, following the trail of blood, and* —

Quinn grabs my arm, pulls me away from the tree. Once my contact with it is broken, I'm back in the here and now, in the wood and the mist.

Carefully, slowly, she leads us through the trees, finding a path I can't see. As we walk and climb, the mist gradually lessens, bit by bit, until we reach the edge of the wood where we came in — the place where a tree appears frozen in flight.

"Without you, we would have been completely lost," Zak says to Quinn. He's right, but for me, in more ways than he means. Without the two of them taking me away from the trees, I'd still be there, somehow lost in that connection with what hungers inside.

Could I ever have pulled away on my own? It was terrifying, and brutal, yes. Yet, somehow . . .

I want to go back.

We climb the twisting slope and walk above the wood. The sun is back on our faces; the wood below us is still shrouded in mist.

"This is a perfect place for our picnic," I say, and Zak starts to get out our rug.

"Couldn't we go up a little farther?" Quinn says, her eyes on the wood below.

"I'm starving," I say, anxious to keep the trees in sight. "Besides, we're out of the wind here."

I shake out our rug on the bracken while Zak gets sandwiches from his pack. We sit down and start to eat.

"All right, Quinn, we're not there anymore! Tell us the legends of the wood," I say, once we've finished eating.

She shrugs. "There are all kinds of stories about Wistman's Wood being haunted. Souls being trapped." She hesitates. "And also that many years ago, it was a place of trial. Gran said that women who were believed to be witches were trapped in a box made of stone, with heavy slabs put into place so they couldn't escape. They'd die slowly, of cold, thirst, starvation. The woods would take their souls."

"Lovely way to go," Zak says. "How was that a trial?"

"If one of them was a witch, she'd use magic to move the stones and escape. Then she'd be caught and burned to death."

"Not much of a choice."

"No." Quinn shrugs. "If you believe in that sort of thing." The way she says it . . . Quinn believes. "Come on. Let's go."

"That's not everything, is it?" I ask.

Quinn starts gathering our lunch things up. "Well, there are legends of the Wild Hunt. That Wisht Hounds are kenneled in the wood. They track the unwary on the moors at night, rip them apart, and make them join the hunt forever." I shiver. My vision, if you can call it that—from the trees. Desperate, all-consuming hunger. Blood.

And my dreams: of running the moors at night, but never being chased, like in Quinn's dream. Never that for me.

The Wild Hunt.

That night I lie awake, staring at the ceiling. Quinn is asleep, Ness, too, but Cat's eyes are wide open and reflect red from the fire. My mind is spinning. Images and sounds and feelings are a mishmash, as if I am staring into a kaleidoscope —or more like I'm in a kaleidoscope myself, and staring out of it.

The trees . . . hunger . . . blood. Fear . . . repulsion . . . blood. Always more blood. It spins round and round in my mind, until I'm falling, down, down, down . . .

It's cold, but there is a growing fire. It's dark, but red eyes can see.

We are trapped.

Frozen.

Waiting.

Hungry, so desperately hungry.

Soon we will be free.

QUINN

Zak and I trudge back up the slope above the house the next morning. I'm going fast, so fast that lack of care soon has me slipping on loose stones. Zak reaches out a steadying hand, but I right myself, and his hand falls back.

At the top I keep going, past Wisht Tor.

"Wait a minute," Zak says, and I pause, turn back. He stands with the tor at his back, the moors sweeping down and then up around us. But he's not looking at the view.

"What is it — can't keep up?"

He shakes his head, a half smile on his lips. "Talk to me, Quinn."

"What about?"

"This place. Your grandmother. What both mean to you. You seem a different person here."

His eyes are intent and curious, but warm — as if he's not driven by a hunger to know like Piper, but by the desire to help a *friend*. And this hooks into the pain inside, the longing to have someone who knows everything about me, someone I can say anything to.

But not like that. Not a friend, and not just someone, but *this* one — the eyes and lips and warm skin, the caring and intelligence and humor, all put together in the tall, fit, Zak-shaped package that now stands so close I could reach out a hand and touch it. Reach out and pull him close.

But that can never happen.

"You'll find out about my grandmother soon enough," I say, and start walking again. We stay silent the rest of the way to the car, but my thoughts race and argue with one another.

Why are we doing this? How does Piper somehow convince me to do just what she wants? Like going to Wistman's Wood yesterday. Despite my fear, despite that strange feeling beforehand that Piper shouldn't go there. Despite Gran's warnings that I convinced myself to ignore.

Piper took my hand and held it to the rough bark of a tree — to feel the anguish, the hunger. I shake my head, not wanting to think what it must mean. And the dream that followed last night? I shiver.

And here I am again, doing exactly what she wants, despite my own judgment.

Something about her dispels fear, makes me believe that things will be all right. There is a magic, an ordinary sort, maybe, but still magic, in her smile. The sort that makes me want what she wants.

Before we came, Piper said all she wanted was to see the house and visit Gran in the hospital. Then last night it all changed. If we go to visit Gran, she said, the shock of seeing the two of us together might be too much for her. We couldn't risk triggering another stroke.

I'd argued; I'd said that when I called, the hospital had told me how strong she was, that she could go home if someone was able to look after her. And I even said if Piper thought we shouldn't go to the hospital together, she could go with Zak and pretend to be me, like I did with our dad in Winchester. I kept to myself that there was no chance of getting that past Gran. She'd know.

Too late I saw my mistake. Piper seized on the hospital saying Gran could go home. She said that we should bring her home, and gently, slowly, let her know we're together here.

Last night, Piper convinced me that everything would be fine, that Gran was just a sick old woman who should be brought home and looked after by us — her family.

Now Zak and I are going to the hospital, without Piper, to collect her.

But without Piper by my side, reason and fear are returning. No matter how I wanted to, I could never leave when Gran was here. I could never stand up to her. What if it is just the same now?

As if she is next to me, Piper whispers in my mind: *Everything will be OK. Things will be different with me here.* And I hold on to that, inside.

"Quinn, isn't it? I'm so happy to see you. But I know someone who will be even happier." The nurse is *very* pleased to see me, but something lurks behind her smile. She glances at Zak. "Who's this?"

"My friend Zak. He's driven me here today. How is my grandmother?"

"Much better. She's still struggling with her speech, and

walking is difficult for her, but she is very keen to go home. We've been trying to reach you, you know." A disapproving look. "The only number we had was at some hotel where you work, and they didn't know where you were. Come along, now; I'll take you to her."

She starts down the hall.

"Do you want to go on your own?" Zak asks.

I shake my head no and, without thought, take his hand. Then I realize what I've done and try to let go, but he holds on firmly. "It's OK," he says.

The nurse pauses at a door, gestures to us, and bustles away. It was in her eyes; she didn't want to go in. Is Gran keen to go home, or are they keen for her to leave?

I open the door. Gran is sitting bolt upright in bed, pillows behind her. Her white hair is twisted into a braid, and she is wearing her own shawl over a hospital gown. She turns her head, looks at me, then Zak, at our hands held together. Her eyes widen. She reaches out her own hand. Is it shaking?

I let go of Zak and force myself to walk across the room to her.

"H-h-hands," she says. Irritation crosses her face at the effort.

"Hands?" I say, and hold mine out. She grips my right hand, tight, and stares at Isobel's bracelet. Was she staring at that, and not at Zak and me holding hands? Are there *tears* in her eyes? No. There couldn't be. Could there?

"Is it all right that I've got Isobel's bracelet?" I ask her, suddenly afraid she'll ask me to take it off—that she'll want it for herself, to remind her of her daughter.

But she nods her head and folds my left hand over the right one with the bracelet. "Keep," she says clearly. "A-a—" She frowns. "Always." She smiles. Her eyes are glistening bright. And something stirs the fear inside me, some other emotion, and now my eyes are stinging. I blink, hard. She *wants* me to keep it?

She turns her head, fixes Zak with a stare, and gestures him forward with her hand.

He walks over, and she points at the chair next to her on the other side of her bed. He sits down.

"Gran, this is my friend Zak."

She holds out her hand again, and he gives her his— a normal, natural gesture, but she is not a normal, natural woman. She holds it a moment, then turns it and stares intently at the palm. Zak looks to me, puzzlement in his eyes, but he doesn't pull away.

Gran releases his hand, reaches out and touches him on the left side of his chest, where his heart beats.

She smiles, and one of the knots inside me loosens— she likes him. I wasn't sure what we'd do if she decided he couldn't come back to the house with us.

"*Zaki,*" she says. "Pure." She taps his chest near his heart. This time her words are clear.

The smile on Zak's face falls away, and his eyes fill with pain and wonder. He shakes his head. "How did you know?"

Gran smiles again, but says nothing more.

Soon the nurse returns with paperwork—apparently it was ready and waiting—for Gran to be released. It's hard to believe they'd release her to me the way she is, but it's what Gran wants. Gran's wishes make all things possible. A doctor is found to sign the papers, and while he is having a word with Gran, Zak draws me aside.

"How did she know my name is Zaki?"

"Your name is Zaki, not Zak?"

He nods. "Only my mother ever called me that." He's shaken. "It means 'pure of heart' in Arabic. Does your gran know Arabic?"

I shake my head.

"She must do, and guessed that's my background, so Zak is Zaki." Zak is looking for the logical reason for the illogical, and I'm tempted to let him grasp for it. But no. He should know.

"Think about it. She's lived in an isolated house on Dartmoor her whole life. How would she have learned this language?"

"How do you explain it, then?"

"She knows things about people. They come to her to learn about themselves, about what has happened, what will happen; to make wishes to change these things."

"Are you saying she's some sort of psychic?"

"She's a wise woman, a healer, a seer."

Before he can ask if that means what his eyes say he thinks it means, the nurse is back.

"Now, Quinn, your grandmother can only walk very short distances, so I've arranged a special loan of a hospital wheelchair. Don't tell anyone." She winks, nervous and anxious for us to go, and go now. We thank her. Gran is helped into the chair by an orderly, and we wheel her down the hall and out a door, then down a ramp. We'll have to go the long way to the house with her in that chair, and even then it will be difficult. I hope the weather holds.

Zak helps Gran into the passenger seat of his car, then the orderly shows us how to collapse the chair. It just fits into the boot.

"How are we going to get her to the house?" Zak says softly, obviously thinking along the same lines as me. "Should we maybe head for the hotel?"

Gran's ears are sharp. "No," she says. This time her voice is strong and clear.

"That's one word she's worked out perfectly," the orderly mutters as he walks off. Gran turns in her seat, gives him a dark look, and he stumbles. He hits his head on the railing and staggers through the door.

"We'll get there," I say. "The long way."

PIPER

I'm watching from Gran's bedroom. I'd searched the house again, sure I wouldn't find anything, but restless and needing to fill the time. I'd left her bedroom for last. When I was done, I'd pushed the heavy wall hanging out of the way, and pulled myself up to sit on the window ledge and watch. I tried to entice Cat to come with me for company, but he wasn't having it, and disappeared downstairs. Even Ness won't come into this room, and is curled up mournfully in the hall outside the open door.

It's late afternoon, the sun low in the October sky. Is something wrong, is there some reason why Gran couldn't come home? Did Quinn change her mind and refuse to bring her?

Ness barks. I hear her light paws scamper down the stairs to the front door. Does her Zak early warning system work here, too?

Again I scan the hill where we walked to this place; nothing. But then, away to the right, light glints off something in the distance, against the sun. I squint, trying to see.

It's a tall figure, pushing something? Moments pass, and they are farther down, nearer, and I can see it is Zak; there is a hunched, slight figure in a wheelchair. Quinn walks alongside, carrying some bags. Ah, of course: our gran is in a wheelchair, so they must have come what Quinn called the long way.

I watch a little longer, then pull myself off the window ledge. It wouldn't do to be spotted. I slip down the stairs and out the back through the kitchen as agreed.

A smile plays on my lips. I've slept so little since we got here that I should be exhausted, but instead I feel wired. Giddy, I laugh and almost skip around the dead vegetable garden under the watchful eye of a bemused Cat, sitting high above me on the roof of the house.

Everything is working just the way I want, like I always knew it would.

QUINN

Zak pushes the wheelchair as far as the gate. There's no way it'll get across the uneven ground that skirts the ruins at the front of the house. It will be hard for Gran on foot even with help.

"Ma'am, I could carry you?" Zak asks.

"No," she says, voice sharp. We have learned on the way that the hospital guy was right; no *is* her best word.

Zak holds the chair while I help her pull herself to her feet, as she's had to on difficult parts of the path along the way. Her face is drawn, exhausted, but her eyes are bright.

She takes my arm, leans on me heavily as we step into her domain. Zak follows behind, carrying her chair. She surveys the ruins of the burning place, as if afraid it has somehow changed. Every crumbled stone receives its own look or touch on the slow way around our ancestors' ruined house; her face is drawn with every contact she makes. What does she feel? The place is forbidden to me, like so many others. Since the fever and the dreaming all those years ago, this place is one I'm glad to avoid.

There's excited barking through the door.

"That's Ness," I say. "Zak's puppy that we told you about. Zak?"

He puts the chair down and goes ahead to open the door,

catching Ness by her collar before she can jump all over us. Gran gives Ness a careful look, then ignores her existence.

I'm nervous as we step through the door. Will Piper have done as she said she would — watched for us, then hidden away? My eyes dart about, but there is no sign of her. This is Piper's plan, after all; there's no reason for her to change it.

Gran's sharp eyes want to see everything — she has me help her into every room downstairs, one at a time. Her eyes linger on the door to her locked reading room, but she walks past it, and we start up the stairs to her bedroom. Can she see Piper's footprints, feel that someone else has been breathing the air in her house?

I help her into bed, settle her pillows behind her.

She catches my hand in hers, so I sit next to her bed. She tries to say something — she must be full of questions about where I've been, how I got Isobel's bracelet, Zak.

She swallows, and tries again.

"S-s-ry." She shakes her head, so distressed when I don't understand that I'm compelled to say something.

"It's all right. Have some sleep. I bet you'll wake up feeling much better tomorrow, and the words will come."

Her eyes are warm. She touches a hand to my cheek and tries again. This time I can make out her word: *sorry*. She taps her chest. "Wrong. Sorry," she says again.

I'm confused, and a little scared. Gran has *never* apologized for anything, or seemed to even consider she could be wrong. I want to ask her what she means, but her eyes are closing.

Soon her breathing is even, and her hand on mine slackens. I ease my fingers away.

I watch her sleep. She is small, frail. This is the woman I've been scared of my whole life? Something has changed and shifted between us, and it isn't just in her. It is in me, too.

Is this Piper's influence, or is it just from me having been away from Gran for a while? The weight of eyes watching me that I felt here for so long is gone. The inbuilt compulsion to do what Gran wants is mysteriously absent, and it gives me a sense of lightness inside, a freedom, as if I could even leave if I wanted to.

But she said she was *wrong*. I want to shake her awake and demand to know about what, and why. Keeping me isolated here? Keeping me hidden away from my sister, my parents? Most of all, I want to demand to know *why*. Why Gran and Isobel never told us about each other. How could they do that to us? But that is a question I can't ask; at least, not yet — not until Piper has tried her plan of masquerading as me to Gran. Until that fails — and it will, I have no doubt about that — I can't admit I know about my twin.

I watch Gran sleep. But only because that is what *I* choose to do.

PIPER

I grip the tray in my hands and climb the stairs, full of a mix of nervous energy, excitement, and something else —something I don't like to name or acknowledge. *Fear.* It's Quinn's fault, infecting me with her fear, with her unspoken but obvious belief that Gran won't be fooled by this masquerade.

At the top of the stairs, I awkwardly shift the tray against my hip, careful not to spill the porridge. I raise one hand and knock lightly.

Turn the knob.

Open the door.

Step through.

She's lying back, eyes closed. I study her. She's small, slight, barely a shape under the quilt. It is pulled up high so I can't see her neck, can't see if the key to the locked room is around it. Her hair is white, her skin so pale I watch closely to make sure that she's still breathing.

Quinn said to leave the tray on the dressing table beside Gran if she was asleep. But Quinn's not here.

I will myself to look and move like Quinn. I've been studying her. She smiles less than I do, rarely makes eye contact. When she does, it is to make a point or to challenge —there is always a reason. She walks a little differently too: doesn't swing her arms as much as I do, moves with less bounce. She's more compact and connected to the earth — less wasted energy, as if energy is something she needs to hoard.

"Good morning, Gran. I've brought you some breakfast," I say, and walk toward her.

She stirs; her eyes open a little, then wide all at once. She stares. Her eyes are a startling, piercing, deep blue. I look down, walk to put the tray next to her, moving as much like Quinn as I can.

Tray on the table, I straighten, raise my eyes. She's sitting bolt upright, still staring.

"Shall I?" I gesture at her pillows and, hearing no reply, lean toward her, pull the pillows up behind her. As I move away, she grabs one of my hands in hers. Her grip is strong, surprisingly so. She turns my hand, studies my palm, then lets go.

"Why are you here?" she says. And I'm surprised after what Zak told me that her speech is so clear.

I gesture at the tray. "To bring you your breakfast."

She raises an eyebrow. "Why are you here, *Piper?*"

I look back at her, considering. Is she guessing, or does she know? But the plan to win her confidence and the key to her reading room as Quinn is only plan A. There will be other ways.

"How did you know?" I say, finally.

"*Knowing* is what I do. And the business of lies is my own; I see through them. Again: why are you here?"

I kneel beside her bed. "I wanted to meet you, to know you. To know the family my mother spoke about."

"I'm surprised she spoke of such things to you. What did she say?"

Can she really see through lies? I consider my answer. "She said she chose to leave you and her heritage behind. She took me with her, but this was not *my* choice."

"And you, Piper. What do you know of this *heritage?* Do you mean this house?" She gestures at the room around us. "You don't want to stay here," she adds, saying the words slowly, drawing them out.

And I don't. Suddenly, I'd rather be anywhere else in the world. A compulsion to stand, to leave this room and this house fills me, and I'm on my feet, poised to run.

I shake my head and risk a lie. "I want to stay." And as I say the words, the compulsion leaves me.

She raises an eyebrow. "I see you know both more and less than you think you do about your *heritage.* But do you know what coming here has cost you? What you have done to find this place?" Her voice is cold. "What you seek would cost far more."

"You must tell me." I put all the honey and persuasion I can into my words. "You're my grandmother; you have to help me."

She smiles, but it is thin and mocking. "Yet I have two granddaughters. Poor Isobel: cursed once, cursed twice. Therein lies the problem. Quinn!" she says, voice raised. "Quinn! Come here now."

Light footsteps run up the stairs, so instantly she must have been waiting for this call.

QUINN

"Come here, Quinn," Gran says. "Stand next to your twin." Her face is unreadable, and dread twists in my stomach. Is she angry that Piper is here, that I let her pretend to be me?

I walk across the room and stand next to Piper by the side of Gran's bed.

I glance at Piper. The way she is standing, the tilt of her head—I can read her now, I realize. She's annoyed about something, but trying to keep it hidden. Not a skill she has practiced often.

Gran studies us; the moment stretches. She finally shakes her head. "So alike, but are you different inside? At birth I read you clear. Your paths were obvious, and tied together. Action was taken to sever this tie, but that obviously didn't work. Now I cannot see."

"Gran!" I say, surprised. "You're talking so much better this morning, just like I said you would."

"Just so. I thank you, Quinn, even as I worry about what it means. Like the two of you: it is half good, half bad." She smiles sadly and shakes her head. I stiffen, shocked that she just straight-out told Piper the truth: that one of us was good, and one bad. And it isn't hard to work out who is which. I was the one hidden away, too dangerous to be let out—just like Isobel always told me.

But Piper doesn't focus on that.

"What do you mean about paths?" Piper asks. "What action was taken? Do you mean us being separated?"

"And what action will be taken by each of you now?" Gran says, and shakes her head again. "Time will show us. On this I will say no more." She fixes her eyes on Piper. "But you should never have come here. How did you find this place?"

I look from one of them to the other. Gran seems to know something she isn't saying; Piper says nothing, but her shoulders are back, her eyes blazing. She's furious.

"I'm sorry, Gran," I say, jumping in before Piper explodes. "I brought her here."

"Oh? I suspect that this fault is not yours. Yet bad blood must rise from it, as it runs through both of you."

I frown, confused. Bad blood runs through *both* of us?

"What do you mean?" Piper says, unable to stay silent any longer. "Our blood is yours."

"And your father's."

Piper shakes her head. "Dad hasn't got a bad freckle on him, let alone anything else."

Gran looks back at her, saying nothing, but there is something else *there,* in her eyes. Piper said that Isobel appeared on Dad's doorstep with her and told him the baby was his. I decided Isobel must have been telling the truth: she warned me for years about the danger of lying, so how could she herself have lied?

But was I wrong?

I stand there, hands together in front of me, one idly stroking the pendant on my bracelet. Staring at Gran. Somehow I can see the truth—the lie revealed—in her eyes.

"He's not our father. Is he?" I ask.

Gran doesn't answer. Half-remembered comments and inferences from years gone by surface in my memory. I'd thought Gran's negative views of my father didn't line up with Piper's dad. I was right: they weren't about him, because he's not our dad.

And I feel like I've lost something I never had.

What about Piper? This must be a far greater shock for her. I turn toward her, but her face is a mask, betraying nothing.

That night I scoop coal onto the fire as Piper arranges our blankets closer to its warmth. The coal is getting low; I'll have to make the trek for more tomorrow.

She settles in, and I lie down next to her, snuggle a blanket around me. Cat is against her back, and Ness against mine.

"Poor Zak. He must be lonely," Piper says. "I wonder if he'll scoot down to visit us?"

"I doubt it. He seemed to get that when Gran says to do something, you do it." He'd moved into my room upstairs without complaint when Gran suggested he shouldn't be sleeping in the same room as Piper and me.

"Who does that woman think she is, lining us up like some sort of freak show and checking us out? I've got a good mind to tell her what I think of her and Mum, keeping us apart all these years when we should have been together."

I feel warm inside. Despite the darkness inside me, Piper still wants to be with me — her sister.

"With Gran, it might be better to keep that to yourself."

"Well. When I'm angry, it *has* to come out. One way or another. But it can wait."

I hesitate, but there is one thing I have to ask her. "Piper, what did you make of Gran's reaction when I said that Dad isn't really our dad?"

She takes my hand, turns so she is on her side. Her face, as familiar as mine, is lit up by the fire, a shadow across it in the flickering light.

"It doesn't matter to me; he'll always be my dad. And when he told me the story of how Mum just appeared with me, I guessed maybe he wasn't our biological father. How about you? Are you OK?"

"I don't know. I don't know why it should bother me. I barely know him. And until a few weeks ago, I never even knew he existed."

She absorbs that, eyes thoughtful. "Maybe that's harder because you went from no father, to maybe having one, and back to no father."

"Yeah. I guess."

"You've still got me." Her eyes are like a cat's, reflecting the light. "You'll always have me." Her hand grips mine tighter.

And I'm afraid she'll ask me more about what Gran said —about good and bad. Bad blood. That if she hasn't already, she'll work out why we were separated.

She doesn't say anything else. Her eyes close; her breathing evens.

But for me, the escape of sleep is harder to find.

Come: run and hunt together!

The words of the summoning are in me, part of me, drawn out of lips that try to stop them. They are in my throat, my ears, reverberating all around until the very woods themselves vibrate with their power.

The trees crack, and break.

We burst free!

We run.

Front paws, back paws; front, back; loping across the moors —flying over gorse, bracken, rocks. They run with me, in desperate joy and hunger, tongues lolling out, side by side.

The Wisht Hounds of death and nightmare.

I'm terrified to be so near them, but it's even worse than that. When I look down, I see great black paws and huge claws as I run.

I'm one of them.

Inside, I'm screaming, NO, NO, NO, *but I can't get away.*

We fan out to form a circle.

Trapping the mindless prey.

We tighten the ring. Bleating, they run in terror, one straight for my waiting teeth.

The first sweet taste of hot blood, spurting down my throat, maddens my senses. It fills me with lust for more.

I sit bolt upright, heart thudding madly. Gradually I become aware of my own body, the blankets underneath—the ordinary, familiar things of this room.

What a nightmare. It was so vivid; it was like I was there, like it all really happened.

And, worst of all, I loved the kill—the blood, hot and sweet. My stomach turns. I try to force out the memory, the taste, and concentrate on breathing to avoid being sick.

Was I even asleep? It was more like the times I fainted when I was a child. The fainting that so alarmed Isobel and Gran. And that other time, when I left my body to listen in to them. Also, more recently, when I was in Winchester with Zak; it felt like I traveled back in time to when that huge dog was sitting on my chest.

I shake my head. Tonight's "dream" felt like all those times. What could it mean?

I look around me. Apart from Ness, I'm alone.

Where's Piper?

PIPER

The sun is nearly here; soon it will steal over the hill and take the night.

I'm not cold. I should be, but my blood is hot, like in that crazy dream I had last night—I was running over the moors, all the way to Wistman's Wood. My hands on the bark called forth the hounds trapped within the dark trees.

When we went to bed last night I was still angry, so angry, with Gran—her saying I should never have come here. When it is my *home.* I'd closed my eyes, stilled my breathing, but inside I stewed, unable to sleep. When the dream finally came, I imagined it was Gran's throat I ripped out.

When I woke up, I was outside, past the gate: am I sleepwalking now? My bare feet were caked in mud, sore; there were scratches on my legs. I walked back through the gate, past the ruins to the front step, and sat there, with only Cat for company.

Not cold, not tired, though I should be both. My spirits sing with the sun as it rises.

It's still very early. I should go in, clean myself up, pretend I've been in my bed asleep all night so no one worries . . .

So no one questions.

"Come on, Cat," I say. "Let's try to catch some z's."

. . .

Later, after breakfast, I pull Zak's hand and drag him out-side. "Alone, at last." He wraps his arms around me. "Your gran must be in cahoots with your dad."

"Ha. As if! And the thing about that is, I'm pretty sure he's not my dad."

"*What?*"

And I tell him the story, what Gran said, what she didn't say.

"Do you think it's true?"

"Probably. I'd kind of guessed it. I mean, Mum was a stunner and, what, twenty years younger than Dad? And she just appeared with me and said I was his. I wonder if even *he* believed her. I don't think he minded, either way, so long as she stayed with him. But I wonder if that's why he didn't want me to come here. Maybe he didn't want me to find out."

"He's still your dad; the one who raised you."

"And he always will be. But that's not all I found out."

"What else could there be?"

"Gran said some weird stuff. The gist of it seems to be that when Quinn and I were born, she could see that we were half good, and half bad. And so we were separated. She seems to think us being together is dangerous." What I don't tell him is that Mum said much the same thing to me.

He shakes his head. "That's crazy."

"Well, there is something about Quinn that isn't quite

right. There always has been, but she seems, I don't know, *weirder* here."

"She's had a lot to deal with."

"I suppose."

"Piper, this is rubbish. Don't let that superstitious stuff from your gran freak you out. Besides, I'm here, so you've got nothing to worry about. But if it'll make you happy, I'll see if I can get Quinn to open up a little." He wraps his arms, warm and solid, around me.

There's a throat-clearing sound behind us. We turn. Quinn is standing in the doorway, an odd look on her face. How much did she hear?

"Anyone want to help me fetch some coal?" she asks.

QUINN

"Quinn, talk to me," Zak says.

"What about?"

"I don't know. The weather, who your father might be, how your gran is freaking Piper out. Anything."

"Well. The sun is out today, but with a northerly wind of about ten knots, I'd say."

Zak laughs. He's taking his turn at pushing the empty wheelbarrow up the path. "Anything else?"

I shrug. "Gran seemed to imply that our father isn't who we thought, but from what you said, Piper must have told you, so why ask me? And as far as Gran freaking Piper out, well. Freaking people out is kind of what Gran does. She freaked you out with that thing about your name, didn't she?" We round a tor. "Stop here," I say, and Zak looks around as if expecting a coal shop to appear.

"Coal? Here?"

"Yes. Here." I find the place under some twigs and dirt, and pull the lid open.

Zak peers in. "Right, so why is there what appears to be a coal bunker dug in the ground in the middle of nowhere?"

I start shoveling coal into the wheelbarrow. "Well, actually, it's not very middle-of-nowhere here. We're not far off a farmer's track." I gesture the opposite direction from the way we came.

"And how does the coal appear here?"

"Well, the farmer keeps it filled up for us, of course!"

"Oh. Obviously. And why does he do that?"

"He kind of owes Gran a favor."

"Forever?"

"That's what owing Gran a favor is like."

We start back. "Do you usually do this on your own?"

"Of course. I'm stronger than I look."

"I get that. But if you want to talk to somebody, Quinn, I'm here."

"And then you can report back to Piper."

"I wouldn't do that."

"Sure."

We continue, in silence. We take a different path from the one we did on the way to the coal, a slightly longer way but easier with the full wheelbarrow. With Zak to help, I put more in than I usually would but insisted on taking equal turns.

We round a corner, and I slow. There is *something* about this place. What is it? I've come this way many, many times, but it's not that bugging me now. It's something else.

Zak turns back. "Tired? Let me take it."

I shake my head, frown. I put the barrow down. Leave it, and take a thin path through some rocks to the side. Zak follows.

"Quinn? Are you OK?"

I don't answer. My blood is racing, as if I've been running. I'm back in that dream, or vision, or whatever it was, from last night—running across the moors. Chasing, circling round, herding them to where the ground dips down, and . . .

There.

This is the place.

The ground is stained with blood. There are three sheep, or what is left of them. Their throats are ripped out, entrails scattered. There are footsteps in the blood—a heel pad and four toes, like a dog's but with long claws, and the whole thing way too big for any normal dog.

Hot, delicious blood.

I'm split between here and now, and then. My stomach rises and I fight not to be sick. Did that really happen? Was it me? I was asleep. It couldn't have been.

Yet here is the grisly scene that remains.

There are footsteps behind me.

"Oh my God." Zak's voice.

I whirl around.

"What could have done this?" His eyes are fixed on the remains, his hand raised to his face, and that is when I notice the smell, the flies. I was seeing it in my mind as if it had just happened, the blood warm and fresh. Not this.

"Let's get out of here," I say, and hurry back to the wheelbarrow, wanting to put as much space between me and *that* as I can.

"Gran? Can we talk?"

She gestures me into her bedroom. I shut the door

behind me. Nervous feet take me across the room to her bedside. I'd waited until Piper was asleep, too freaked out to sleep myself. I *have* to know. Did I really do that? How?

Only Gran will know, and I'm more afraid of myself than I am of her now.

I sit next to her.

"You're frightened," she says.

"Yes. Something happened. It doesn't make sense, but I'm afraid I did something bad."

"Tell me."

I describe the dream of the night before, the scene of the sheep today. Gran remains silent, her face grave.

"Well? At first I thought it was a dream. But I saw the sheep; Zak did, too. It couldn't have been a dream. So what was it?"

Gran's face is etched with sadness. "It wasn't a dream. What you have described is spirit traveling—when you leave your body behind and go somewhere in another form. From what you've told me, I believe you were present this way when the hunt was summoned. Whether you led or merely followed, I cannot say. If you led, you will be marked to the hunt now."

I look back at her in horror. "Spirit traveling? *Me?* But I can't do stuff like that." I deny it even though, deep inside, I know: those other times weren't dreams or imaginings, either.

"It's in your blood, Quinn, and it always has been

—as my granddaughter. And you did travel when you were younger. I stopped you for a time using various means—spells and herbs. Do you remember?"

This means . . . no. It can't be true. Am I . . . like Gran? Am I a witch? I shake my head, in denial of all I have been remembering since I got back here.

"It is true. And now the hunt has been awakened, for the first time in many years: a call I have resisted my whole life. None are safe on the moors."

My blood chills and slows in my veins. "What did you mean when you said if I led I'm marked to the hunt now?"

"That you are part of them, fated to join them over and over again, whether by traveling or death. I tried, Quinn." Her hand touches my cheek, then falls away. "I shielded you from your powers and stopped you traveling out of your body. I used every charm and spell I could come up with. It was hard staying one step ahead of you. But wearing Isobel's bracelet blocks spells—it broke the protective shield I had around you. Yet still I hoped that your fear of dogs would keep you away from the Wisht Hounds."

I stare at her, shocked. That's why she made me terrified of dogs when I was a small child.

I touch the bracelet on my wrist. "Should I take it off?"

"No! Don't ever take it off. The shield is broken, and I lack the strength to replace it now. You would be at far more risk without it."

"What about the pendant?" I say, and touch it: smooth

stone on one side, markings on the other that not everyone can see. "Is it really a pendant of power? Is it part of what the bracelet does, or something else?"

Gran's eyes widen at the words *pendant of power*—the name Wendy told me. She nods. "That is what it is. But I can't say for sure what the pendant will do for you: it varies with the wearer. It will help you with whatever is most important to you. You'll have to work that out for yourself."

"What can I do to put things right?"

"Quinn, I have told you your whole life, you must guard against the darkness. Don't let it take hold of you. There is nothing I can do to save you if it does."

"How can I stop it?" I whisper.

"Only you can answer that." She shakes her head. "I've done all I can."

"This is why I was separated from Piper and kept here. Isn't it?"

"Yes."

One word that confirms every fear I ever had.

"Quinn, when you were born, I saw your path. That you would destroy your family and steal your sister's life. Your mother and I separated you and Piper in an attempt to break the tie between you, the tie that would lead to this path. By finding your twin, you have taken the first steps to destroying your family. All I have done your whole life is try to prevent this." She shakes her head. "Don't make me a failure. Now go."

Her eyes are kind and full of pity, but her face is repelled.

Like she can't bear to look at me any longer. The same way Isobel always looked at me.

I stand, knees shaking, and walk to the door.

Downstairs, I slip back under the covers next to Piper. I watch her chest gently rise and fall. We may look the same, but somehow she has a spark that I don't have, that makes her beautiful. Even in sleep, she is so alive. *My sister.* Something I thought I would never have.

Could it really be so dangerous for us to be together? My hand reaches out, strokes her hair. She murmurs in her sleep, moves toward me. I'm shaking; hungry for warmth, for life.

For love.

I hold my hand up in the firelight. The pendant on my bracelet glistens. What is most important to me? I don't know. Freedom, maybe. Or being loved for who I am.

Or even just working out who I am, or what I should do. I sigh.

My fingers stroke the pendant and close around it, and all at once I know: *the truth.* That is what is most impor-tant to me. Truth and half-truths, too — the sort that hide behind lies, that I must fight to reveal.

Though my truth just now is straightforward: I want to leave this place. I *must* leave this place, alone, for all our sakes. Winchester and Dad and the lovely house there fill my mind. But if he isn't our father, I have nowhere to go.

PIPER

Gran pulls the key from under her clothes and unlocks the only locked door in her house: the one to her reading room.

"Come in, both of you," she says.

Quinn is pale, with dark smudges under her eyes. I gesture for her to go first, so she shields me. She steps in slowly. I turn and cough by the door, then follow her in.

I stand there, trying to take it all in at once. A small room, or does it just feel that way because it is so full? Of chairs, a table. Shelves everywhere, packed with books, ornaments. Crystals and drawings hang on the walls.

While there are some books, I'm guessing this isn't called a *reading room* because of that.

"Sit," Gran says. There are two seats in front of the table, one behind. Gran lowers herself into that one.

I sit down. Quinn sits next to me slowly, as if she is reluctant to be here. I look at her, but her eyes are cast down.

"Quinn, Piper," Gran says, and Quinn's eyes are drawn up to her along with mine. "I've given this situation some thought. I've decided that if you find the right questions to ask me, I will answer them, in hope it will help you find your way. But there is a cost."

"What is it?" Quinn asks, her voice quiet.

"The truth. Only the truth can be spoken in this room."

"I have a question," Quinn says. Her voice is stronger. We both look at her.

"Go on," Gran says.

"Who is our father?"

Gran looks back at her and sighs. "Not who you thought he was." Distaste crosses her face.

"That isn't much of an answer," Quinn says.

"True. My room, my rules."

"My turn," I say. "Mum said something about there being an inheritance."

"Only speak truth," Gran admonishes, an eyebrow raised.

"It is the truth! Well, Dad said Mum said that. That there is an inheritance, one only a Blackwood can have. What is it?"

"Straight to the point." Gran smiles thinly. "There is. Only a direct blood descendant can inherit, and women of our family do not change the Blackwood name. Now that Isobel is gone, it will come to one of you when I die. Only one of you can inherit. You cannot imagine how high the cost. Or maybe you can." She stares at Piper. "Think about that."

"What could it be?" I ask Quinn.

"What?"

"The inheritance." Could she really be that indifferent to it?

"I don't care."

"Really?"

"It's true! I want to leave this place. You can have it, whatever it is."

"Do you mean it? Will you help me find it?"

"Yes."

I throw my arms around Quinn. Her shoulders are stiff at first, but relent. She droops against me.

"What is that stuff about not changing the Blackwood name?"

Quinn shrugs. "I've heard Gran say before that names are powerful, that some power is tied up in our name. I don't know what it is."

"What can I do for you in return?" I ask her.

She shrugs.

"There must be something you want . . . wait. I have it!"

Quinn pulls away, looks in my eyes. "What?"

"Our father. You want to know who our biological father is. If you help me find my inheritance, I'll help you find him." I hold out a hand. "Deal?"

Quinn pauses, as if digesting what I said, and the words I used to claim it — *my* inheritance.

Then she shrugs. "Yes. Deal." She puts her cold hand in mine.

QUINN

Isobel's bracelet itches on my wrist as Piper drags me back toward Gran's reading room. It felt so *wrong* to be in here before, when Gran was opening the door and beckoning us in. That's nothing to how it feels now.

"Come *on*," Piper says, impatient. "She left the door unlocked, didn't she? That's practically a written invitation. We need to search her room. She's asleep, and Zak won't be back for ages yet." He volunteered to walk to the car and go on a supply run when Gran professed a craving for lemon cake this morning, knowing we didn't have any eggs or lemons—a craving I was sure she'd invented to have us alone with her this morning.

I pause at the threshold. The last time I entered this room uninvited, I got locked alone in the dark for two days.

But this time I'm sure Piper is right. Gran took us in there this morning, then left it unlocked? I can't believe that was an accident; she must have done it on purpose. I finally follow Piper in.

"What are we looking for?" I ask Piper.

"I was hoping you'd know. For now, let's just check out *everything*." Piper starts on one side of the room; I take the other. I'm randomly looking on shelves, in drawers, at drawings of strange symbols, etched crystals, tied charms of dried herbs and grasses that Gran had me collect for her.

The time I was here on my own as a child, I had barely a moment to admire the shiny crystals before Gran caught me, my hand on a book I'd just taken from the shelf. My bracelet itches again, and I scratch at my wrist. The book that had the same symbol on the front as the pendant on this bracelet. The book Gran reacted so strongly to seeing in my hand, even though I promised her I'd never even opened it.

With more purpose now, I scan the shelves, searching my memory for details. The book had a dark red cover of ancient, worn leather; the binding was hand sewn. It's not here.

I sigh and sit on Gran's chair, fiddling with Isobel's bracelet. My fingers stroke the surface of the pendant and close around it. What are we really looking for? Two things: information about our father and whatever it is that Piper wants to inherit. Once we find these things, I can leave this place and never come back.

With everything else that is going on, why do I feel so desperate to find out about my father? Gran's face earlier said it all: she didn't think much of him. But even if he is a total waste of a human being, I feel almost compelled to find him. Is it because I feel cheated that I thought I'd found a real parent in Winchester, and I was wrong?

I lean back in Gran's chair. Things look different from here. My eyes drift around the room, as Piper goes through a shelf on the other side of the table. I twist to look behind me. There is an ancient, dusty box not visible from the other chairs, hidden by shelves and tucked in a back corner. I turn and lean down to pick it up, then put it on the table.

"What have you got there?" Piper comes to stand next to me.

"I don't know. Some box. I haven't seen it before."

The lid is tight on top, and I wiggle it a bit to get it off. Inside are drawings of faces, newspaper clippings, photographs, bits of paper with notes. Some of the paper is so old, it feels as if it might crumble to dust if handled too much. Careful not to disturb the order, I start looking through, but it seems mixed up, random.

"Is it family stuff?" Piper asks.

I shake my head. "I don't think so; there are no Blackwoods mentioned. It's about some other family. Name of Hamley." I scan the newspaper clippings. "A very unlucky family, by the look of things. Stuff kept happening to them, even as recently as a few decades ago and going right back. Hunting accidents, disasters, murder, bankruptcy. You name it. It's like they were cursed." Hairs prickle on the backs of my hands.

I start looking through the drawings and photographs, and Piper watches over my shoulder. "That's weird," she says.

"What?"

"It's like the photos are exposed funny. They've all got a shadow on their faces." I look again, but don't see what Piper does. I shrug.

There are initials and dates on the backs of the

photographs. Some are very old, some from this century. I go through a fistful of them. I wish I could just find *something* I want! A couple of loose photographs flutter down from the pile in my hand.

I study them closely. A red-haired lad. On the moors, on a sunny day. A summer's day, judging by what he is wearing. He's smiling in a warm, intimate way, as if he really likes whoever is holding the camera. Goose bumps prickle my back. Written on the reverse of both photos is *W.H.* and a date about forty years ago, open-ended with a dash. Is that when he was born? If so, he was just a few years older than Isobel. And *missing* is marked after the date—in Gran's handwriting.

"What do you make of these two?" I ask Piper.

She comes around, takes the photos, and studies them. "His hair is red, like ours. And those cheekbones. Do you think he could be—"

"Your father?" Gran stands in the doorway. Her face is ice cold; her eyes flash fury. "Yes. He is."

PIPER

"How did you get in here?" Gran demands. Her face is enraged, and I hate that I involuntarily take a step back.

"You left it unlocked," I say.

"I did not."

Quinn's face goes pale. She looks at me. "Piper?" she says, uncertainly.

"It was unlocked," I insist. "We thought you left it unlocked for us. How else could we have got in?"

Gran turns, examines the lock. "It's been tampered with. Very impressive, Piper. How did you manage that this morning when we were both in the room with you?" She shakes her head, a grudging respect in her eyes. "Now, both of you: get out. And don't ever come in here again without an invitation."

Quinn rushes to obey; I follow more slowly.

"And, girls?" We turn. She gestures at the photograph still clutched in my hand. "You will regret it greatly if you find him. Let the past lie where it will." I hold it out and she takes it, then goes back into her reading room and shuts the door.

Quinn follows me to the front room. She looks at me oddly. "You lied to me. You said the door was unlocked."

"I didn't lie; it *was* unlocked."

Quinn shakes her head impatiently. "But *how* was it unlocked?"

"I cast a spell on it," I say, and shock fills her eyes. I roll mine. "No, Quinn. I shoved some gum in the lock mechanism as we went in this morning. Remember, I got you to go in first, so you shielded me. It is an old, simple lock. Jamming it was all it took to stop it from locking when she turned the key."

"You're mad."

"At least now we have a lead to our father. Isn't that what you wanted?"

"Not much to go on without the photograph."

I smile, reach into my pocket, and hold out the second photo. "I hid this one earlier."

Quinn finally succumbs to tiredness after her sleepless night and curls up on the sofa for a nap. I slip out onto the moors with Ness. It's only early afternoon, though with everything that has happened, the day feels like it's had too many hours, that they've stretched out and become bigger to hold all the thoughts, feelings, and events.

I climb the hill we came down to get here, then pause by Wisht Tor at the top. All this talk of fathers has reminded me—if I don't call home soon, Dad's likely to appear and ruin everything. This is one of the highest places around here: will there be any signal? I take out my phone. There is one bar that fades in and out; I walk around the tor to find the place where it is the most stable. A number of missed texts and calls ping in—most from Dad.

I hit Return Call; it rings twice. "Hello, Piper?"

"Hi, Dad."

"Is everything all right? I've been trying to call."

"All is fine. There's really poor network here; I've had to climb a tor to find a signal."

He chuckles, as if the thought of me climbing a tor is funny. Well, I suppose it is. I smile, and he chatters on and asks me questions, and I do my best to put his mind at ease. It's not his fault, any of this. Whether or not he doubted Mum's claims, he has always treated me like his daughter, one he cherished. What was Dad really, to Mum? A place to run? Finally I interrupt. "Dad, my battery is low. There's nowhere to charge it, so don't freak if I don't answer calls, all right?"

"Don't forget—be back for school on Monday."

"I'll try. But promise you won't worry if we're late. All right?"

"Just be back for Monday."

We say our goodbyes, and I slip my phone back into my pocket.

I start down the tricky slope on the other side of the tor, heading away from the house, eyes searching for the path Zak would take back from the car. I struggle down, not as adept at finding my way as Quinn or Zak. Ness runs ahead and back and ahead again. She's loving the space here, not having to be on a lead. *Running free.* I know how she feels. There is something about being here that speaks to some-where inside me, a place that always longed for something without knowing what it was.

If—I mean, *when*—we go back to Winchester, it will seem small. Contained and civilized.

Zak appears in the distance. I wave and hurry down to meet him before he starts up the hill with a pack and bags in his hands.

"Hello there!" he says. "Piper?"

I roll my eyes. "Yes, it's me."

"Sorry. I thought it was, unless you two did a complete clothing swap since I left this morning. I'm just surprised to see you walking on your own. Did you come to meet me?"

"Sort of. Do you mind if we go back to the car with that for now? There's something I want to do."

"I know that look in your eyes, and it makes me ner-vous," he says, and grins. "Come on, then. At least you caught me before I went up the hill with all this."

I explain on the way—that Gran confirmed our dad wasn't who we thought, and that I have a photo of the real deal. We reach the car, and Zak stuffs the pack and bags in the boot.

I take out the photo. Zak holds it, studies it closely. He whistles. "All right, maybe I can see the family resemblance. What now?"

I grin. "We need to find some locals to ask about the photo, so I thought we'd go to the hotel for a drink."

"I like the way you think. Though Quinn worked at that hotel; they'll think you're her, won't they?"

I shrug. "She's masqueraded as me often enough in Winchester. It's my turn to be her for a while."

"Have you thought about how your dad—you know, the one who raised you and loved you all your life—will take it if you find this guy?"

"He wouldn't be happy if he knew about it. I just called him, by the way. There's a bit of signal at the top by Wisht Tor."

"How are things back home?"

"He misses me, of course. But he's fine. And you don't have to worry about Dad. I don't plan to tell him about any of this."

"Kiss for luck?" He pulls me close. It almost feels the same, like it used to before Quinn came along. But nothing can ever be the same with her in my life, can it? Everything has changed, forever.

So this is Two Bridges Hotel.

It has all different bits stuck together—roof height and windows not lining up—in that haphazard way that old country inns often have, but it's still pleasing to the eye. I know from checking the website before we left Winchester that it is over two hundred years old and started as a coaching inn. It has changed names and hands a number of times. It is a prettied-up version of what I expected. The grounds as well. They are lovely for this time of year, with scattered benches and a gazebo.

Green grass slopes down, and a small army of white geese troop about below by the hotel. They notice us and start squawking noisily among themselves, as if they're trying to decide whether to run or attack.

Ness growls, and Zak picks her up. "Trust me," he says. "You don't want to take on that lot."

We walk across the lawn, and I concentrate on moving like Quinn while my eyes drink this place in. Where my mother worked, years ago, where she met the man who raised me, the one I thought was my father. Where Quinn worked until recently, too.

We go through the front door. It's warm here after being outside. Zak puts Ness down. There is a woman at a desk on the phone; another person waiting there. The woman looks up and waves excitedly when she sees me.

"Let's look around?" I say to Zak, my voice low.

The public rooms are rambling and interconnected, full of mismatched, faded, grand furniture, a weird mix of paintings on the walls. Clocks stopped at different times, all the wrong time, in different sizes, shapes. There are fireplaces, bookshelves, cozy nooks. The whole place is sort of gleaming and posh, and old and worn, at the same time.

A painting in a corner draws my attention. Huge black dogs stare from the canvas. Their eyes are red, their claws long and sharp. Wisht Hounds? Around it are framed stories and reports: *Howling heard at midnight, deaths by heart attack; hounds sighted, three missing. Bodies found, torn to pieces.* None are recent.

"Quinn! There you are. It's so good to see you." I turn, and the woman from the desk bustles over. She reaches around, gives me a hug. Her eyes get wider and wider as she takes in what I'm wearing, Zak next to me, and Ness.

"Are you coming back to us? How is your grandmother? Oh, sorry, my manners. Sit. I'll bring you some tea and then we can talk." She ushers us toward a sofa by the fire and disappears. We sit down, and I wonder: does the cleaner usually get tea in front of the fire? She seemed so happy to see me, and not just in a way that said they were short on cleaning staff. She must genuinely like Quinn.

Another woman comes over. "Karen said you were here, Quinn. So good to see you. I've got some more books for you." She holds them out; I take them.

I say thank you and study the novels in my hands to explain why I'm not introducing Zak. They're old and worn —one a detective story by someone I've never heard of; the other *Emma,* which put me to sleep in English class last year.

Zak takes the initiative. "Hi, I'm Zak." He holds out his hand.

"I'm Lyndsay," she says, and smiles. "It's lovely to meet any friend of Quinn's." I look up, and her eyes are bulging with curiosity. Ness barks.

The woman from the desk—Karen?—returns with tea

things and a bowl of water for Ness, and I give Zak an apologetic glance. This won't be quite what he had in mind for a drink at the pub.

Lyndsay goes to check in some guests, and Karen sits with us. "So, tell me everything," she says. "How is your grandmother?" The way she says the words, the hesitation—like so many others, she's nervous of Gran.

"She's much better. She's out of the hospital now, and at home. I can't come back to work because I'm looking after her."

Karen's eyes are on Zak. "And you—where did you spring from?"

He looks at me, uncertain what to say. I opt for vague. "Oh, we met when Gran was in the hospital. He's visiting for a while."

"Have you been seeing the sights of Dartmoor?" She chatters on about the moors, walking, and some craft market that is on next weekend while my hand touches the photo in my pocket and I try to think of a way to ask about it that won't be too weird.

She pauses for air and I dive in. "Karen, I was wondering if you could help me with something."

"Of course. What is it?"

"Gran's memory isn't so good now since she had the stroke. I've been going through old photos with her, to remind her who people are."

"Oh, dear." Sympathy replaces the discomfort in her eyes.

"And we found this one of someone I don't know, and she can't remember who he is. It's upsetting Gran that she can't remember. I wonder if you might know who it is. It says 'W.H.' on the back." I hold out the photo.

She takes it, studies it, and frowns. She finally shakes her head. "No, sorry. You should come by tonight; ask some of the regulars. They might know."

QUINN

When I wake up, I'm alone. I check the house. Gran is asleep in her room, and there is no sign of Piper or Zak. I wander outside. The sun says it's late afternoon.

I call for Ness, but she doesn't come. Is Zak back; has he taken Ness for a walk with Piper? I try not to mind.

My bracelet is itching, like it did earlier in Gran's room when I was looking for her book, the one with the same symbol on it. Is the missing book the inheritance Piper seems to want so desperately?

I should find it and give it to Piper, and leave this place — leave Piper. The thought is a wrench, deep inside. We're part of each other. We always were tied together; we didn't know it, but we were. My mirror image. To think of leaving her is to think of losing my reflection.

But there was a reason we weren't together. It was because of me, I'm sure of it: I'm dangerous, just like Isobel always said. Everything Gran said about me spirit traveling with the hunt confirms this. I should leave Piper before it's too late.

I sit on the front step to watch for their return, leaning against the door. Thinking of leaving makes we want to see Piper, *right now,* so much. My sister, so like me but not like me at the same time. I picture her smile, the spark she has, and then —

Everything changes. My stomach lurches in fright. I'm not by Gran's house, not anymore. I'm floating above the moors. The ground moves past at speed; I'm afraid.

All at once, I stop. I can hear voices.

I focus below me, and drop lower. It's Piper and Zak. Ness, too. They're walking away from the hotel to the car. Opening the boot to get out bags of supplies. The ones Zak went out to get, not Piper. Whatever are they up to?

Never mind where they've been, *where am I?*

I'm not in my body. I start to panic: what if I can't get back to it?

How did I leave it in the first place? I wanted to see Piper, and I did. Now I concentrate on my body on Gran's front step, will myself to go back there, to do it *now.*

Fear speeds me along so fast that the moors blur past below. Gran's house appears, my body slumped on the step.

I slam into it, hard. So hard it's like being hit by a truck. I gasp air into my lungs; tears spring into my eyes. I hold out my hand in front of my eyes. My hand. My face. My body. All back together again, the way it should be.

I did that. I wanted to see Piper . . . and I did.

This is crazy.

I get to my feet, start pacing around the ruins at the front of the house. Back and forth, back and forth. To move and feel and breathe, to feel connected to my body once again.

Finally, I stop, and lean against the stone fence under a tree by the gate. Idly my hand pulls lightly at a tree root.

Something stings, and I pull my hand away. There's a bright spot of blood on my finger.

I brush aside some dead leaves, and there, twisting around a tree root: a thorny green plant, green even in October. With red berries.

Like the plant that used to grow in Gran's garden. The one I crushed berries from to color red eyes in the dirt, and then made a monster. The plant vanished from the garden after that happened, but Gran must have replanted it here, hidden under roots and leaves.

I stare at the berries, remembering: it wasn't a dream. Just like traveling without my body wasn't a dream. It is real; I did it today.

What am I?

And what about the hunt, and the blood? Even though Gran said it was real, it seemed too crazy to believe. Then.

Panic twists my belly. I run back into the house. I need to get away from this place, and I need to do it soon, or . . . or . . . I don't know what, but it'll be *bad*.

Like me.

I need to find the book for Piper so I can go. Or *try* to find it. If I try and fail, that is enough.

The door to Gran's bedroom is still closed; she must be asleep. Piper and Zak will get back soon. I rush through the rest of the house — the kitchen, the front room, the spare room upstairs — hunting for the book in earnest. I even peek into my room, the one Zak is sleeping in now. The blankets are mussed where his body has been. I fight the urge to go there, to lie down in the same place and hide.

I don't find the book, but somehow I knew I wouldn't. At least I tried.

"Quinn?" Piper's voice floats up the stairs. I hurry down.

They're in the kitchen. Zak is unpacking the supplies he's bought — lemons and all.

"Where's Gran?" Piper asks.

"Asleep, last I checked." I look at Piper again. Where did they go? She's bursting with something; her smile is wide on her face. "What have you done?"

"Well. We — Zak, Ness, and I — paid a visit to Two Bridges Hotel. Of course, they thought I was you. I think I covered that pretty well."

"You did *what?*" I'm shocked. "Why?"

She draws the photo out of her pocket. "To see if anyone knew who this is."

My blood quickens. "And? Did they?"

"No. But someone named Karen suggested we go back tonight and ask around at the bar. Do you want to go, or shall I?"

"I . . . I don't know," I say.

Piper reaches across, hugs me. She's in happy, excited mode, so pleased she's done this for me. If Gran knew, she'd be furious. Despite that, I'm gripped again by this compulsion. I stare at the photo. "I want to find him," I say.

"I know," she says, but I can see that Piper isn't as bothered about wanting to find our dad as I am. Is it because she has a dad already, one she's always had?

But she said she'd find him — that she'd do it for me.

Everything inside me says to leave this place, and do it now. But I need to find our father, too.

"Shhh," Zak says. He gestures toward the door. There are footsteps outside it, and they are getting closer.

Piper stuffs the photo back in her pocket.

The door opens. Gran steps in.

PIPER

Quinn hands me a small metal whatsit and a lemon. I study the metal thing for a moment, but am none the wiser. It looks too modern for this kitchen of museum pieces.

"What's this?" I ask.

"Are you serious?" Quinn says. "It's a lemon zester. Here, I'll show you." She runs it across the lemon over a bowl, and neat shavings of yellow come away.

I try, and it skims too light. Then I overcompensate, and it gouges in too deep. Gran peers over, shakes her head. "Try an even, firm touch—drag it across without pushing in," she says.

I try again, and this time get the pressure right. Sprinkles of yellow drop into the bowl.

Ness is curled in front of the kitchen fireplace. Zak is beating butter and sugar, carefully measured by Quinn using metal cups instead of scales. Gran surveys it all from a chair to make sure we do it right—a matriarch and her clan, matching granddaughters, a dog, and a boy. What would it have been like if Quinn and I had grown up here, together, with Gran and Mum?

At least Gran seems to have got over her anger at my door tampering earlier—though that would soon change if she knew about the second photograph and my trip with Zak to the hotel.

Gran looks in Zak's bowl. "Yes, it's ready. Eggs next." Quinn carefully cracks an egg into his bowl.

"Mix it in slowly," Gran says, and Zak stirs while Quinn adds another egg, and another. Then flour and the lemon zest, and I watch over Zak's shoulder as they become part of the batter.

"Haven't you ever made a cake before?" Quinn asks.

"Of course not. Cakes come in boxes from bakeries."

"What was Isobel thinking?" Gran shakes her head, and sadness overtakes her face.

"Did Mum make cakes here with you?" I ask.

"Of course."

"She never did at home." Now that I think about it, Mum never seemed comfortable in our big, bright, modern kitchen.

The cake mixture is poured into a greased pan. Quinn proclaims the oven—if you can call that box over the fire an oven—to be at the right temperature, and in it goes.

"Now we wait," Gran says.

Zak goes to build up the fire in the other room against the night while we settle around the table. Quinn puts the kettle on a stand over the fire, gets out teacups. The small kitchen is cozy with the fire raging, and it all feels a bit Happy Families, like an occasion, like baking a cake is a big deal. And I try to picture the mother I knew—the elegant, distant one with the perfect hair and designer clothes—in this place, but I can't.

"What was our mum like when she was young?" I ask.

Gran stirs sugar into the tea Quinn has handed to her. "Isobel, ah. She was a sunny child, always into mischief. Always trying to get out of things. I was too lenient on her."

"How about when she was our age?" Quinn asks.

Gran doesn't answer for so long that I think she won't. She shakes her head at last. "She rebelled; she wouldn't see sense. It got her into trouble."

"Into trouble, meaning us?" I say.

"Yes. You shouldn't have come here, Piper."

The warmth eases out of the kitchen for me, even as there is a blast of heat when Quinn turns the cake around. She closes the oven door, straightens, and looks at me.

"I just wanted to find Quinn, to be with my sister, and my family," I say. "Is that so wrong?"

Quinn's brow wrinkles. She shakes her head. "But I found *you*. I saw that article about Isobel in a paper at the hotel, and I came and found you. And you said you didn't know about me until I showed up at Isobel's funeral. So what do you mean you wanted to find me?"

"Piper knew about you from Isobel," Gran says. "Isobel shouldn't have told her, but she did."

I shake my head. "No, no; it's not true. I—"

Quinn interrupts. "Stop it, Piper. Stop lying to me. When we first met, I thought you must have known about me: you didn't seem shocked enough to see me. But when I asked, you told me you hadn't, and I believed you. Why did you lie to me, Piper?"

I take Quinn's hand. *Why* doesn't she believe me? "I *begged* Mum to take me to you. But she wouldn't."

Quinn pulls her hand away.

"Piper, do you see what damage lies cause?" Gran's face is grave. "Lying is dangerous. Especially for women in our family. Didn't Isobel teach you this?"

Whispers from the past say she tried. But I would never listen, would I?

Quinn leaves the kitchen, and a moment later, I follow her. She's standing by the fire in the front room.

"Leave us for a moment, will you?" I say to Zak.

I wait until the door shuts behind him.

"You lied to me, Piper," Quinn says. "Why?"

"What I did, I did for love. To find you, the sister I wanted to know and love."

"I don't understand. How did lying help achieve that? I was already there with you. Tell me the truth."

And I'm scared of the look in Quinn's eyes—the hurt, and disappointment, and where they might lead.

"I'm sorry, I thought it was harmless. I did it because I didn't want to upset you." *I wanted you to like me. Please like me.*

"Have you done anything else? Are there any more lies?"

My hands are clenched in fists. Can't Quinn see that

what I've done, I've done for us? To bring us together, here, the way we should be.

But what else have I done?

Full of unease, I push the question away. I don't answer Quinn; I don't answer myself.

QUINN

Zak and I walk to the hotel in the dark. He has a torch, but I don't need one. The moon and stars are out tonight, and I know the path very well. I lead the way.

"Is everything all right, Quinn?" Zak asks.

I shrug. "Just Piper stretching the truth again."

"Ah, I see. Do you want to talk about it?"

I pause in my steps, and turn to face him. Yes, I want to talk, but I shouldn't. He'd run a mile if I told him everything, and didn't I vow to keep this distance with Zak, to guard against my feelings? Because of Piper, and her forgiving me. But my certainty about that is wavering.

Moonlight and Zak go well together, and my hand aches to reach up — to touch his cheek, to put my fingers in his dark hair and pull him close. To kiss him, like the first, last, and only time. But it isn't just that, is it? I'm not *just* attracted to him, even though I am. It's more than that. And he waits to hear what I might say, his dark eyes on mine — interested and concerned for a *friend.* He may be close to me now, but for all he really sees of what is inside me, I might as well be Cathy's ghost, lost and cold on the moors.

But he's not my Heathcliff — he doesn't want *me.* I sigh.

"Quinn?" he says.

"I don't think so. But thank you."

I turn away, continue down the path. We walk in silence, and I can hear his steps behind me, fewer than mine with his longer legs. His breathing. His heart that beats *th-thump, th-thump* for Piper — always for Piper.

Piper and her lies. She lied about Gran's room being unlocked. She lied to me back in Winchester when she said she hadn't known about me. At least today she finally told the truth about that, but only because Gran made her.

Gran said that lying is dangerous, especially for women in our family. Why? Is this yet another way we are different, or is it something about our lies?

All my life I've had a distrust of lying drummed into me over and over again by Gran. And fear of the darkness it could bring from inside of me. But Piper does it all the time. And here I was thinking *I* was the one who had to leave *her*, to keep her safe.

Piper says we are family; she says she wants me in her life. She also wants her life in Winchester and her dad who isn't her dad; she wants Zak. She wants this place, too — she wants to inherit whatever there is to inherit. She wants it all — Piper, who has always had whatever she wanted.

Why should she have everything and leave me with nothing?

It seems strange to be here at night. The bar is warm, too warm with the fire and bodies and their drinks.

It's easy to tell the locals from the visitors. The latter are in couples or small groups, settled into sofas and chairs. The locals—farmers, mostly—are standing by the bar, talking of crops and sheep, waving their hands about and laughing about some incident involving a tractor, a tourist, and a passing place. A few of the older ones see me and lower their voices so I can't hear. What are they saying?

I'm not comfortable here, in this part of the hotel. As if he knows it, Zak takes my hand. His warm fingers squeeze my hand lightly and don't let go. He pulls me toward the bar, orders drinks for both of us from someone I don't know. They're either new or only work at night.

I stand there, awkward. How can I just go up to these strangers, and ask about the photograph in my pocket?

Then the two I thought were talking about me walk over to us. "Say, aren't you Isobel Blackwood's daughter, Quinn?"

"I . . . yes. I am," I say.

"Your hair is brighter, but you're the spit of her when she used to work at the bar. She moved away years ago, didn't she? How is she?"

I look at Zak, not sure what to say.

"Sadly, Isobel died recently," Zak says.

"Ah. So sorry to hear that," one of them says, and buys a round for his friends and us.

They're raising their glasses. "To Isobel!" they say, and clink them together.

And the older ones are talking about her, remembering

a lively girl who flirted behind the bar, and I'm thinking —is this the cold mother I barely knew? It's hard to believe.

A sudden surge of inventiveness hits me.

"Before she died, my mother wrote a letter to a friend she had back then," I say to them. "But I don't know where to post it. I've got his photo here." I take it out. "Do you know him?"

A few of them peer at it, and if him having red hair like mine raises any suspicions, they keep them to themselves. "That's the Hamley boy, isn't it?" one of them says, with a disapproving look on his face. "They moved away, years ago. I don't know where they got to."

Another one is listening in. "Didn't they move down Exeter way after they lost the farm?" He goes to ask someone else, who gets out a phone and makes a call.

He comes over. "My cousin thinks a friend has their number. They'll ring back if—"

His phone rings. He waves for a pen and paper, writes something down, then hands the paper to me. "There you go. Don't know the address, but that's his name—Will Hamley —and his number. Call him if you want to, but be careful. That Hamley lot are nothing but trouble."

As easy as that. All it took was a lie about a letter. Gran said lying is dangerous, but nothing happened—lightning didn't crash down, the gates of hell didn't open at my feet.

Piper has shown me that lying is easy. And it gets you what you want.

• • •

We head out for the long walk back in the darkness. I clutch the paper in my hand; my belly churns. Should we call him, this Will Hamley? Suddenly I'm not sure. First, there was Gran's warning. And *nothing but trouble,* they said tonight.

But he's my father.

I give the paper to Zak. "Can you keep it? I'm not sure what I want to do with it."

He nods and tucks it away in his pocket.

When we finally reach the gate to the house, I pause and turn to look back at the slope above in the moonlight. Wisht Tor is high above us.

And next to the tor: a movement, an outline.

The fox.

The call comes: to hunt!

No . . . No . . . Not again.

But there is no way to stop it. The Wisht Hounds are released, and I'm swept along as one of them. We run free on the moors.

I'm terrified what will come.

I'm exhilarated, too: flying across the dark moors. Not sated by the last kill; never sated. Desperate hunger drives us on.

Arrrroooooo! We howl as one when we catch the sweet scent of prey on the wind.

This prey doesn't run or bleat in fear as we encircle and trap it. It sleeps, cocooned inside a tent.

First we rip that down.

The prey—two of them, a man and a woman—are awake now and screaming, calling out to their god to save them.

But gods have no power here.

I'm repelled, horrified . . .

Excited. The eyes of the hounds opposite me — *horrible, red-rimmed* — *mirror my own.*

We rip out their throats and still their cries.

Beautiful, joyous blood spurts in rhythm — th-thump, th-thump — *gradually lessening as their hearts stop beating.*

We feast.

PIPER

"I'm not sure about this," Zak says.

"Come on, Zak. You know finding our biological father is what Quinn really wants. She's just scared."

"I still think we should have checked with her first and made sure she's OK with us calling him."

"Well, apart from Quinn, he's my father, too. And I want to call him."

Zak considers what I said, then finally nods. He holds out the piece of paper with the name and number. "Go on, then," he says.

I move around, trying to find the place on the hill with the best signal. But no matter where I stand, it's really low —as is my battery. As if to spite me, my phone chooses that moment to power off.

"My phone is dead. Ack . . . ! How do they live here without phones and chargers? I should have charged it when we were at the hotel."

Zak laughs and takes out his phone. "Try mine?"

The signal on Zak's phone is just as low, but the battery is marginally better. I dial the number.

It rings once . . . twice . . . three times.

"Hello?" a man's voice answers.

"Hello, is that Will Hamley?"

"Who wants to know?" Suspicion in his voice.

"I'm Quinn Blackwood." Zak frowns at me, but I move away. "Isobel Blackwood was my mother."

"Oh, wow. That's a blast from the past. How is Izzy?"

Izzy? "I'm sorry to have to tell you this, but she died recently."

Long pause. "Oh. I see. I'm sorry, too." His voice is weighed down with sadness. "But why are you calling me?"

"I'd really like to see you to tell you. Can we meet?"

"Tell me now. What is this about?"

"I think . . . well, I'm pretty sure . . . that I'm your daughter."

The silence is so long, I'm afraid the phone has been disconnected. "Hello?" I say, finally.

"I'm still here."

"So, can we meet up?"

"I don't know. I haven't got any money if that's what you're after."

"No. I've got plenty of my own."

He digests that. "Where are you? Still on the moors?"

"Yes. Can we meet at Two Bridges Hotel?"

"S'pose so. If you're buying."

"Fine."

"When?"

"How about tomorrow afternoon? Two p.m."

Another pause. "Yeah, well, I ain't got nothing better to do. I'll see what I can do."

"Promise me you'll be there."

"For what it's worth, yeah, I promise. I'll be there." Then the phone clicks—it's dead. He's gone.

I hand the phone back to Zak, and smile. "It's all sorted," I say.

He raises an eyebrow. "I really hope you know what you're doing."

"Don't worry, it'll be fine."

We walk back down to the house. Quinn was angry with me, and last night I was angry right back at her. How can she not see that we're in things together?

I had another almost sleepless night. I've slept so little since we got to Dartmoor, I wonder why I'm not exhausted. Instead, I'm exhilarated. My mind seems sharper; colors and smells and touch all so heightened and clear that they almost hurt. Everything is turned up a few notches.

When I finally drifted away, then came another of those mad dreams, where I called the hunt and ran with it on the moors. The kill, the feast. If I close my eyes, I'm there again: the power, the blood. I half shudder, half shiver, a tingle going down my tongue and throat just to think of it.

And when I woke up and went out to watch the sunrise again, I realized what I needed to do.

Quinn is doubting me now, because of Gran pointing out my lies. I need to do something to show Quinn I'm on her side—I need to give her something she wants. Something she *thinks* she wants, anyhow.

Then she will *have* to give me what I want—she'll have to stick to her promise to help me find my inheritance.

QUINN

Running on the moors . . . the taste of blood.

I shake my head, trying to dislodge the memory and struggling not to be sick. Those people in that tent. A man and a woman, camping on the moors. I can still hear their screams; still taste their terror, along with their blood.

I'm going crazy.

The front door opens; there are footsteps, voices. Zak and Piper are back from their walk.

Ness runs in, jumps up on the sofa next to me, and licks my face.

"You don't look like you've moved all morning," Zak says. "Are you—"

A shrill scream from upstairs interrupts him.

"Gran?" I leap off the sofa and run up the stairs, Zak and Piper close behind.

She's collapsed on the floor of her bedroom, face ashen. I go to help her, but she slaps my hand away.

"I see," she says, but she's not looking at us.

"Zak!" she says, and holds out her hand. He kneels next to her, and she grips his hand tight. "Listen to me, Zak."

"I'm listening," he says.

"Leave. Leave this room, this house, the moors. Get in your car and drive far away, and never come back. It's too late for us, but you can escape the fire."

"The fire? What fire?" He looks up, shrugs, mouths *Do we need an ambulance?*

I shake my head.

"I tried to stop it, all those years ago," Gran says. "I should have known it could never be stopped. What started in fire must end in fire. Go now, Zak. Before it's too late. Go!" she says, agitated.

Go downstairs, I mouth silently to Zak, and he slips out of the room.

"He's gone now, Gran," I say. And Piper and I help her up, into bed. She's cold, shaking.

"You both know, in here," she says, and taps her chest. "Even if you don't know in here." She taps her head.

"We know what?" Piper says.

"Where it all began, and must end. In fire."

Gran droops back in bed, her eyes closing. Soon she falls asleep.

We tiptoe out of the room, shut the door.

"Well, that was a major attack of the crazies," Piper says, but I can tell she is shaken.

"Gran has visions sometimes. They shouldn't be ignored."

"That stuff she said about fire . . ." Piper starts to say, hesitant, and doesn't finish the sentence.

I nod. "You remember the fire, don't you? When we both had the fever when we were thirteen. I don't think it was a dream, or a hallucination. I think we were spirit traveling into the past," I say. The truth is coming in and fusing with what has happened lately and what was then —they were the same sort of experience. And *so much* I want to ask Piper if she has been dreaming the hunt, too—the sheep, the campers . . . the blood. But I can't bring myself to do it. If it is just me, it would confirm to her what I've always known: that I'm the bad one. I don't want her to know.

We stare at each other on the stairs. I fancy I can see echoes of the dream that wasn't a dream from all those years ago in her eyes: the house, the burning. Fury not destroyed, but strengthened.

"That was for real?" Piper whispers, her eyes open wide.

"Yes. It happened close by. The burning place is the ruins in front of the house. They are forbidden to us."

The three of us are subdued that evening. Zak is nervous that if Gran realizes he's still here, she'll flip out again, but he doesn't believe the rest of it.

He should. He should leave; we should all leave this place behind. But no matter where I go, the darkness will come along inside me. Even if I leave this place, at night the hunt will find me.

I slip upstairs to get Zak's things; he'd better stay down here with us tonight.

The three of us settle down to sleep.

I sense a movement and open my eyes. Piper is sitting

up. "Oh my God, Quinn. Even after all that happened today, I can't believe I forgot to tell you."

"You forgot to tell me what?"

"About our biological father. I called him, and he's coming to Two Bridges tomorrow afternoon to meet the daughter he never knew he had. Do you want to go, or shall I?"

PIPER

I slip out into the night once Zak and Quinn are asleep. Nothing could stop me; the word *forbidden* holds no meaning, not to me.

Without thinking about it very much, I've skirted around these ruins ever since we got here. I mean, it is easier to walk around them than across, but I've avoided touching any bit of them, without really wondering why.

The ruins outline a small house; where we live now was once the barn behind it. The rundown outbuildings and the remains of fences here and there all say that once this was a farm — a small one, but a farm.

Quinn called the ruins *the burning place.*

I first had the dream — what I thought was a dream, or a hallucination from fever — when I was thirteen. I'd been ill, so very ill, but I remember Isobel wouldn't send for a doctor. Recently I've wondered if it was because she knew what was wrong with me and that a doctor couldn't help. That it would pass. She said she and her mother experienced the same thing themselves at that age.

And Quinn had the same dream.

I try to remember the details, but strangely, it is both imprinted on my memory forever and forgotten. Almost like I tried to erase it, but only managed to get rid of some of the edges.

And it was around then that I started to understand how different Mum and I were from everyone around us: how we knew things other people didn't that we had no way of knowing, and how easy it was to make everyone agree with what we wanted. In fact, it was really only because this ability of mine didn't work on Mum that I first realized I was different from other people — that how I interacted with them was different.

I started to want to know more. I was desperate to understand how and why we could do the things we did, and to find out what else I could do. There was a conviction inside me that this was only the beginning; there could be more, so much more. Then Mum and I started not getting along. She looked at me oddly, watched me all the time.

Why is this ground forbidden to us? There is an unease, a fear, inside me.

I step forward, over what was once a wall. I reach out with both hands, grip its stone, and fall to the ground.

I run on the moors, tangled in my skirts, tripping in haste, scratched by gorse, cut, bleeding. Chill howls hang in twilight air; the hounds are close. They hunt me like an animal, herd me to the place they would take — my home. But if they want me there, it is no sanctuary.

Gasping for breath, I bolt the door behind me and retrieve the book from the hidden place. I caress the worn cover, red as blood, the symbol of the women of my family. The source of our slight power—the twisting of words, the shaping of belief.

I take a knife and dip a feather into the most special ink—my own blood. I make myself hold the pen steady, and begin.

If you destroy me, I will return stronger and destroy you. My daughter and my daughter's daughter, and on and on, the strongest one of each generation, will grow in power and spite. You and yours will be marked by shadow. We, the women of the black woods, will hunt you down forever until no Hamleys remain, and trap you in the hunt for all eternity.

The trees are burning. The peat of my walls will soon follow. Fear grips and twists me inside, but more, there is anger. Does that Hamley scoundrel dare take by force what he could not buy?

Even now, I could escape the flames. All the Hamleys want is to destroy the farm.

But the ending of this old life will make my last lie—my last words, written in blood in the Book of Lies—the most power-ful of all. My death will twist my lies into a curse. The Hamleys will be destroyed and imprisoned with the hunt in the wood where my ancestors were put on trial. And the hunt will run on the moors when we call it.

I take off my bracelet and hide it and the book in the secret place, replace the stones to save them from the flames. My daughter will know where to find them.

. . .

It is some time later when I come to, crumpled on the ground. My face is covered with tears, my body twisted with pain and fear.

And *anger.*

She was alone, an old woman alone. But she wasn't defenseless—oh no. She was a wise woman, an enchantress, the keeper of the book.

I've long known that the power to shape belief is in my blood: when I twist the truth, listeners believe. But the Book of Lies will give me *so* much more: lies written in it become true to all.

If I have the book, any lies I write in it will become the truth. *This* is my inheritance.

She wrote the curse of the Hamleys in the book. With her death, it came true, like she knew it would. It has plagued the Hamleys every generation since then. That box Quinn found in Gran's reading room with all the notes, drawings, and photos shows what has happened to them over the years, generation after generation. And as we've grown in power— each generation stronger than the last—their suffering has continued. And so it must: one comes with the other, forever entwined.

It *will* continue.

My family are the women of the black woods. Now I understand why Mum wouldn't change her name. How could she, when the Blackwood name defines everything about who we are?

Now, too, I know our enemy. In the photographs in

Gran's box, the Hamleys were all marked by shadow. I saw this without knowing what it meant.

And now, at last, I understand what is imprisoned in the black woods of Wistman's Wood—why the hounds of the hunt were unleashed when I went back there at night, when I felt the hunger in the trees again and called it forth.

That was no dream. When Quinn said earlier that we were spirit traveling all those years ago, I understood. Like a puzzle suddenly clicking together, making the hidden pattern obvious.

The dreams that were not dreams: *I* called the hunt. Me, not Quinn. I commanded it.

Now I'm shaking. The *fear* of those campers when we ripped down their tent; their cries echo in my ears. Their blood: we feasted on their blood. All because of *me.*

What am I?

I'm freaked out, horrified: a scream is building. Panic is taking over. I'm going back; I'm remembering. Other times, other blood . . .

Be still. All that you have done has brought you to this moment.

I breathe: in, out, in, out. These were things that must be. They show that *I* am the strongest of our generation. I cannot deny this part of me.

Everything I've done to get here has led to this moment of truth.

The book must be mine.

And I can use it to fix things, can't I? I can make things better and forget what came before.

My beautiful Zak. I tell him that he loves me, and he believes me. Of course he does; he has no choice. But that isn't the same as him *truly* loving me, is it? If it were, he could never have kissed Quinn.

If I have the book, lies written in it will become true. And the very first lies I will write are these: Zak loves me with all his heart and soul. Quinn loves me as her sister. Quinn doesn't love Zak.

Then we can all be happy together. Together, forever.

The book *will* be mine.

I sense a movement, a presence, and turn.

By the fence in the moonlight stands a fox, unlike any I've seen before. It's big and has a huge bushy black tail. It tips its head to one side and stares.

QUINN

"I really can't believe we're doing this. Thanks for coming with me." I look sideways at Zak. We're sitting in the gazebo out front of the Two Bridges Hotel.

"It's not something you should do alone. Though I really think Piper should be here, too. She's the one who arranged to meet him."

"Well, it makes sense that we can't be seen around here together without creating a massive fuss. Also, twins might be a shock to him, since she didn't mention it. And she thought I should be the one, as it was me who wanted to find him originally."

"Being seen together is something you and Piper will have to face eventually."

I shrug, a little uneasy. I parroted Piper's reasons without knowing *why* she didn't tell Hamley that there are two of us. Gran knows, and the promise Piper extracted that we not let anyone else know we are twins until her dad knows as well seems like it shouldn't apply to our real father. I shake my head; it doesn't matter. I still plan to leave — meet my father, then find the book, give it to Piper, and leave. Alone.

If no one but Gran knows we are twins, no one but Gran will know I am missing. A shiver runs down my back; I shake it off. I can go somewhere nobody knows me and try to start over

—to grasp at the slim hope that if I leave the moors, the hunt will sleep again.

Piper may not be with us, but she is the reason we decided the gazebo would be a good place to meet. She's watching. We left her and Ness a safe distance away, binoculars from Zak's car in her hand.

"Are you ready?" Zak asks.

"Yes. As ready as I'm going to get."

Zak slips a comforting hand on mine, then gets up and walks across the lawn, past the marauding geese, and through the door.

He is gone for a while. Maybe Will Hamley didn't turn up? I'm cold, and wrap my arms around myself. Just when I think I'll give up and join Zak in the hotel, the door opens. Zak steps out, followed by a man.

Will Hamley's hair is still red, what there is of it. He sees me in the gazebo, says something to Zak, and they start to walk toward me. They've got pints in their hands. Was that the cause of the delay?

Will's steps seem a little unsteady.

When they get closer, I stand up. He walks over to me. Zak hangs back, but as I asked, close enough to listen—to help me if I can't work out what to say.

"Oh my God," he says. "You're so like my darling Izzy. But with my hair." He smiles wryly. "Sorry about that."

I don't say anything. I don't know what to say.

"Quinn, is it?"

I nod.

"Weird name. Can't blame that on me."

"No," I say, finding my voice. "You're Will Hamley, is that right?"

"Guilty as charged."

"Did you know about me? I mean, did you know . . ."

"That Izzy was pregnant? No." He sighs. "Her mother hated me; I never knew why. Izzy seemed to like that, sneaking out and meeting me on the moors. But then one day we'd arranged to meet and she didn't show. I saw her at the hotel, and she blanked me. I waited until her shift was over, and followed behind as she walked home to make her talk to me. I'll never forget that night. The wind was wild; it was raining. She stared at me and said it was over. I thought she was crying; maybe it was just the rain on her cheeks. She said she never wanted to see me again; that I should move away and never come back. She seemed almost afraid. I always thought her mum had got to her somehow."

I stare back at him, the sadness in his eyes and story taking hold. Isobel, his Izzy: she who always hated the rain. Was this why?

His eyes drop to my wrist. "Is that Izzy's bracelet?"

I raise my hand self-consciously so he can see it, then let it drop again. "Did she wear it back then?"

"Always. She'd never take it off. Said it was important, that she needed it to be safe." He shrugs. "Crazy stuff she said sometimes, but when she said something, somehow I always believed her. Anyway, how have things been for you all these years? Have you been all right?"

And for some reason, I lie. I tell him I've had a wonderful childhood with his *Izzy,* and everything has been fine. Lying is easy; it's becoming a habit.

"How about you?" I ask.

"I did what Izzy wanted me to do. Like I always did. I left. I'm sorry. If I'd known . . . well. Things might have been different." He shrugs. "Then again, they might not have been."

He looks around us and shivers, takes a long drink from his pint. "There's something about the moors that gets to me."

"It's not a safe place. You should leave; you should get away from here, as far away as you can." My belly is twisting. The words came from a certainty so strong, it is all I can do not to grab his hand and drag him away. A flash of something from the night fills my mind. I push it away and focus on here, now.

"That sounds a lot like what Izzy said to me all those years ago. I can take a hint." He finishes his pint. "Thanks for the drink," he says, turning to Zak. He walks slowly back to the hotel, and disappears inside.

Zak and I head back to Gran's house, collecting Piper on the way. Zak tells me that Will had downed two pints, one after the other, before he'd come out to see me. He seemed genuinely shaken by Izzy's death — funny how I'm thinking of her as *Izzy,* now. She seems more like a real, three-dimensional person to me than she ever did when she was alive. I'm getting a sense of her being this rebel who flirted in bars and went out with Will to annoy her mother. What made her into the cold woman I knew?

Despite how it ended, maybe their relationship meant something to her—maybe there *were* tears on her cheeks with the raindrops, and she really loved him. It's hard to see it as possible, with him as he is now. But even if it wasn't real to her, it was to him. And she told him to go and broke his heart. She never told him about us, not in all these years. How could she do that?

Piper asks about the meeting as we walk, and I let Zak answer her questions. She seems as subdued as I feel. She doesn't ask why I sent him away, much like his *Izzy* did all those years ago, and I'm glad. How can I answer that when I don't know myself?

I'd wanted to meet my real father, and there he was. And I told him to go. Not because I never wanted to see him again; somehow, I was *compelled* to do it.

Gran comes down for dinner and doesn't seem surprised that Zak is still here. She doesn't comment on it one way or the other. Just looks at him sadly.

PIPER

This night has *a purpose, a target—work that must be done.*

Come. Hunt with me tonight!

I call them from the trees, and we become one again.

Clouds hide the moon. The moors are dark, dangerous. But not to us.

We run side by side. This prey is slow and stumbles in the dark. The sharp stink of his fear is on the wind, and easy to follow.

Make him run. Make him suffer, like she did.

And so we hang back, steer him where I want him to go.

He falls, pulls himself up, falls again, but this time there is no getting up. He is caught fast in the bog we'd been herding him toward. Struggling, he sinks ever deeper, held tighter.

We wait until the clouds pull back. Moonlight reveals the shadow of death, stark and oozing, on his skin.

He sees our eyes gleaming around him. His scream is short-lived as we rip out his throat, maddened by blood.

Hot, intoxicating blood.

QUINN

That night, I run with the hunt again.

I try to leave it, to travel back to myself, but I can't —
I'm held in its grip.

When it's finally over, I come back to myself, and cry.

PIPER

I slip out the front door into the darkness, finally giving up on sleep. I'm full of nervous energy and walk along the fence. There is a damp chill in the air that promises winter. The last leaves have given up their hold on bare branches, to join their rotting friends on the ground—the dead and dying that crunch under my feet. So it must always be: the old die, to allow the young to live.

I'd been furious at what my ancestor had gone through.

And at that Will Hamley, too. When I'd held the binoculars yesterday, even at that distance, I could see it. He was *filth*. The thought of him touching my mother makes me ill. How could she let him near her?

The sky is just starting to lighten. The sun struggles to come up, casting streaks of pink in low cloud. It's going to be a spectacular sunrise.

I slip back inside and rouse Zak. His hair is tousled, his eyes half open. I'm tempted to slip under the warm covers with him—to lie against his warm skin, feel the hot blood *th- thump, th-thump* that rushes through his body as his heart beats.

Hot, joyous blood. Dark hunger inside . . .

I shake my head, hard, and take his hand, and lead him outside.

We stand in silence in the shadows, arms around each other, and watch. Orange and pink soon stretch across the sky, streaked with cloud, white, gray, and blue.

"All right, Piper," Zak murmurs in my ear. "I guess that was worth getting up and freezing half to death for. Now, how about some tea?"

"You're soft. It's not that cold. But if you insist . . ."

We walk to the door, pause on the step, and look back at the sky.

"Wait a minute," Zak says. "I think we've got company." Zak shades his eyes with his hand, peers up the hill. "Yes. One person — a woman, I think — heading this way."

I find where he is looking: a lone figure walking down the hill.

"That's interesting. I wonder who it could be? Stay here and watch. I'll wake Quinn. If they come here, one of us has to hide."

Quinn is still under the covers, but when I go to her, her eyes are open, staring at the ceiling.

"Quinn?" She doesn't stir. "Quinn?" I say again.

Her head moves slowly. Her eyes are red. "What?"

"There's someone walking down the hill. It looks like they're heading here."

She doesn't answer.

"Any idea who it could be?"

She sighs. "Of course. I should have realized it would start again, now that they know Gran is back."

"Well, who is it, and what should we do? Do you want to hide, or shall I?"

She shrugs. "Hide if you want to. You'll be all right if you stay in this room; they never come in here. But we need to ask Gran if she wants to take visitors or not."

"I'll do it. Get yourself up or something."

I skip up the stairs, knock on Gran's door, then open it and peer in. She's up, dressed, pinning her white hair. She speaks without turning. "Yes, I know who approaches. I'll be down in a moment."

I stay in the front room as Quinn suggested, and listen. The door opens; Zak comes in with whoever it is. Quinn says hello, and thank you, and she'll be with you soon.

Footsteps come down the stairs; there are murmuring voices. Then a door opens, shuts, and I can hear them no more.

Quinn and Zak come in and shut the door. She has a bag on her arm.

"What is that?" I ask her.

She shrugs. "Payment." She peers inside. "Let's see: money. Tea, fresh bread. Eggs."

"Payment for what?" Zak says.

"Whatever she wants: a fortune, a wish?" She shrugs. "She's a regular. She must have heard that Gran is back after you went to the hotel and told Karen and Lyndsay."

"How long will they be in there?" I ask.

Quinn shrugs again. "About an hour, usually. Probably longer, as she hasn't been for a while."

I clap my hands. "I fancy scrambled eggs for breakfast. Zak, can you get the kitchen fire going?"

Quinn hands him the eggs. As soon as he's gone, I smile at Quinn. "An hour? That gives us some time."

"For what?"

"To search Gran's bedroom, obviously. You promised to help find my inheritance; let's go upstairs while Gran is busy. Come on."

I peer into the hall; the door to Gran's reading room is safely shut. Then I gesture for Quinn to follow me up the stairs.

I step into Gran's room, but Quinn pauses in the doorway.

"Don't just stand there; help me."

I've been through this room before, but then I didn't know what I was looking for. Now, I do: the Book of Lies.

I start opening drawers, rifling through, and feel underneath each drawer in case a book is hidden there, taped to the wood. Quinn walks across slowly, stands next to me.

Does she know? "It'd help if we knew what we are searching for," I say, looking closely at Quinn. Is she keeping anything from me? "Do you know what it is?"

She sighs. "It might be a book." A door opens below.

Footsteps start up the stairs, careful and slow: it's Gran. We exchange a look.

"It hasn't been even close to an hour," I say.

"The bed," Quinn whispers. "We're changing the sheets."

In a swoop she has the bedding off and new sheets out of a drawer. I rush to help her as the door opens.

Gran stands there, takes in what we are doing.

Quinn's face is flushed. "I thought you'd be longer," she says. "Just sorting this out for you."

Gran's face is thunder. "I've heard some things. Things that disturb me greatly."

"Oh? What about?" I say.

"Apparently for the first time in many years, an old resident returned for a visit. He was at Two Bridges yesterday. I don't suppose you know anything about that?"

"Of course not. Who was it?" I say, answering quickly to stop Quinn from speaking. With Quinn, there is no knowing what she might say.

"I think you do," Gran says.

"Our father," Quinn says softly, not catching my *keep quiet* look.

"Yes. That Hamley boy," Gran says, almost spitting out the name. "But that's not all. He stumbled out for a walk last night after too many pints. His car is still at the hotel, and no one knows what happened to him. A search is being organized. What will they find?"

Quinn's face is pale, pained.

"He's probably sleeping it off someplace," I say, and

shrug, face carefully blank, even though I'm shaken. What *will* they find?

"There are also reports of livestock being savaged, and a few walkers who were camping out on the moors have been reported missing. Search and Rescue have been out looking for them. The superstitious are saying that the hunt has been unleashed." Gran holds out her hands. "Come here," she says.

Quinn walks to her slowly. I want to ignore Gran's command, but again there is this compulsion inside to do as she says, and the more I resist, the stronger it gets. I shrug. What does it matter? I follow, and stand next to Quinn. Gran takes Quinn's left hand, my right one, and holds them in hers. Her fingers are hard, bony. Her eyes are fierce as she looks first into mine, then Quinn's.

She lets go of our hands and slumps down into herself. "Please, for your own sakes, listen to me. Don't access the darkness again. Its power grows. If you can't control it, it will control you."

Later, the sky is darkening, the wind picking up. Dartmoor is like the storm capital of the *world*. Zak and I wander outside to stretch our legs and check the weather.

I cling to his hand. No matter how real the hunt had seemed at the time, I'd still been freaked by Gran's confirmation that Hamley is missing, and those campers.

The hunt really happened. Those people really died.

What am I? Panic is twisting my gut; my heart is racing with fear, revulsion, and—

You are strong. Strong and powerful. Embrace what you are; be strong now. Protect yourself.

The panic eases. My heart rate slows.

Whatever I am, no one must find out. Someone else must be to blame.

"Piper, what's wrong?"

"Zak, I'm scared."

He slips an arm around my shoulders. "Don't worry, Piper. I'll protect you from anything Mother Nature throws at us."

"Not of the weather, doofus."

"What, then?"

"Gran's freaked me out. She told Quinn and me that Will Hamley is missing from the hotel." I relay what she said. "And she gave all these dire warnings about not accessing the darkness. That if we do, it can control us." I pretend to shiver.

"It's just superstitious weirdness. Don't let her get to you."

"It's not just that. It's Quinn. She looks like she didn't sleep all night, and she had this strange look about her. She wouldn't meet my eyes, or Gran's. It's like she's hiding something."

Zak frowns, shakes his head.

"You know something. What is it? You must tell me."

"There was this weird thing that happened when we

went for the coal. We were bringing it back, and Quinn suddenly stopped. Put the barrow down, went off the path. I followed her, and . . ."

"And what?"

"There were these sheep. Dead, and in a right state. They'd been savaged by some animals, I guess. Though I don't know what could be big enough to do that."

"And she just went straight to them?"

"Yes."

I shudder, real shock shaking me to the core. "How did she know where they were?" I say, without meaning to say the words out loud. It was *my* hunt; how did Quinn know where to go? Did she witness the hunt? She must have. How or why she traveled along, I don't know—is it because of the tie between us that Gran spoke of?

"I don't know," Zak says. "Maybe she just found them by chance. It's crazy to think she had anything to do with that, or with Hamley going missing. Totally crazy."

"Yeah. But sometimes crazy things happen." I should know.

His arms close around me. "Why don't we leave? You've done what you wanted to do—seen the place where your mum and Quinn lived, met your grandmother. Let's go home."

"Not just yet." *My inheritance* itches inside; I have to find it. But will I ever want to leave, even then? I think of Dad, and all at once I'm twisted with homesickness—for him, my friends, my normal life. Or at least the *pretense* of being normal, like everyone else. Tears prick in the backs of my eyes.

This is your home now.

Yes. I blink the tears away. This is my home now. My home, my inheritance. But what about Quinn?

"Zak, promise me something. Watch Quinn; keep an eye on her. Make sure she's all right, and not getting into anything weird. Will you do that for me?"

"Will it make you feel better?"

I nod. If Quinn has been following me on the hunt and said nothing about it, she must be up to something. Is she after the Book of Lies for herself? She can't find it on her own if one of us is always with her.

Zak leans down and kisses my forehead. "Then of course I will."

QUINN

Finally my chance comes. Gran is still upstairs, where she's been all day; Zak and Piper have gone for a walk.

I slip out, not stopping to find a coat even though the air says a storm is on the way. They're likely to be heading back soon; I don't want to be spotted and stopped.

I have to do this. *I have to know.*

A sick certainty in my guts already does know. I shake my head; push it away.

I follow the path we took to go to Wistman's Wood. As I walk, the wind is picking up even more, raising faint noises all around me as if the whole of the moors is in pursuit. I go faster.

I've nearly reached it — the bog I showed Zak and Piper. The one where I planted my stick to show them the danger. But the will to go on leaves me, and I stop. Is knowing better than not knowing? I could go back. If my eyes don't confirm what I fear, I could pretend it never happened.

I stand there, my hair whipping around me in the wind, the cold plucking through my thin sweater. The moors are alive, everything moving, rustling, speaking to me in accusing voices.

One step forward. Another. I'm numb with cold and fear. I walk with my eyes focused on my feet, willing them forward but afraid to look up.

Finally, I stop. I force myself to raise my eyes slowly.

They refuse to identify what they see. My eyes are sending a patchwork of details to my brain, and the pieces are floating around, unconnected.

Try one thing at a time.

Colors: the green of the bog. The red of his hair — matted with the darkness of blood in the fading light.

His face is savaged, unrecognizable, but I know it's him. I was there.

My father.

He ran as fast as he could. He stumbled, fell, got up, and ran again, blind with fear.

He loved Izzy.

We held back, led him to this place, to his death.

He was terrified. But not for long.

He came to see me.

I warned him; I told him to go.

He didn't listen. And now, he's dead. The father I only just discovered I had is dead.

The darkness Gran always warned me about has found me, hasn't it? It has claimed me for its own at last. There's nothing I can do; there was nothing I could do to stop it.

"Quinn? Oh my God."

I whirl around, tears wet on my cheeks. Zak stands there, his eyes wide with horror.

"Is that . . . Is he . . ."

"Yes. It's our father, and he's dead."

"What happened?"

"I don't know," I answer, truthfully. I know how he died, but not *how* it came to be — how I came to be here, in another form, how I could do this. I'm shaking, and the tears run more freely.

Zak hesitates, then steps toward me. He puts a hand on my shoulder, draws me close, and holds me a moment.

He takes his phone out of his pocket, looks at the screen. "No signal. Come on, let's get away from here to somewhere we can call the police."

He takes my cold hand, gets me to start walking away from this place. I glance back. The fox is on the rocks above, watching.

"Quinn, there is something I have to ask you."

"What?"

"How did you know where to find him?"

I don't answer.

A moment later, I ask, "How did you find me?"

"I followed you."

After that, there doesn't seem to be anything else to say.

We walk to Wisht Tor. The wind is ever more wild; the sky is dark, but not because the sun has gone down.

Zak takes out his phone, dials. What will he tell the police? I don't even care.

"Hello, this is —"

He stops, and curses under his breath.

"What is it?"

"The battery's dead. We'll have to walk to the hotel and call from there."

But even as he says the words, violent streaks of light cross the sky. There is an immense crash of thunder—a massive *boom* so near we are thrown from our feet.

Wisht Tor—the high point, just meters from where we stood—was struck by lightning. Rocks are scorched, smoking. The air has a strange, singed smell to it.

"Are you all right?" Zak says. He helps me up as the rain starts pelting down.

He looks at the sky and curses again. "It's too dangerous to walk to the hotel in this storm. We'll have to wait until it passes. Come on. Let's get back to the house."

PIPER

Sometimes it pays to be direct.

I arrange tea things and lemon cake on a tray, and carry it up the stairs. I knock once and open the door.

"Hi, Gran. Brought you some cake." I smile, as if she never freaked out on us about darkness or anything. I walk across the room with it before she can tell me to leave.

I put it on the table next to her bed. She glances, sees there are two cups, and shakes her head. "Leave it and go."

I smile again, shake my head in turn, and sit in the chair next to her. "You and I need to have a talk."

She glances at the door. "Where are Quinn and Zak?"

I shrug. "Quinn went for a walk, and Zak followed her."

"In this weather?" The howling wind seems to whistle into the house, through the stone walls. The wall hangings are living things, swaying slightly with the cold air that seeps around their edges into the room.

I pour the tea, angle a cup toward her, and pick the other up in my hands. I take a sip and look at her over the rim.

Something about Will Hamley and what she heard has knocked the stuffing out of her. She looks old, tired — ordinary, and not frightening like she usually does.

"Gran, I was hoping we could be straight with each other. Can you tell me what the inheritance is?"

She shakes her head. "That is for you to discover."

"Perhaps it would help if I tell you what I know."

She raises her eyes to mine. "Go on."

"I know about the burning place."

"From the 'dreams' you and Quinn had, years ago?"

"Not just that. I went there last night, you see."

She shakes her head again. "You shouldn't have done that. It'll have you now. But perhaps that makes no difference. Perhaps it always had you."

"Why can't you ever speak plainly?" I frown, shake my head, then smile again. "Anyhow, I know what happened, Gran. It was our ancestor, wasn't it?"

"Yes. Aggie of-the-Black-Woods. She was treated like an animal by those Hamleys." She spits out their name.

"Tell me — why did they do it?"

"They wanted this land to have free run for their fox hunting, over three hundred years ago. She wouldn't sell it to them. They chased her with their hounds and burned the house down with her in it."

"But that isn't the whole story, is it? There was a book, one she wrote in before she died. To get her revenge against them and their family. And that's what is in that box in your room — all the grim details of what happened to them, generation after generation."

"Yes. They have all paid the price since then. As have we. One comes at the expense of the other. So high a price, Piper." She shakes her head. "And what has happened to Will

Hamley? Poor Isobel. She loved him, you know. She sent him away to try to save him."

I shudder. How could she love *that* man, of all men? "How does the book work, Gran?"

"Whatever is written in the Book of Lies becomes true. It started with simple things—good fortune, health, love—but it got darker. Write in the book that someone who still lives is dead, and they will die. Write a curse like Aggie did, and it will be so. The book strengthens any lie written in it, beyond what you can do by merely speaking the lie out loud, as you so often do. Spoken lies only affect the belief of those who listen."

I ignore the condemnation in her eyes. "And as you told us the other day, only one of us can inherit the book."

"Yes, one in each generation."

"Where is it now?"

She shrugs. "It was in Aggie's house when it burned."

"But that wasn't the end of it."

"No. It was hidden safely. Her daughter came and found it. Years later she rebuilt the barn into this house we live in now."

"Where is the book?" I ask again.

"I don't know."

"You're lying."

"Am I?" Now she smiles. "Perhaps I am, perhaps not. But there is something else I know that you may not."

"What's that?"

"Isobel sent me a message just before she died."

This I wasn't expecting. "She did? What about?"

"She said we'd got it wrong, and she needed to see me. But she never came. What happened to your mother, Piper? Tell me the truth."

"You know the story from the news, the clipping Quinn showed you. The one that landed you in the hospital."

"You tell me—I want to hear it from you."

"I wasn't there." I sip my tea. "But it was a pack of dogs. Guard dogs, big and vicious. They escaped and went wild. They hunted her down and attacked."

Gran's eyes are full of tears. "My Isobel. The horror of how she died; hounds, like Hamley's hounds, all those years ago. Like Wisht Hounds then and today."

"She didn't die then, not straightaway. She was still alive when the police found her the next morning. She died later at the hospital."

Gran looks at me, head tilted as if considering something. Her eyes widen.

The door opens downstairs. "Quinn!" she calls out, her voice stronger than I would have thought it could be.

Then she starts to shake. The color drains from her face, and she clutches her chest.

QUINN

I open the door. Piper is there, by Gran's bedside. She turns. "I think she might be having another stroke or something."

"Gran!" I run across the room to her. She's lying back in bed, and her eyes are shut.

"Gran, Gran," I say again. No response. I take her hand, and it's limp. I hold a finger lightly to her neck, feel for her pulse, her breath, and sigh with relief. "She's breathing; her heart is beating," I say. "What happened?"

"I don't know! One minute we were talking, and then she clutched at her chest and collapsed back in bed."

"She needs an ambulance."

Thunder crashes — *boom* — outside; the rain on the roof is almost deafening.

"You can't go out in that," Piper says. "It's too dangerous. Get Zak to call?"

I shake my head. "His phone is dead."

I smooth Gran's hair, and hold her hand. "Gran, please be all right," I whisper, shaken by how much I care.

It's a revelation. Despite everything, these feelings I have for her were buried somewhere deep inside. Is that why I phoned the hospital from Winchester to make sure she was all right? Maybe even without Piper wanting to come here, Gran would eventually have drawn me back.

Perhaps I'm able to admit this now because I've seen it reflected in Gran's own eyes. Right from when we went to the hospital, and she said I could keep Isobel's bracelet, to the first night, when she said something I never thought I'd hear her say — that she was sorry. She'd seemed cruel for so many years, but did it all stem from her *caring* for me, wanting to protect me from the darkness? However misguided she may have been, I'm finally starting to understand her reasons.

Piper goes downstairs to fill Zak in on what is happening.

A moment later, Gran stirs. Her eyes open, she looks wildly around the room, then relaxes. "Quinn," she says.

"Yes, Gran, I'm here. You're going to be all right."

She shrugs. "Old. I'm old. Maybe I've had enough." She half smiles, and the smile falls away.

I take her hand and look down when she winces. "Gran, you're bleeding. Have you hurt yourself? I'll get a bandage." I start to get up.

"Never mind that now, it's just a nick." She shakes her head. "Piper."

"Do you want me to get her?"

"No! Quinn, you must listen to me."

"I'm listening, Gran."

"Piper, the dogs, and Isobel started it all. You must stop the hounds."

Is she wandering in the past in her mind? "Isobel is at peace now, Gran."

"No, no; you must stop the Wisht Hounds. Our ancestor, Aggie of-the-Black-Woods, imprisoned her enemies as Wisht Hounds. They thought they had destroyed her, but she returned in the form of a fox. She led them to the wood, destroyed and imprisoned them there. And so it has continued."

There are footsteps downstairs.

"Listen," Gran says fiercely. "I had a vision when you were born that one of you — Piper — would be dangerous to us all. I told Isobel only that one of you was dangerous, that I would keep the dangerous one and guard against her always. But I didn't take Piper. I kept you instead, so I could keep you safe. I never thought that the moors would call to Piper from so far away, that she would be able to command her power away from here. Poor Isobel. I thought the bracelet she stole from me all those years ago was enough to protect her, but I was wrong."

"What do you mean, you *kept me instead?*" I stare back at Gran, more shocked to hear this than anything else. Could it be that the way Isobel treated me all these years was because of mistaken identity?

"I told Isobel you would destroy your family and steal your sister's life. She assumed that meant you were the dangerous one, the one we needed to guard against. She was wrong."

"Then it isn't true? That I'm the bad half?"

She doesn't answer. "Quinn, you have to be strong. Cut the tie with Piper, or you'll both die."

I stare back at her, unable to process her words. A door opens downstairs.

"And, Quinn, I hope you have the courage to do what I didn't."

"What do you mean?"

There are footsteps on the stairs.

"Take the bracelet off and go to the ruins — then you'll understand," Gran whispers hurriedly. "But you *must* put the bracelet back on after. It will protect you."

She says the words like she believes them, but the bracelet didn't protect Isobel.

PIPER

Zak is changing into dry clothes when I get down-stairs, just pulling a shirt over his head. I reach for him, put my hands on his warm skin, and his arms go around me.

"Everything OK up there?"

"Gran isn't well. She had some sort of attack, then passed out. She needs a doctor."

"Oh no. We won't be able to go for help until this storm passes."

"Quinn said something about your phone battery being dead. Were you trying to call someone?"

"Yes—the police. I've got something to tell you. It may be a shock." He takes my hands and leads me to the sofa to sit down next to him.

"What is it?"

"I followed Quinn like you asked. You remember that place with the bog she showed us? She went there. But it was weird. First she was almost running; then, when she was nearly there, she stopped. Just stood there, like a statue. And finally she started walking forward again, not looking up. One step at a time, really slowly."

"And?"

Zak shudders. "And there, in the bog—it was Will Hamley. Your father."

I stare back at Zak. So Quinn came along on the hunt

again. Has she been spying on me? I remind myself that I shouldn't know any of this and make my face look shocked.

"What do you mean? Was he stuck in the bog — is he OK?"

"No, Piper. He was dead."

"What?"

"It looked like he'd been attacked by something. Like those sheep we saw that I told you about."

"Oh my God. And Quinn just went straight there, like she did with the sheep?"

"Yes."

"She knew where he was. She must have. But *how?*" Is she following me everywhere I go, even as a spirit hunter in the dead of night? She hasn't told me she was there; she *must* be plotting against me. Maybe she is trying to gather evidence to betray me. I have to stop her.

"I don't know." He runs his hands through his hair. "I can't begin to believe Quinn had anything to do with what happened to Hamley, but if she didn't, how did she know where to find him? And the way she walked at the end. It was like she knew there was something horrible ahead of her, and she was making herself go on."

"Listen to me, Zak." I take his hands and stare intently into his eyes. "Quinn is dangerous."

"I can't believe that she —"

"She's a witch." *Like I am,* I add silently. "Like her grandmother, but Quinn is out of control. I don't know how or why, but I'm certain she killed our father. And I might be next. Don't ever leave me alone with her." She can't travel if she is always watched; I know no other way to stop her.

"That can't be true," he says, but his face is a war between horror and disbelief. He doesn't want to believe it, but he does. When I say the words, he has no choice.

"Gran told us a few days ago that the real reason Quinn and I were separated is because Gran had a vision: that we were half good, half evil. Quinn was hidden away because she is dangerous. We have to watch her until we can get out of here when this storm clears."

"What about your gran? Is she safe?"

"You're right. We shouldn't leave them alone together, either." I stand. "Wait here. I'll take over sitting with Gran. Keep an eye on Quinn, Zak."

"I still can't believe any of this," he says, though his face and his words contradict each other. "But I'll do it."

QUINN

The door opens, and Piper peeks in. "Any change?"

Gran's eyes are closed again, her breathing even. My head is whirling with what she told me.

"No change. She's still unconscious," I lie.

"Let me take a turn watching her for a while. You need to get out of those wet clothes."

I'm reluctant to leave Gran, but what was it she said? *Go to the ruins — then you'll understand.* The burning place is forbidden to me no longer, but it is not a place I want to go to.

I stand slowly. "All right. Call if you need me."

"Of course." Piper's eyes are odd. She watches me cross the room, step out the door.

I walk down the stairs, and Zak is waiting at the bottom. "How is she?" he asks.

"Still unconscious," I say — lying again.

He follows me into the front room. I open the door to the closet where I'd stuffed my things. "I'm freezing. I need to change into some dry clothes. Could you maybe make some tea?" I fake a coughing fit.

"Of course. I'll be back in a sec."

"And some toast, please?" I say, trying to think of something that will take longer than a *second.* Has Piper told him to keep an eye on me? Or maybe it's Zak who doesn't trust me, a pain that twists inside.

He dashes out of the room so fast that I'm sure of it.

No time for a change of clothes. I wait seconds only, long enough for him to get to the kitchen, then I creep out into the hall and carefully, quietly, open the front door. Hoping the sound of the door is masked by the howling wind and rain, I shut it behind me.

I want to think about this. I want to work out whether the desire to know is enough to make me go through whatever this will be. Most of all, I'm scared — of the burning place, and of taking off Isobel's bracelet, not knowing what will happen if I do.

But there is no time for thinking, or talking myself out of it. Whether I want to do this or not, I'm certain that I *must*.

Now is the time for doing. I'm shaking, with both fear and cold. Icy rain pours down, really more sleet than rain. I step forward. My numb fingers struggle with the clasp on the bracelet.

It clicks open. The bracelet slips off my wrist and dangles in my hand, still half around my fingers. I force myself to shove it into my jeans pocket.

And everything *shifts*. Changes. There is a murmuring in my mind, whispered voices I can't quite make out. Something is urging me forward.

I step over what was a wall, around to what is left of a fireplace.

Yes, sighs a voice in my mind. *It is time.*

I kneel down, the remains of the fireplace between me

and the door. Hopefully it will block me from sight of the house when they realize I'm gone. The rain is freezing, but the ground under my knees is warm, and getting warmer. I reach out with my hands to clasp the stones . . .

And collapse to the ground.

I live it all. The chase on the moors.

The book, the lies written there, lies that become true. The fire.

The fear and pain are Aggie's, and mine.

And the anger.

I see and feel each death.

Aggie's is first. And then she returns. She is the fox — the black brush fox. She tempts her murderer and his hounds to chase her into Wistman's Wood. They are the first to fall, to become trapped in the black woods — to become part of the Wild Hunt.

And the deaths of every other Hamley that follow. Hunted, chased. Throats ripped out, souls trapped as Wisht Hounds. Doomed to join the hunt whenever a descendant of Aggie demands it.

Gran.

Or Piper.

Or me.

I scream and scream. Open my eyes and wrench my hands away from the ruins. They're red, raw red — burned from the stones? I stagger to my feet, stare at my hands, and hold them out to the cold rain.

Everything that happened since we came here was set in motion in Aggie's book all those years ago. That is why the hunt has returned to Dartmoor. The Wisht Hounds have been released and hunted their prey: first the sheep, then those campers, and finally, our father. Our enemy. A Hamley.

Was it Piper touching my hand to the tree that made this happen? Did I summon them, or did Piper?

My stomach is twisting in horror. I was there. *Was it me?*

And at last I understand about lies, about what they do —why Gran warned me never to lie. *Shaping belief by words is in our blood.* If I lie, I am believed. Piper too. Is this why Zak always believes her? But write in the book, and lies go beyond changing the belief of those who listen—they come true.

I'm aware of a blur of motion, of voices, through the rain. Piper and Zak are coming toward me, calling my name.

Rage rushes through my veins. Pain. *Hate* so black and deep it twists my soul. I stagger out of the ruin.

"Quinn? What's wrong?" Zak reaches out to me, but he looks scared. What has Piper been telling him? She lies to him, and he believes.

Now she's reached his side. There is a disgusting mark on her, a shadow. She's one of *them:* she has Hamley blood in her veins.

As do I. Do I have this shadow marking my skin? My stomach twists with self-loathing.

Gran's words from before penetrate my anger. *You must put the bracelet back on after. It will protect you.*

I hesitate. Wearing the bracelet blocks spells. I've never seen the shadow on Piper before; was it blocked by the bracelet? Does that mean the shadow is a spell? I slip my hand into my pocket and put my fingers through the bracelet. The burn on my hands is instantly soothed.

I look up, and the shadow on Piper is gone, too: both it and the burn must be spells.

I hold the pendant in my hand, and Gran's other words —the dogs, Isobel, and Piper—slam the truth home. I gasp, and let go of the bracelet.

"*You* did it!" I reach for Piper, but she springs away.

She laughs. "Did what?"

"The dogs. You controlled the dogs—you killed our mother!"

Denial is on her face, a struggle deep inside, fear.

"I wouldn't do that!" Piper shouts. Her lie hangs in the air, dark and ugly, like the shadow that is back on her skin.

I scream and lunge at her. Zak grabs me, holds me away from her. "This is crazy. Calm down, Quinn."

But this is what I wanted to happen. Zak *must* see the truth, and he can't so long as he believes every word Piper says. I let myself relax, stop fighting to get away. Zak's arms loosen. I move a little so he is blocking Piper's view.

And I slip the bracelet onto his wrist. He looks down at it, then at me.

"Zak, listen to me: Piper can control dogs. Isobel was killed by dogs. Put it together!"

PIPER

Zak turns, lets go of Quinn. He looks confused, dazed, as if he's just woken up.

"Piper?" he says. "Did you control the dogs that killed your mother?"

I shake my head. "Of course not. Why would I do that?" My words echo inside my mind, but have no certainty behind them.

"Do you even believe your own lies now?" Quinn says, and I shake my head again—am I denying that I'm lying, or that I believe? "Remember what you did!" Quinn says.

I try to push her words away, but they won't leave me alone. *Remember . . .*

I was so angry with Mum. She finally admitted I had a sister, a twin, but refused to take me to Quinn. I was *furious* to my core. We were walking Ness, and I ran off, leaving Ness with Mum. I went to a place I visited when I needed to get away—the training place for guard dogs. I knew a way in through the back when it was closed. I guess with those dogs there they never worried too much about security.

But the dogs didn't soothe me this time. It was like they soaked up my anger—and then ran away. I hadn't latched the gate, and they jumped at it to push it open and were gone.

I knew it was my fault they got out, so I never told anyone I'd been there.

But the rest of it . . . ?

Did my fury infect them, lead them to its cause? Did they rip her apart because in that moment of rage I wanted them to?

No. Not Mum. "No! I didn't do it! I couldn't," I say, denying it. Denying the truth.

"She's lying, Zak," Quinn says. "Isobel wouldn't help her find me, so she killed her. She was after me all along."

"And why would I be after you?" I face Quinn. It is finally there, in plain sight, marking her face—the shadow I'd sensed and glimpsed for so long is making its ugly self plain on her skin. The Hamley blood oozing through her veins marks her for death. Quinn had said she'd help me, that she didn't want to inherit. But it was lies, all of it; lies. Anger fills me.

"You know why," Quinn says. "You want our inheritance: the Book of Lies, the source of our family's power. You needed me to find it."

"That's crazy! I didn't even know it existed until we got here." I reach for Zak's hand, but he pulls away.

"Oh, really?" Quinn says. "Is that why you asked Gran what our inheritance was the first chance you got?"

"Piper? Did you really do it?" Zak says. "Your mum and those guard dogs?"

I turn to him, confused. "What has got into you?" My eyes shift, focus on his wrist. He's wearing Mum's bracelet? I frown, remembering: Aggie had saved a bracelet with the book. Is it *this* bracelet?

I was never able to control Mum or Quinn—is the bracelet the reason?

But she's not wearing it now. I smile.

I stare at Quinn. "You know where the book is, don't you? Tell me where it is, Quinn. Do it now." I drip persuasion into the words.

Quinn frowns, as if her head hurts. Then her face clears. "Don't try that trick on me again."

"Don't worry. If that one doesn't work, I have other tricks we can try. Where is the book?"

"If I knew, I wouldn't tell you."

There. She confirms what I suspected all along—she wants the book for herself. She never meant to help me.

She lied. And she will *pay.*

Call the hunt.

Against my sister? And Zak? I shake my head. No, I can't, I can't, I—

You must. You are stronger: prove it.

I reach out with my mind to the desperation hidden in the wood. I *feel* the trapped souls; they are a part of me.

Before, it was anger and dreams—my unconscious wishes—that made them hunt. This time, I call them knowing what I do. *Come. Come to me, and hunt.*

"Piper?" Zak's face is twisting with pain. "My mother. Her horse bolted at a dog; that's why she fell and died. Did you make that happen?"

"Of course not! It was an accident," I say, and this time, I know it is true . . . sort of. There was that little dog, but I just wanted Zak's mother to get hurt, so he'd come home.

Zak's eyes are staring at me, eyes I love—I'd have done *anything* to have him with me.

I did.

"I didn't mean for her to die! It was an accident."

Zak is shaking his head, stepping away—stunned. But anger will follow.

No. This isn't how things are meant to be. No!

"You're a murderer!" Quinn screams in fury, and flies toward me. She swings a fist that I deflect with my arm. I stagger, pretend to fall, and pick up a stone from the ruins. It burns my hand. I smile and swing it hard at Quinn's head.

Zak jumps between us, and the stone hits him instead. He drops to his knees, blood dripping down his ear.

I want to throw my arms around him, to take it back, but he's not mine anymore. And it is Quinn's doing. Rage flashes through me.

She will pay.

And Zak *will* be mine again, no matter what Quinn has done. With the hunt, Zak's blood will be part of me.

I lunge at Quinn, but then light flashes above us, and we both turn.

Gran stands in her bedroom window. She must have pulled the hangings back. Light flickers behind her. She holds out her hands, and there, between them, is the Book of Lies.

QUINN

Piper runs for the house, and I spring after her. She mustn't get the book.

The door is open. Smoke: there is smoke coming through the door. I push into the house after Piper and cough. The flickering I saw behind Gran: is there a fire? Was the house struck by lightning in the storm? We'd have heard that; it couldn't have been.

What started in fire must end in fire: Gran's words. Is this her doing?

Piper is heading for the stairs. I throw myself at her, knock her off her feet. I jump up and get a foot on the stairs myself, but she is up again too and grabs my arm, pulls me back by the hair.

Zak has followed us, unsteady on his feet. "Quinn, Piper —you have to get out of here. The house is on fire. Get out!"

Piper is closest to him now; he grabs her other arm, and she lets go of my hair. She turns and shoves Zak. He falls to the ground and struggles to get up, but then collapses and lies still.

Ness barks, runs around our feet as if trying to herd us out of the house.

"Forget it, Piper," I say. "The book is mine. Not yours! It was always mine."

"You should have grabbed it years ago when you had the chance. It's too late now, Quinn."

"You can't inherit from our family—I won't let you. You killed Zak's mother, and Isobel. *Our mother.*"

This time, Piper doesn't deny it. "And you. You're next. No one knows you exist; no one will care."

And there it is, the ugly truth in her eyes: the real reason Piper made sure no one knew there were two of us. No one will look for me if no one knows I exist.

PIPER

Quinn is coughing. The smoke is thicker; my eyes burn. I try to crawl up the stairs, but Quinn's hands are a vise grip on my ankles.

"Did you kill our father, too?" Quinn says.

"That was you, wasn't it, Quinn? You were there. You hunted him down with the Wisht Hounds; you lunged at his throat. You tasted the warm blood."

"No! I wouldn't. I couldn't."

"But you traveled along with the hounds and me. You hunted. The sheep, the tasty campers, then our dear *father*. You enjoyed it."

"No! I didn't want to be there. Never. It was *you* who awakened the hunt. Please tell me it was you."

Quinn's voice is anguished, and I laugh. "You're too weak—too soft to do what must be done. Of course it was me," I say, owning what is mine. Why deny it? It is part of who I am. At my call, the Wisht Hounds are getting closer, even now.

"But *why* did you kill our father?"

"That filth. Couldn't you see the shadow marking him? Like it marks you. Like it marks all Hamleys."

I stop trying to shake her off, turn, and see the dripping shadow that marks her skin.

And attack.

QUINN

Piper swings a fist. It connects with my jaw, and I crumple to the floor. But not before I see the shadow on her that I saw before.

She said *I* am marked? No! She is the one; she is the one who must die.

I stagger to my feet and lunge for Piper — reach for her throat. My fingers tighten; my thumbs push into her windpipe. She struggles, claws at my hands, but I'm not letting go.

Her eyes shift focus.

And then there is pain in my ankle.

I look down; Ness's teeth are digging into my ankle. I swing my other foot around to kick her, not letting go of Piper's throat. She's starting to weaken.

Ness: the first dog I let get close to me, the puppy whose boundless energy and unconditional love have made me happy, whom I love in return. It isn't my Ness doing this; somehow Piper has made her attack. I drop my foot, stopping myself just in time from kicking her, and let go of Piper. I pour love out of myself to Ness.

Ness lets go of my ankle and looks up at me, scared, confused.

And past her, lying on the floor, is Zak.

Behind me, Piper is crawling up the stairs.

I cough; the smoke is thicker. My head is spinning. I drop to the floor.

This is the moment.

This is the choice.

The hate is a wave inside me that wants to wash me up the stairs — to stop Piper, to have the book for myself. To end her life.

But there is something else, something stronger: Zak.

PIPER

When Quinn lets go of my throat, my lungs want air, badly. I can't stop myself from gulping it in in a rush, but it makes me cough.

I want to go after Quinn, but the book must come first. The hounds are nearly here; they'll have Quinn and Zak soon enough.

I must hurry, but the smoke is worse. I force my body to crawl up the stairs when I want to stand and run.

I reach the landing.

Gran's door is closed. I stay low and reach up for the handle, open the door.

More smoke billows out.

I crawl into the room.

By feel, I find her body on the floor in front of the window. I grab her. Some cloth is wrapped around her face. She might still live.

I rip it off and slap her. "Where is the book?" I try to yell, but it's more of a croak.

She stirs and coughs. "Somewhere you'll never find it."

I feel around her on the floor. My hand connects with something hard. My fingers close around it.

I laugh. "The book! The book is mine!"

QUINN

I crawl to Zak, shake him. He murmurs, but doesn't wake up.

"You have to help me, Zak. Come on."

I start trying to drag him toward the door. "Ness, come!" I say, and she follows us. Zak comes to, crawls along next to me. Out into the night.

We're both coughing in the cold fresh air. The rain has stopped. We crawl in the mud farther away from the house, to the stone fence, and lean against it together. Zak sags against my shoulder, unconscious again.

"Please, Zak, please come back to me," I beg, but he doesn't open his eyes. Ness licks my hands as if to say sorry, but it wasn't really her that bit me, was it? It's this strange hold Piper has on all dogs—even Wisht Hounds.

Arooo-ooooo! Howling fills the night, as if to answer my thoughts. Howls of hunger, despair, and death ring inside me, vibrate into my bones, so terrifying I want to scream, to curl into a ball and will my heart to stop beating. Die now so they can't have me. Ness whimpers, shaking at my side.

The fox is here. It stares steadily into my eyes. Rage, Aggie's rage, pushes against me and tries to get in. The Wisht Hounds could be *mine* to control, not Piper's. I could run with them in the hunt; I could taste blood and survive. But how many others would die?

And what about Zak and Ness? I can't leave them to the hounds. I wrap my arms around Zak.

There must be *something* I can do to stop the hounds without controlling them myself. And all at once I know what it is.

I ease Zak gently to the ground, then get up and run along the fence toward the gate. I feel along the bottom of the fence until I find the thorns. I stand and grab a twig off the tree above, twist it, and break it off. Then I kneel down on the ground and brush the leaves aside.

The howls of the hounds are close now.

Frantic, I scratch a form in the dirt, and another, and another, as fast as I can.

I pluck the red berries, stab my finger with a thorn, and smear a mix of blood, dirt, and berries into the eyes of my monsters.

Like that time before, the shapes I've drawn shimmer. They move, grow, and begin to pull away from the earth.

Arooooo! Arooooo! Wisht Hounds are all around us now. I can feel their hunger. My protectors are nearly ready. I'm about to spring up and run to Zak . . .

But I'm too late.

There are hounds between Zak and me. I'm cut off from him.

Ness stands between Zak's unconscious form and an

approaching ring of hounds, a growl deep in her throat even as she shakes. Another ring of hounds is forming around me, but farther away, their eyes on my creations.

The monsters I made shake off the earth and stand: they are many times taller than the hounds, as I wished, with the long claws and teeth I drew. They're a frightening sight, even to Wisht Hounds. But there aren't enough of them to protect all of us. I feel limp, cold, as if the life is draining out of me even now.

They look to me, and I command them.

"Protect Zak and Ness!" I say. In a flash, they are there, between Zak and Ness and the hounds. The hounds move away from them, uncertain; I don't know how long that will last.

Longer than I will. Hounds now edge close enough for me to smell death on their rank breath. They're huge, black. Red eyes gleam; black tongues drip over yellow fangs.

Above us, flames shoot higher. Will Piper emerge from the door with the book in her hands — gloat, and then feast on my blood with her hounds? Maybe my monsters can delay the hounds long enough for Piper to see and repent — to save Zak and Ness.

The hounds around me are poised to attack. What are they waiting for?

Their eyes shimmer, and inside each I can see a trapped soul — tortured, captive, forced to hunt.

And one of them is my father.

Many are Hamleys, but not all—some of them are my ancestors, too. Gran said that the ones who called the hunt when they lived were trapped within it when they died. Did they know that when they called it, but the tortured hunger of the hounds was too much for them to resist? Like it was to Piper. She wouldn't have known the consequences. If she had, would that have stopped her?

If I'd never brought her to Dartmoor—never taken her to the wood—it wouldn't have happened.

A movement above draws my eyes.

Piper stands in the window, holding the book above her head in triumph.

There is a rumble; she turns to look behind her.

The roof of the house collapses. A fountain of sparks and flames shoots into the sky.

Pain. Smoke. Flames.

Death is close.

The tie between us pulls my spirit to Piper. The same way the tie between us pulled me to her in the hunt—a passenger, not a participant. I know that now.

The fire has taken the shadow from both of us. Despite all she's done, she is still my sister: the other half that makes me whole. And she's afraid.

"Piper! It isn't too late, it can't be. Get out of here. Crawl to the door."

"I can't." Piper is crying, scared. Her body was broken by the

fall of the roof. Even if she could move, the door is blocked by burning timber.

The Wisht Hounds are with her now, here, in the fire. Ready to take her to join them forever.

With me tied to Piper—they will take both of us.

I'm crying, too. "Twins are cursed. Tied together. We live or die together."

"Unless you cut the tie."

"No. I can't. I won't leave you."

"After everything I've done, you still tried to save me. And now you won't leave?" Piper is full of wonder. "Why?"

"You taught me that. That's what sisters are. We forgive each other, no matter what."

"Listen to me, Quinn." She's weakening, struggling for words. "I didn't mean it. I didn't want Mum to die. Or Zak's mum, either. It was my fault, my anger did it, but I didn't mean for it to happen. And I'm sorry."

"I believe you," I say, and I do: I know she speaks the truth . . . as she sees it now.

"I'm sorry about fighting over the book. I needed it. I needed to write in it that Zak loves me. That you love me, and . . ." She pauses; she's fading, fighting to go on. "And that you don't love Zak. I wanted us all to be happy, together. But everything started to go wrong when I summoned the hunt."

"That isn't all lies. I do love you, Piper. I tried not to, but I do." How can I not love my shadow, my reflection, the images I don't want to see and do see, both at once? The good and the bad halves of me are both part of me.

Then, on the moment of death, Piper tells her last lies:

"I never loved you. I don't want you. I want you to leave me, forever."

The lies that set me free.

I gasp as cold air rushes into my lungs. Back outside, on a cold night — not burning, not any longer.

The tie is broken. I'm back in my body. It's whole.

I'm alive.

The Wisht Hounds are gone, and they've taken Piper.

I get up and stagger toward Zak. The hounds are gone. But my monsters are still here. They rear up in front of me, blocking my way to Zak.

I commanded them to protect Zak and Ness: do they think *I'm* dangerous to those I love? I flick dirt in their eyes to return them to dust, and they vanish.

I sink next to Zak and watch as the rest of the house is consumed by fire. And while I might doubt my eyes or fear some trick, I can feel it — the surge of rage and power in my veins. It says that no matter what happened to that book in Piper's hands, I have inherited.

Power settles uncomfortably, a weight on my soul. It is now mine.

And mine alone. Piper and Gran are no more.

Zak moans. Ness presses against him, and I cradle his head in my arms. His color isn't good, not at all. With all there has been to be scared of, I'm scared for him, most of all.

But I can lie. Piper taught me that, too.

"Tomorrow, Zak, you'll have a headache, and your memory of what happened will be muddled up, but you'll be all right."

I kiss his forehead and know it will come true. Even without the book, my lies are strong.

Early the next morning, I hold Zak's hand as he sleeps, and stare at Isobel's bracelet on his wrist. I hesitate, then undo it and slip it back onto my own wrist. All at once the rage that kept trying to take over subsides. It is still there, but held away.

Piper had no shield, nothing to protect her. First I had Gran, then I had the bracelet. For whatever reason, Gran chose me to save. She shielded me in every way she could. Did the self-hatred and rage from being half Blackwood and half Hamley twist and change Piper all her life? She didn't seem to understand the things she did, or even remember them most of the time — she even lied to herself. Only at the very end did she acknowledge the pain she'd caused to those she loved.

Zak stirs, groans. His eyelids flutter partway, then snap the rest of the way open. He stares at the still-smoking house.

"Piper?"

Half startled, I stare at Zak. He thinks I'm Piper? Of course he does.

If I'm Piper, I can leave this place. I can go home to the dad who raised her and step into her life.

"Yes. I'm here." I say the lie and know he will believe me.

"I thought it was a bad dream," he says. He reaches a hand to his head, and winces. "But my thoughts are all mixed up. Tell me what happened."

I tell him there was a lightning strike; the house burned down. He tried to save Quinn and Gran, but a beam fell and hit him on the head. All the rest was a fevered dream in the night.

And as I tell him, the tears come. I cry for Gran. I cry for the sister I so desperately wanted to love me. She did, but by the time I knew it, she was gone. I cry for Aggie, my father, and all those who died and became Wisht Hounds. Piper released them, but they are back in their prisons in the woods now, tormented and trapped. And Piper is trapped with them. The only way they can be free is if I summon them to hunt, something I will never do. If I lose myself in the darkness, I risk losing myself altogether—like Piper did.

And I cry for me: for Quinn. The girl who is no more.

Zak holds me, soothes me. Does he deal with my pain to avoid his own shock at what has happened? Either my lies made him forget, or he doesn't want to believe what he remembers. He kisses away my tears as though they were Piper's tears—tears of the one he thought he loved. But she deceived him, and now I'm doing the same.

We walk to the car. The storm has gone; the world is fresh and new.

Our packs go into the boot. I was confused when we found them against the fence near the gate. How did they get there?

I convince Zak we have to leave, go home, not go to the police. If it came out now that I had a secret twin and she died, it would destroy Dad. There's nothing useful we can do here.

Zak believes me. But he always did believe Piper, didn't he? Except when he wore Isobel's bracelet.

I feel guilty, but not enough to tell him the truth. His girlfriend — my sister — killed his mother and then ours. He doesn't want or need to know this.

And I want her life. First it was Gran and Isobel who kept me hidden from the world. Later, it was Piper who took pains to make sure we weren't seen together. Piper may have kept my existence a secret for her own ends, but now the secret suits mine.

When we get back to Winchester, I don't go home. Not yet. I stay at Zak's the first night, not ready to face anyone else.

I open my pack late at night in his mother's room, still mystified by how our packs came to be where we found them. Inside, carefully folded, are clothes—Piper's clothes, not mine. And in their midst?

A cold, hard shape, wrapped in a sweater. I unwrap it and hold it up by the window in the moonlight.

Faded red leather, hand sewn. The symbols on the front are as I remember them from when I held the book as a child, the same as on the pendant on my bracelet.

The Book of Lies.

Movement draws my eyes to the garden through the window. There, by the fence—the black brush fox.

So the book didn't burn in the fire. The one Gran held in the window must have been a fake. Piper didn't know what the true one looked like, and it was too far away for me to see the deception.

Gran: she did this. She must have planned it all, hidden the book and the packs. She sent me to the ruins, knowing that I'd put it all together. That Piper and I would fight.

And she set the house on fire and held the fake book in the window.

But how could she know what would happen? We could all have died along with her—me, Piper, Zak, even Ness.

Did she trust me to work out what was most important, or did she gamble with all of us? She sacrificed her life to pass this book along to me.

Or maybe she just left it there for the winner.

I open the book and read it through the night. It starts

with simple things, in old handwriting and funny misspellings; wishes for love, good crops, a healthy child.

Things changed the night of the first burning — Aggie changed us all. Her fate made us stronger, yes, but cursed us to hunt the Hamleys all these years.

And now everything has changed again, on the night of the second burning. Gran's handwriting slopes strong across the page, written in a dusky red brown. A small knife and a feather are tucked in the back cover of the book, the quill of the feather darkened. That cut I saw on her hand — is this written in her own blood?

She who is selfless at the end will prevail and inherit.

But was I selfless?

I turned away from Piper and the Book of Lies to save Zak and Ness. That is true. But I did it for very selfish reasons — I wanted them for myself.

I did try to save Piper at the very end, but it was she who cut our tie to save me. She could have held me close, had me as company in her Wistman's Wood prison. With no one left from our line to call the hunt, it would have been forever.

I can go around in circles about *why:* why I survived, why I was the one. Was it because I was prepared to sacrifice myself to save Zak and Ness, or because I wouldn't leave Piper?

Gran's dying words—written in her blood, in the Book of Lies—must have come true with her death. They are all I have to cling to at the end.

And Gran's vision, all those years ago, came true. She saw that to possess this book, I'd destroy my family and steal my sister's life. And I did it. Not on purpose maybe, but I did it.

She was right.

Five years ago, Gran said she hoped I had the courage to do what she didn't.

I didn't have it — not at first. But the cost of living with lies is too high, now more than ever. It's time for truth to prevail.

It took me a while to fully understand that Piper and I were cursed. Once by Aggie of-the-Black-Woods, our ancestor: cursed by power and the spite that went with it. And once by Isobel, our mother.

Izzy wore the bracelet she stole from Gran to escape Gran's control, to keep Gran from quelling Izzy's fun and teenage rebellions, but it had another effect. It stopped Isobel from seeing the shadow that marked Will Hamley as her sworn enemy, just as it stopped me from seeing the shadow on Piper and her seeing it on me. That all changed when I took off the bracelet. When Isobel realized what she'd done, she sent Will away. But it was too late for her daughters.

With a Hamley for a father and a Blackwood for a mother, there was never any other possible result for Piper and me. We would try to destroy each other.

Gran and Isobel separated us, hoping to keep that from happening.

Gran said we were half good and half bad. I'd thought I was the bad half and Piper the good. But Gran said she always knew that Piper was the dangerous one, and she kept this from Isobel. Does that mean I was really the good half?

I can be honest, at least with myself. Both of us were half good, half bad. It was half a truth, half a lie — the worst lie of all — that had one of us painted good, and one painted bad.

Maybe the real reason Gran kept me with her was because she thought I'd win.

It's hard even now to accept how Isobel treated me. Pregnant by a Hamley, she was in an impossible situation. She segmented Piper and me in her mind, as if we were one good child and one bad, not grasping that we were a mix of each.

I refuse to believe our paths were always set. Why Piper chose the path she did is a question that haunts me. She caused the deaths of Zak's mother and our own mother. Could I have done the things Piper did if I'd been with Isobel instead of with Gran? Once I met Piper, was there anything I could have done to change her? Could loving her enough have kept her from summoning the Wisht Hounds?

At the very end, Piper chose to save me. She let me go. She let me live.

Gran had her own kind of courage. I understand now how much pain I caused her. How every time she looked at me, she saw her enemy. How she both loved me and hated me. It was much, much harder for her than it was for Isobel. Isobel had the bracelet.

Gran tried as hard as she could to teach me never to lie

—did she think if I never lied, I'd be safe from it all? She must have foreseen that the Wisht Hounds would be running the moors when Piper and I were both there in the future, so she made sure I was afraid of all dogs, as if that could somehow stop me from joining the hunt.

Gran was wrong about one thing: there was nothing she could do to keep me from lying. It's in my blood.

The lies I'm living now are many.

Dad still thinks I'm his Piper, his daughter, and I'm neither of those things. Perhaps it would be a kindness to leave those lies in place.

I lived with Dad, went to Piper's school. Zak finished at Cambridge. We're living together now while he works and I go to university. And the basis of it all is lies.

Will Zak still love me when he knows the truth about who I am, about how his mother died, and the other things I haven't told him all these years?

I have to find the courage: so much depends on it.

I start a small fire with the kindling and wood I brought in my pack.

Then I open the Book of Lies and take out the knife and feather. I make myself cut the palm of my hand.

I dip the feather into my blood, open the book, and write. Slowly, letter by letter.

As this book returns to fire and ash, my power, and
that of my children and all future generations, will
vanish in its smoke as if it never was. And all the

trapped souls of Hamleys and Blackwoods will be released from Wistman's Wood, and they and Aggie Blackwood will rest in peace forever.

My little fire is roaring. It's time.

I know that after I do this, I'll be ordinary. I won't be able to make things happen or know things I shouldn't.

But it must be done.

I hold out the Book of Lies and drop it into the flames.

For a moment, it threatens to smother the fire. But then it catches and burns bright.

As the book slowly turns to ash, I feel the power drain away from me, bit by bit, until it is gone. I feel light, released.

Free.

"Goodbye, Piper," I whisper.

I can't make Zak forgive me. I can't know if he'll be there for us when he knows the truth.

I put my hand on my belly. It is too soon to feel a kick, but I fancy that I do — that I can feel another heartbeat through my own skin and blood; a heart, body, and soul that are part of me and part of Zak. Our child. Our daughter, for I know it is a girl, the same way I know many things I shouldn't.

She is the one who gave me the courage. Without our power and the curse it brings, I can love my daughter, completely and unreservedly — in a way that Isobel and Gran could never love Piper and me.

And I can hope.

ACKNOWLEDGMENTS

I'm a little obsessed with the art of lying, something I'm personally not very good at — I seem to have an inbuilt compulsion to tell the truth, even when it would be better to stay silent. Not always a good thing, and a strange trait for someone who makes things up for a living. *Book of Lies* takes a study of lying to an extreme: two girls, outwardly identical, yet when it begins, one seems to have a compulsion for truth, and the other for lying.

Special thanks to Jo Wyton. *Book of Lies* began over a few glasses of red with her at a Scooby (SCBWI) writing retreat, and may never have happened without her. And also to Addy Farmer, who said to make it scarier: blame any nightmares on her!

Thanks to my agent Caroline Sheldon, who read the first chapter at lunch and said, "I love the voice. Write this one!"

Thanks also to my editors, Megan Larkin and Emily Sharratt, and everyone at Orchard Books and Hachette Children's Group for their enthusiasm and hard work.

Two Bridges Hotel and Wistman's Wood are real places. Wisht Tor and the setting around Gran's house are not. There is a Dartmoor legend of a landowner who burned out a farm for fox hunting and a wise woman who returns as a black brush fox, as on legendarydart moor.co.uk. Wisht Hounds are the legendary hounds of the moors, thought by some sources to be kenneled at Wistman's Wood. The hounds and the wild hunt are known by a number of names and appear in many legends across the UK and Europe.

Thanks to Karen Murray and Lyndsay Stone for coming along on my research trip, and making sure I didn't get lost on the moors. We stayed at Two Bridges Hotel, and I borrowed their names for fictitious staff members. We had such a wonderful time there, and the food was awesome! There was talk of another trip, so we may be back.

And first, last, and always, thanks to Graham for putting up with all the endless writerly angst and dramas through this one, and holding the home fort.

Finally, to Banrock, Hobie, and muses everywhere: *cheers!*